A DREAM OF STARS AND CURSES

Chaos of Esta Anderson
Book 2

SARINA LANGER

All books by this author

Relics of Ar'Zac
Rise of the Sparrows
Wardens of Archos
Blood of the Dragon
Shadow in Ar'Sanciond (#0.5)
The Relics of Ar'Zac Box Set

Darkened Light
Darkened Light
Brightened Shadows

Blood Wisp
Blood Wisp
Blood Song
Blood Vow

Chaos of Esta Anderson
A Dream of Death and Magic
A Dream of Stars and Curses

Anthologies
Once Upon a Name
Twice Upon a Name
Third Name's a Charm
I Gave You My Heart (discontinued)
Shifting Fate
Magic Discovered

Find out more about Sarina's books at
sarinalanger.com

Content Warning

Please be aware that this book contains blood/gore, violence, death/dying, torture, and one mention of a pet's death in a fear-driven dream, though please be assured that no fictional animals were harmed in the making of this book.

Please also note that the slow-burn romance is heating up in this book and will turn spicy from Book 3.

If these things are not for you, it's unlikely that you would enjoy this book/series.

To my Familiar
Selina/Selly/Kitten/Cat,
the best cat that's ever catted
who returned to Bastet's side during the edit of this book.

CHAPTER ONE

My life isn't the same since I jumped into the void lake, the Dreamcatcher invaded my dreams, and Leverett touched me.

Okay, so, no, that last one didn't technically happen, but he did carry me to bed. Which I missed. Completely.

But it did happen.

A week has passed since I made peace with the Dreamcatcher and the Mara, and I'm still a little shaken from everything: the Veiled's existence, their need for secrecy, Bonnie seeing them too, my neighbour Kate teaching me basic magick anyone can do, and, yes, my feelings for Leverett. I'm coping, but it's a lot.

Which is why, at nine a.m., I'm getting the box of tea bags from the cupboard for my second cup of tea.

I cannot handle caffeine. One tea is usually enough. Two give my steps a definite bounce. Three? *All* of me will be bouncing off the walls and swinging from the ceiling. I'm going for two today because Kate has a lot to teach me and I don't want to miss any of it.

I've also deluded myself into thinking that the more hyper

I am, the more I can distract myself from Leverett. He's not even here and all I can think about is how he carried me—*in his arms*—to my *bed*. Never mind that I missed it because I was passed out at the time. His hands were on my body. How am I supposed to pretend that never happened?

I sigh and put the kettle on. It doesn't matter, because Leverett doesn't have feelings for me. Why would he? I'm a thirty-year-old human and probably very immature in his eyes. He's a several-hundred-year-old vampire. Of course he doesn't have feelings for me, to say nothing of possible love.

So, I focus entirely on my first real lesson with Kate as I put the tea bag into my cup, spoon in some sugar, and nearly place the sugar bag into the fridge because I *really need this tea* to focus. Or maybe all this caffeine will make it infinitely worse. I guess I'll see.

Kate volunteered to teach me about the Veiled when we all talked it out with the dream monsters in our living room. Except I can't get myself to think of either the Mara or the Dreamcatcher as monsters. They're all just trying to survive. We've met up once since, and Kate briefly went over everything she wants to teach me: everything about the Veiled from their variations to their cultures to their habits, herbalism, scrying…

I've started to think of it as Magick 101.

I take the mug over to the kettle, set it down on the worktop—

And lose my grip on the handle.

The mug falls to the floor and breaks in two. Little chips of smashed pottery lie around it, the handle broken clean in half.

'*Fuck.*'

This is either proof that I need this second tea, or the universe is telling me that the last thing I need is a second tea.

I gather the shards that are large enough to glue back together and place them on the worktop. The smaller pieces I quickly hoover up. I rummage through our drawer full of little useful things like emergency thread and needle, new batteries… and hopefully instant glue, but I don't see any. Fitting this mug back together will need to wait. At least it's off the floor now and I got rid of the smallest shards, so my rottweiler daughter Lady won't hurt herself on them.

I get another mug and lean against the worktop with a sigh, a warm tea finally in my hands. The weather has cooled down a little over the last few days. It's still hot since it's July, but the heatwave has broken and I couldn't be more grateful. Until the next one hits. But right now I can breathe again, and I don't come home a sweaty mess when I walk Lady.

Bonnie and I have walked Lady together a few times lately. We don't know how or why, but my best friend and found sister can see the Veiled now, too. I gained this sight when I walked into that void lake in my dreamscape, but Bonnie didn't do anything. She did join me in my dream to fight the Dreamcatcher, though. Maybe that was enough? Whatever did it, I'm glad. It's nice to be able to share this knowledge with my sister. Kate sees the Veiled who trust her enough to have revealed themselves to her, and Leverett, as a vampire, is one of the Veiled himself. It's not the same. I didn't grow up with Kate or Leverett. I haven't always shared everything with them until this big secret I couldn't talk about came around—I didn't even know Leverett until a few weeks ago. I told Bonnie because we tell each other everything, but it wasn't the same for her. She didn't see what I see. Now that she does, we're determined to help the Veiled. We just don't know how.

After everything that happened, the worst thing to do would be to walk up to someone and say 'Hey, I see your wings but it's cool, I want to help you,' so we're just observing for now. Kate told me she's a witch and Leverett revealed himself as a vampire on their own terms. I'm happy to respect the boundaries of other Veiled and let them do the same thing.

My photography idea is well and truly gone, too. I got carried away in the moment as I usually do, but now that I've had time to think, I know it was a terrible idea. Bonnie and I have since taken a few pictures here and there in the park as we always do, but nothing out of the ordinary shows in any of them. We look up and see gorgeous winged fairies, but the photos look perfectly normal… or rather, they look *human*. The Veiled are normal, too. I just didn't know they existed until recently. Maybe it's because the photos are of Lady so the Veiled are merely in the background, or maybe they have some kind of magic over all technology that stops cameras from picking them up, but either way, there's nothing to see. So my photography project would never have gone anywhere anyway.

Of course, my photography project was never the real problem; my disrespect of their boundaries was. I can see that now, and I feel awful. I realised years ago that I easily get carried away when I'm excited, but it's never endangered anyone's safety before.

Our plan now is to approach the Veiled like we'd approach anyone else: rarely and with every intention of leaving the conversation unless we really hit it off.

Lady trots into the kitchen, sits in front of me, and whines up at me.

'Sorry, but you were sleeping,' I say. 'I'll pour you one now, okay?'

She gives me one brief, happy bark and watches my every move as I take another mug out of the cupboard, place a tea bag in it, and pour warm water on it. Lady loves her tea as much as Bonnie and I do, and she won't drink it unless one of us makes it. Usually we share our first tea of the day, but the ordeal with the Mara and the Dreamcatcher has tired her out, too. She's been sleeping more all week while I've been getting up earlier, too excited about whatever I might learn that day to sleep.

I place the tea on the floor for Lady. She immediately laps it up like she needs it as much as I do.

'Is Bonnie still in bed?' I ask Lady.

She gives me a look that definitely says *yes*.

My sister has just finished her second year at uni as a marine biology student. Her internship starts in one week, so she's been using this chance to sleep in. Besides, she was an awesome supportive sister when everything with the Dreamcatcher went down and even saved my life by throwing a shoe at my boobs—I mean, at the Mara, who was on my chest at the time. So, Bonnie deserves all the rest.

'She'll walk you once she's up, okay?'

I'd do it, but I need to get to my lesson with Kate. She's a wonderfully patient teacher, but I don't want to be late—these lessons are part of our agreement, and I am excited to learn. Today is my first real lesson after her introduction. I want to be a good student.

Lady's low whine tells me she doesn't approve.

'Do you want to come with me? You can play with her dogs.'

Lady smiles at me—yes, dogs smile, deal with it—and I put our mugs into the dishwasher.

'Let's go, then.'

She keeps step next to me as we head next door, where Kate is waiting to teach me Magick 101.

CHAPTER TWO

Kate opens the door just as I walk up to her porch. Her two dogs, Keano and Bruin, greet Lady first, bouncing around each other like it's been years.

'I was just about to come to you,' Kate says. 'Since it's so lovely out and my dogs are asking for exercise, why don't we go for a walk for our first lesson?'

All three dogs pant their adoration at her for the idea.

'Sure, I don't mind,' I say, 'but will that work? I mean, if we discuss *the Veiled*—I whisper those two words in case any are listening from neighbouring houses—'won't that be a problem?'

One of the reasons the Mara and the Dreamcatcher were sent to take me out was because my boundaries needed work. If we go for a stroll through the park and openly discuss the Veiled with several Veiled around… It doesn't sound like I'd be sticking to my end of the bargain. Kate usually knows best, but I don't see her reasoning here.

She smiles her warm, patient teacher smile at me. 'We don't have to discuss their different types today. There are so many other things that would make excellent starting points and raise no more than an eyebrow, perhaps. I thought we could walk through the park and make our way to the adjacent forest.'

'The what now?'

How long have we lived here? If there was a forest nearby, we'd have found it by now.

Kate laughs lightly. 'I guess I'm about to show you several new things today. The forest is much more private. We can start with something like scrying, since you asked me about it, and then move on to different Veiled once we're out of earshot. Does that sound good?'

I mean, she's the teacher. It's *her* lesson plan.

I asked her about scrying when I first found the void lake in my dreamscape. As it turned out, it wasn't relevant at all, so we didn't get into it at the time. Neither I nor Kate forgot about my request though.

'Sounds amazing. Thank you again for this.'

'It's my pleasure, Esta. This won't be very different to the chats we've already had about herbalism and tarot, for example, except I'll ask you to do some homework now.'

I smile at her. 'Will there be a test, ma'am?'

Her smile grows more mysterious, and I get the feeling that the test has already begun. I don't know what will happen if I fail. Maybe whoever sent the Dreamcatcher after me will kill me after all? I have no idea who's really behind all this, only that the Dreamcatcher and Mara were hesitant about going behind her back. That's all I know—that someone who identifies as female is scared I'll destroy the balance the Veiled have created. It's not much to go on, but if all I need to do to stay off her shit list is abide by the rules we set in my living room that night, then I can do that.

We take our dogs into the park. They nearly fall over themselves and each other in their excitement, and I feel some of it, too. Or a lot of it, actually—I've been looking forward to these lessons since Kate promised them.

'How have you been feeling?' Kate asks as we cross the road. 'Are you sleeping better again?'

'Much better,' I say. 'It really helps that the nightmares are gone.' Funny that. Of course, these weren't regular nightmares, either. These were horrors controlled by the Dreamcatcher. 'It took me a few nights to feel… safe… to fall asleep again. Mischief helped.' My kitty dream guide's sarcasm could get me through just about anything. Seeing her "alive"—sort of—and well helped, too. The Dreamcatcher knew my fears and how to get to me through them, but nothing he did was real. That I can hold Mischief and cuddle her again is soft, purring proof of that.

Kate and I begin to follow our dogs towards the other end of the park. Still no forests in sight though.

'I'm glad to hear it,' Kate says. 'I can't imagine how jarring it must have been to have your unconscious invaded, even violated, like that. How are you feeling overall?'

'I feel fine,' I say, just as I trip over my own feet. 'Been a bit clumsy, maybe. More than usual, I mean. I broke a mug this morning.'

The truth is, I'm usually a little clumsy anyway, but I haven't broken a mug in… I don't even know how long. I know it's nothing unusual to drop things, least of all for me, but after everything that happened, I have this stupid paranoia that grows stronger every time something goes wrong… which has been three times in the last week: one dropped mug, and tripping over my own feet twice, once just now and once three days ago as I was walking down the stairs. I *could* have fallen and broken more than pottery.

Okay, so maybe I'm overreacting. I'm not exactly on edge, but after what the Dreamcatcher did to me and how badly his employer seemed to want my mind destroyed, I can't help wondering if someone has cursed me.

'It's only natural to feel out of sorts after what you've gone through,' Kate says. 'If it helps ease your mind, I can't sense any negative energies on your home.'

I asked her to check the day after the Mara and Dreamcatcher left. I wonder if she would have sensed them if she'd tried before that, though. They are both ancient beings. What's to say they can't mask their presence? I adore Kate, but the woman isn't a goddess or something equally powerful. She's one human witch. She grows herbs and sometimes does prosperity rituals under the full moon or… something. I don't think I've ever asked her for details. Maybe it'll be part of my curriculum now she's officially teaching me?

'That's a relief,' I say. 'Thank you for checking. So, what should we talk about?'

I'll take anything that distracts me from the few Veiled around this morning. There aren't many people in the park and most look perfectly human to me, but the fairy family I saw before is here again. My heart warms slightly. The two mothers and their children were the first Veiled I noticed. I'd thought the heatwave got to me then. I want to help all the Veiled, but I feel especially protective of them since they were the first I identified as not human. It's silly, but there it is. They're special to me.

Of course, they can't know that I know unless it somehow comes up naturally in conversation—which it won't, because why would it?—or they choose to tell me. I have no reason to talk to them or become good enough friends with them that they might tell me, so that's not going to happen either. So, I'll do what I promised I'd do and protect them from a distance. Not that anyone seems to be threatening them. Would I even know? I'll do a pretty bad job if I can't tell, but I don't think supernatural spy training is part of Kate's lesson plan. Shame. It sounds awesome.

'Why don't we start with scrying?' Kate asks.

My heart beats a little faster. 'Yes, please!'

I picture myself going crystal ball shopping with Kate.

'There's not as much to it as you might think,' she says. 'You could even start right now.'

I look at her like I'm expecting her to pass me a scrying mirror or something.

'Don't I need, I don't know, a crystal ball?'

I blush. I must sound like a terribly naïve pupil, but I honestly don't know.

'Don't feel bad,' Kate says. 'It's a common misconception I imagine some of us put in place, though I can't imagine why.' The way she says *us* tells me she means all the Veiled. Technically, she isn't part of that community herself since anyone can learn witchcraft, but it's the easiest way to hint at who she means without saying it out loud. I'll have to be careful with this, too.

'Isn't it dangerous?' I think I read something along those lines once, or I saw it in a movie, probably.

'Another misconception. Most scrying is perfectly safe and easy to practice. You're an air sign, are you not?'

I nod. 'January Aquarian.'

'Then perhaps you would take best to cloud scrying to start with. Smoke scrying can work well, too, since the slightest air currents affect the shape.'

I squint at the sun. 'You mean… you want me to watch clouds?'

'Yes, exactly.'

Well, call me Estelle and slap me sideways, I've always done that. Who knew I was such a natural? It's not the exciting crystal ball shopping trip I pictured, but it's free and she's right—I can start right now. No complaints from me.

'I didn't know it was so easy.'

Our dogs chase one another across the large meadow, jumping around like they're puppies again. I notice the fairy mothers look at our dogs and exchange a look with a secretive smile. The last time I met them, they mentioned that they were thinking about getting their kids their first puppy next year. I'm glad my dog helped sway them towards it.

'It's easy to hide, too,' Kate says. 'Not every young witch is lucky enough to have accepting parents. Gazing at clouds can easily pass as simple boredom or daydreaming.'

'So what do I do?'

'Take this cloud, for instance.' Kate points at a large fluffy cloud ahead. 'What do you see?'

'Erm…' I don't really see any shapes, but I don't want to tell her that. It's all just a smooth mass of white to me.

'Take your time,' Kate says. 'The beauty of cloud scrying is that you can practice every day without any tools or much effort. Let your gaze soften and your mind ease.'

I do like the sound of *without much effort*.

Kate whistles once, and our dogs come bounding back to us. 'Make sure you clear your mind before you try. If you look up when you're in a negative or fearful mindset, you're more likely to see those thoughts mirrored. You get the clearest answers when you have no expectations. Always remember that there is a fine line between allowing your unconscious to speak to you and wishful thinking—don't confuse the two. It's the same for tarot and all other forms of divination.'

So if I look up and see Leverett kissing me, it probably won't mean anything. Not that clouds could be that specific anyway. Or maybe they could? As Kate said, I can practice easily enough. I guess I'll see.

'Maybe I should learn tarot, too,' I say. 'I mean, if there are similarities, would it make sense to pick up both?'

Kate thinks for a moment. 'I don't see why not.' She smiles at me. 'I know you're serious, so if you show me the deck you'd like, I'll buy it for you.'

I smile, too. Kate is like my witch mum. 'It's true, then, that my first deck needs to be a gift?'

Kate dismisses it with a flick of her hand. 'More misconceptions. Some witches like the idea of being chosen, that someone gifting them a deck out of the blue is a sign, but it's really not necessary. I find it's a much stronger sign when you see a deck and feel an instant pull to it. If it calls to you, there's no harm in buying your own. You also have the certainty that you like the deck. It's never pleasant to receive a present you simply don't like, especially when it was so well-meant.'

I guess my earlier vision of going crystal ball shopping with Kate wasn't far off after all, only we'll be looking for cards instead.

'Where do we go to buy cards?'

Eastport doesn't have any metaphysical shops that I'm aware of. Kate would know the area much better in that regard, though. It's not like I know every little corner and narrow side alley in this city—I only know what a quick internet search told me.

Kate gives me a prodding smile. 'If you find one you like online, I'm sure Leverett wouldn't mind ordering it for you.'

I blush. Does she know how I feel about him? She couldn't. I haven't been *that* obvious. Have I?

Kate laughs. 'Don't worry, I simply have a feel for such things.'

Apparently I'm being very obvious. I doubt that's the full truth, but I appreciate that she doesn't spell it out. If she can pretend that Leverett has no idea, so can I.

'I've been wanting to ask him for ideas of how to help *them*... you know. I just haven't been back yet.'

I bite my lip and look around at nothing in particular. I hate how tongue-tied I feel. He isn't even here.

'I went to his shop two days ago,' Kate says. 'He asked about you.'

My heart skips a beat. 'He's wondering how I'm doing?'

Of course he is—that doesn't make it a personal concern. It's natural to wonder how I'm adjusting. It doesn't mean anything.

'He is,' Kate says. 'I told him you're doing well, but I'm sure he'd appreciate you coming by and telling him yourself.'

I suppose if I'm ordering a tarot deck through him, I'll have a good excuse to go. I'll be looking up decks as soon as I'm home.

I do feel bad that I haven't been back, but I didn't know how to face him. I feel like I've made the biggest idiot of myself, and I know I'll do no better next time I'm around him. Being near him makes it hard to think. The Dreamcatcher was a real threat to my mental health, but it's Leverett who'll take my sanity.

And against him, I have zero defences.

'It's just through here.' Kate nods towards a narrow path leading away from the park. No way there's a forest through there. The main path runs alongside most of it, and that's going straight into a neighbourhood. This smaller path dips down slightly, sure, but that doesn't mean it can't go up again seconds later. It doesn't mean there's a whole forest just off to the left.

I follow Kate down and stop to stare at the trees around us.

'Well, I'll be damned.'

There actually is a forest here. I can see the park right behind me and get a peek at someone's garden through the trees, but otherwise they're so thick and overhung that I can pretend we're in a genuine forest. The path ahead leads farther in, and there's a tiny brook running alongside the path. It's like something out of a fairy tale.

Kate laughs. 'I'm glad our first lesson is proving so fruitful!'

I'm learning scrying, I'm getting into tarot, and now I've found a whole part of this neighbourhood I didn't know we had.

What a day.

And true to her word, the path ahead is empty except for our dogs. Keano and Bruin are leading the way while Lady is following them, tail wagging and head going left and right and left again. Neither of us know where to look. I still can't believe all this is here.

'You probably don't realise it,' Kate says, 'but we're surrounded by all kinds of Veiled every day. Elemental spirits, for instance, are very good at blending in. Household spirits, too.'

Now it's getting interesting. The leaves rustle as if in response.

'And they don't mind us discussing them?' I ask.

'How many do you see right now?'

I look around, but there's nothing but foliage and our dogs. While it wouldn't surprise me to learn that my dog is a benevolent cuddle spirit of love, I don't think that's what Kate means.

Kate has a way of making me realise how little I know without making me feel stupid… or at least not very stupid. This isn't the first time today that I feel like I'm missing the obvious.

'I want to say none, but that's not the right answer, is it?'

Kate laughs. 'You're correct, actually. You won't see elemental spirits if they don't want to be seen. Most seamlessly blend into their natural habitats. That doesn't mean they can't make themselves visible, but it'll be rare that you see them. Household spirits, on the other hand, can be spotted by accident, and most don't appreciate it. Some even turn violent. It's best to— Esta, are you paying attention?'

My head snaps back to Kate from Lady, who's been splashing around the brook like she's trying to catch the water with her teeth.

'Sorry. I'm still a little surprised that I never knew we had a forest right here.' My eyes flick to Lady. 'She isn't hurting any water spirits, is she?'

Kate shakes her head. 'No, but I expect you to pay better attention from now on. This is part of our deal with the Mara, after all.'

I blush at being scolded. 'Yes, sorry.' Like I could forget the agreement we came to. 'So I take it each of the four elements has its own spirits?'

I'm hoping that asking a question will make her less angry with me again. Kate doesn't have to teach me but suggested this herself, and I really do want to know.

'There are five elements,' Kate says, 'but we will start with the four everyone knows beyond question: air, water, earth... and fire.'

She draws a pentagram in the air, naming the four corners as she does so. She gives me a knowing look when she doesn't say anything at the top point—I guess that's the fifth element.

'We will cover the basics for this first lesson to give you a good starting point,' Kate says. 'Air elementals are known as sylphs, water elementals as undines, earth elementals are gnomes, and fire elementals are called salamanders. We can call on each of these easily enough, but you need to remember that they are ancient forces. If you wrong them, they will let you feel it.'

I got hung up on *sylphs*. My grandpa once called me his little sylph when I was very young, but I doubt he meant anything by it. I've simply always loved a strong breeze, and most of the elementals Kate named aren't exactly unknown words; although, I half expected water elementals to be mermaids.

'Household spirits are just as varied,' Kate explains, 'and many are of the fae family. There are hobgoblins, brownies—'

'Is *that* how you say it?' I've heard of them before, but I've pronounced them like the chocolate bake. I didn't realise they were pronounced *broo-nie*.

'Their name comes from the Scottish–Gaelic dialect. You wouldn't know if you've only ever seen it written down.'

I nod. 'I wish I'd brought a notebook. There's so much to remember, and it's only been a day.'

The more Kate tells me, the more questions I have, but I don't want her to have to repeat herself when I ask her everything again once I have a notebook in my hand.

'Your homework will be to practice cloud scrying, find a tarot deck that speaks to you, and research the different elemental spirits I just told you about. Can you remember all four?'

I repeat the names, prouder of myself than I should be that I didn't forget anything. It *is* only four words, but it's been a very informative morning.

'Very good. We will leave it here, I think, so we don't overdo it. We will meet once every week to discuss your homework and add to what you've learned.'

It doesn't seem like often enough, but I have a feeling I'll fall down the rabbit hole as soon as I stick my head in.

'Can I still ask you things when I see you in the garden?'

Kate smiles. 'Of course. You can ask me anything anytime.'

'Thank you.'

A breeze sighs around my arms and neck. I put my head back and close my eyes for a moment. It's so much to remember, but I'm not put off by any of it. If anything, I want to learn more. Kate and Leverett could have taken my memory of the Veiled, but I didn't want it then and I don't regret my decision now. The two of them, the Mara, and the Dreamcatcher have chosen to trust me. Now it's my turn to put in the work.

'Shall I send you the link when I've found a deck? I don't think I have your email address.'

Kate considers it for a moment. 'No, just take it straight to Leverett. I can leave my payment details with him next time I'm over there, or he can call me when it's arrived.'

I swallow and nod. I have been acting childishly by avoiding him. The longer I put it off, the harder it'll be, and I really don't want him to think that I don't want to be his friend anymore.

'I'll have a look today and visit him tomorrow.'

I'll need to get over myself to be his friend, so I may as well rip the plaster off.

Kate and I finish our walk in companionable silence. When we leave the forest the same way we entered, the bright sun dazzles me for a moment before my eyes adjust. There are fewer clouds around now—looks like we're heading into the next heatwave; awesome—but the few that are there almost look like…

Fangs. One even looks like blood is dripping off it.

I blush. We *were* just talking about Leverett, and when am I not thinking about him? I remember what Kate said about not confusing intuition with wishful thinking. I haven't been wishing that he bites me, exactly—I know he doesn't drink blood—but I'd be lying if I said that I never wondered what it might feel like. If it would hurt, or if he'd be gentle, hold me in his arms as he runs his tongue over the wound…

The clouds move, I blink, and they look like candy floss again.

So it's probably nothing.

CHAPTER
THREE

Lady yawns even before I close the front door and wanders over to the sofa for a nap. I guess exploring this exciting new place with Kate's dogs has really tired her out, bless her.

The shower's running, so I knock on the bathroom door and shout a 'Good morning!' to my sister, then I sit on my bed and open my laptop. Kate has given me so much homework to do, but for the first time in my life I'm actually excited for it. Who knew that was possible? I flick open my notebook and write down everything I remember. I leave one double page free for scrying research, one for elemental spirits, and one for tarot. These are just for my initial notes and questions, though. I know I won't be able to summarise everything in so little space. Since I can start with cloud scrying anytime and Kate has told me a little about different elementals, I search the internet for tarot cards.

There are *so many*.

I knew there were a few different decks, but I didn't realise there were hundreds. I see oracle cards mentioned, too, and make a note to ask Kate about them.

How does anyone pick just one? Would it be terrible if I bought decks just for the art? Kate did say to buy a deck that calls to me, but I've no idea how any one of these is supposed to stand out when there are so many vying for attention. I see one recommended for beginners a lot, but the art doesn't speak to me. There's nothing wrong with it, it's just not my style. I guess I can start eliminating them one by one like that…

And I'd still be here a few days at least.

I start a list in my notebook with decks I like. Whether I'll still remember what any of the names are tomorrow, though, is another matter.

The bathroom door opens. Bonnie, wrapped in towels, sticks her head into my room. 'Hello.'

'Late night yesterday?' I ask with a smile.

She breaks into a grin. 'I'll tell you all about it, just let me get dressed first.'

Bonnie had a date last night. With Sunitha, the diving instructor lady.

I grin, too, and get back to my research while Bonnie gets dressed, or I try to, anyway. I quickly suffer from choice overwhelm. Maybe I should have asked Kate for a recommendation? I worry I won't feel a connection to any of these just from looking at pictures online. Wouldn't it make more sense to find a shop that sells them, look through the cards, hold them in my hands? But we don't have anywhere nearby that sells them, and complaining won't fix that.

Bonnie comes in and sits on my bed. 'I saw your note. Thank you for walking Lady.'

I shrug. 'Always a pleasure. Kate came with me; we did our first lesson while Lady tired herself out. Did you know there's a forest just around the corner?'

Her eyes go wide. 'Seriously?'

I nod. 'I'll show you! But first, how was your date?'

I still feel like the worst sister ever because we've barely talked about her and Sunitha at all, but with the Dreamcatcher messing with my dreams… my mind was elsewhere. This was only their second date. I'll do better.

Bonnie can't help grinning, and she blushes. 'It was great. She's so sweet, Esta! I can't wait for you to meet her. I know you'll love her.'

I wiggle my eyebrows. 'Not as much as you do, hopefully.'

This is the happiest I've seen Bonnie in a while. She does love her degree, but deadline pressure isn't the natural habitat of joy. It's nice to see her like this.

'What did you guys do?' I watch for any signs on her face that I don't want details.

But Bonnie relaxes against the bed frame. 'We went for drinks. We talked until about two a.m. I only actually got home around three-thirty.' She sighs happily. 'She asked me out again, to Brighton this time. She suggested we go swimming together.'

'Sounds serious,' I say. 'I'm excited to meet her, too.'

She gives me a careful look. 'So, how's it going with Leverett?'

I freeze. It's not that I don't want to talk about him or even daydream about him—it's difficult to stop, actually—I just don't know what to say. Or rather, I don't have anything *new* to say.

'It's not.' I turn the laptop around so Bonnie can see. 'Kate has offered to teach me tarot and said she'll buy my first deck if I order it through him.' She hasn't technically made that a requirement, but I have. I could order whatever deck I'll choose quite easily online, but ordering it through him will give me a reason to see him. Hopefully I can behave like a normal person who isn't constantly wondering what he looks like naked. How his hands would feel on my skin. Between my—

Hopefully, I'll simply move on soon.

'Oh wow!' Bonnie takes the laptop from me. 'These are gorgeous! Which one are you getting?'

'Haven't decided yet. I'm not sure— Are you scrolling?'

She freezes with her finger on the laptop. 'Sorry. Do you remember where you stopped?'

'No, but I don't think it matters.' There's one name I keep coming back to. Maybe I'll have another look at that one. 'There are so many, I'm not convinced the list ever ends.'

Bonnie giggles. 'You could ask Leverett for a recommendation. I bet he'd have an idea.'

The idea crossed my mind, too, but would it seem too much like I walked into his shop only because I wanted an excuse to talk to him? That's exactly what's happening, but I don't want it to feel like that. I want it to feel natural. Casual. Although…

Will it seem forced since I haven't visited in a week? I don't want him to think that I'm only coming by because Kate made me.

I'm shocked by how hard I've fallen for him, and how

quickly. This isn't like me.

'You know,' Bonnie starts, 'when he picked you up and carried you upstairs, he looked so gentle with you. Like you are the most precious thing to him.'

I blush and swallow the awkward lump in my throat.

'I doubt that was it,' I say. 'I mean, we were both tired, right? You and me? Maybe you imagined it.'

Bonnie raises an eyebrow. 'Nu-uh, I don't think so. Just talk to him, okay? He was a huge help with the Dreamcatcher. At the very least you should tell him how you're doing.'

I swallow again, out of shame this time. She's right. Leverett went out of his way to help me with the nightmares, and he's answered every question about the Veiled and vampires I've asked him. And I've turned my back on him, or it feels like I have. He deserves better than that.

I'm itching to go right now, but if I do that it'll definitely be awkward. If I find a deck first, it'll give us something to talk about, and hopefully it'll be fine from there.

I nod. 'Yeah, I know. I'll go. When are *you* going swimming with Sunitha?'

Bonnie beams at me. 'She's busy today and tomorrow, but we've made plans for two days from now.' She gets up. 'I'd better apologise to Lady, so I'll leave you to your research. Is she downstairs?'

'Passed out on the sofa.' At least, I assume she's sleeping. It never takes her long, and she seemed exhausted.

Bonnie leaves me to it, and I turn back to my laptop to see where she stopped scrolling. I don't like the feel of the deck on the screen and next up is an oracle deck, but the one after that…

It's all bright pinks and blues with golden highlights. Pastels or pinks in general aren't my thing, but this deck… This deck, though. It's absolutely stunning, and it feels comforting, like it's reaching out. Like it's offering. And it just so happens to be the deck whose name I kept thinking about.

I guess that means I've found the one.

I type the name into YouTube, then I open the shortest flick-through video. Every card is prettier than the last, and I get different feelings from all of them: Joy. Hope. Disaster. If I can read them like this, in two-second bursts, surely I'll cope when they are mine? I can't wait to hold them in my hands and take in every detail on every card. Maybe buying them for the pretty pictures isn't the right way to do this, but I feel like they're calling my name. Who am I to argue?

I've recently learned a hard lesson about getting carried away when I'm excited, though, so I put a little star next to the name in my notebook and close the laptop. If I still feel this strongly tomorrow, I'll know this is my deck. It's not like I need to buy it right now or it'll be gone forever. And if I don't feel like this anymore tomorrow, it'll be a good thing that I waited.

I turn the page in my notebook and get lost in scrying and elemental research. I write down to ask Kate and Leverett for book recommendations. I make notes like the good student I want to be. All the while, I can't get that tarot deck out of my head. I know waiting is the mature thing to do, and I have every intention of doing just that, but part of me has already decided.

And when I fall asleep that night, the last thing I think of is the beautiful colours and artwork, all other decks forgotten.

My dreamscape has become a whole new kind of nightmare, and I don't know how to stop it.

I created this whole forest specifically for shadow work. The tree trunks and leaves are black, the canopies wide. The grass is a muted shade of yellow here. Golden light filters through the leaves. A slight breeze strokes through the forest, gently teasing my hair and caressing my skin. Bamboo and glass wind chimes ring through the trees, but besides that, it's quiet. Honestly, it's beautiful, if I do say so myself. It's the kind of comfort and peace I need when I do shadow work. In here, it's just me, my demons, and Mischief.

And today, visions of Leverett making me his in any number of ways.

Mischief keeps poking fun at me over it, and my unconscious keeps conjuring more visions despite my protests. Frankly, it's hard to focus. I keep brushing the visions aside, but they don't stay gone for long. While I can generally control my lucid dreams just fine, it's still difficult to convince my unconscious to not do its thing, especially when my emotions and hormones are running so wild. Since I'm struggling to work through my feelings for Leverett when I'm awake, my unconscious is here to help me face my feelings while I'm dreaming. That's why I'm in my shadow forest tonight: to help me get over him so I can at least think straight around him.

And maybe, if I'm lucky, it'll stop my unconscious from

creating Leveretts that throw themselves at me.

'Maybe you should just get it over with,' Mischief, my dream guide cat, says. 'Isn't that what dreams are there for?'

I frown at her. 'You can't be—'

'Maybe sleeping with him here will get it out of your system. I won't look, I promise.'

Okay, so, the thought *had* occurred to me—clearly, or Mischief wouldn't have had it. She's part of my unconscious and therefore has a talent for guiding me towards clarity. Of course, this also means that she knows my every thought and wish… which is usually a blessing since it helps us communicate, but with this, I really wish she didn't.

The point is, I did think of it. Everyone has sex dreams, but this wouldn't be like that. Not when I'm lucid. I wouldn't wake up and go 'whoa, where did *that* come from?' because *I* would have *made* it happen. It's one thing when it happens when you have zero control over it. But I *would* be controlling it, which means I'd feel too much like I'm taking advantage of dream-Leverett. Like I'm making him do something he doesn't want to do.

And I just can't bring myself to do that.

'It's still just a dream, you know,' Mischief purrs around my legs. 'It's not real. He'd never know.'

'But it *is* real,' I argue. 'Sort of. It's *my* decision. It doesn't happen *to* me. Don't you see the difference?'

'Are you sure?' Leverett murmurs into my ear. My vision goes fuzzy. He puts an arm around my waist and pulls me to him. His erection presses against my back. His arms are very naked, too. 'I'm right here,' he whispers.

His breath against my neck is one thing too many. I sigh and push myself away from him. I don't turn around, though, because I'm not sure I could resist if I saw him naked right now. I'm kinda impressed with my own willpower, but I don't want to find out today where my breaking point is.

I'm pretty sure a naked and hard Leverett is my breaking point. I'm only human with very real limits.

'This is ridiculous,' I say to Mischief. Maybe he'll go away if I pretend that I don't see him. 'I don't even know what he looks like naked. Where is this'—I almost gesture behind myself at him but don't want to accidentally touch something I'm not supposed to—'body coming from?'

'Wish fulfilment,' Mischief purrs. 'He wouldn't be here if you didn't want—'

'*I know!*' I hug a tree because I'm afraid he'll still be there if I turn around to face Mischief. It's easier to pretend that he's not if I can't actually see him, so I hide my face in the bark. 'Help me. How do I address this? How do I fix it?'

I look down. Mischief sits upright by my feet. 'You could be a grown-up and tell him you're not interested.'

'I don't think my unconscious will fall for that.'

I'm not a great liar at the best of times, and lying to yourself—your unconscious—only really works when you believe the lie yourself. I don't think there's anything I can say that'll trick me into believing I don't have feelings for Leverett.

'You won't know if you don't try,' Mischief says. 'You didn't fight the Dreamcatcher for control only to lose it to Leverett.'

And yet, under different circumstances I would give him complete control over me in a heartbeat. But that kind of thinking doesn't help right now, so I take a deep breath and decide that Leverett is fully clothed before I turn around.

Thank fuck that worked.

I walk towards him on weak legs. 'Please, leave. I don't want you here.'

It's hard to get the words out when I mean the exact opposite. I hope that the bit of truth in there helps: I don't want him *here*. I want him in real life on his sofa, in my bed, in *his* bed, in—

Leverett smirks at me, and I melt. He reaches out to pull me to him again, but I take a forced step back. I need distance between us or I'll never survive ten minutes in his bookshop.

'*Please*,' I whimper. When he smiles and walks towards me, I add, 'Leave.'

Gods. Why is this so difficult?

It shouldn't be. I haven't known him that long, and he is a vampire. Maybe I should focus on that. Maybe if I see him rip my throat out or something…

I look to my right, where another version of me is being shoved against a tree. His claws have grown more than enough to run me through, but instead, he cradles me in them. When he rams his fangs into my throat, the other Esta moans, fists his hair, and thrusts him closer by her legs wrapped around his waist. I don't look away as fast as I should.

'Damn it.'

Apparently my unconscious couldn't care less that he doesn't drink blood.

'Would that even work?' Mischief asks. 'Surely his claws would saw you to ribbons?'

I take another deep breath and will the pretty vision to go away.

But of course, my unconscious knows better. Usually I can create just about anything I want in my dreams, but my emotions are getting in the way a little where Leverett is concerned.

I lean against a different tree and slide to the ground. 'How do I do this, Mischief? I'm supposed to order a tarot deck through him tomorrow, but I don't… How can I be around him when *this* plays in my head on a loop?' I gesture towards the other tree, where dream-Leverett violated Other-Me in *the sexiest* way I've never known possible a moment ago. Turns out, I do have an idea what his fangs would feel like. Judging by Other-Me's reaction, it's *good*.

And it's not just this, either. I can't close my eyes without seeing his smile. I've caught myself spacing out several times because he keeps entering my daydreams, usually by entering *me*. It turns out my daydreams are very creative. How am I supposed to talk to him like this?

'They say when you meet your soul mate, you know,' Mischief says. 'Maybe that's why you've got it so bad.'

'That's not helping.' I create a glass of icy water and drink it in three big gulps. The temptation to empty another over my head is strong. My heart clenches when a thought occurs to me. 'Is it possible to be someone's soul mate but they aren't yours?'

Mischief hops onto my lap and gets comfy. 'I wasn't prepared for the big questions tonight.'

I stroke her back. Pet her head. Rub her ears.

It helps.

'But what do you think?'

Mischief waits a moment to enjoy the cuddles. 'I think that would defeat the point of soul mates.'

I nod. 'Then I don't think that's it.' If Mischief is right and you just *know*, then he would know as well, wouldn't he? Something would keep bringing us together.

'Have you asked him why he chose Eastport?' Mischief asks. 'Maybe some invisible pull he couldn't explain drew him here?'

I smile, but it doesn't get far. 'We're not soul mates. I'll just need to figure out a way to live with it.'

Mischief squints at me. 'Or you could grow up and tell him how you feel—for real this time. What's the worst that could happen?'

I frown. 'It could ruin our friendship and a perfectly wonderful bookshop. I don't want to lose either, definitely not both.'

Mischief does her cat equivalent of a shrug. 'You do you. Although, if *he* did you it would—'

'Oh, gods. Stop. I created this forest to work through my shadows, not to be teased about them.' Or by them.

Mischief laughs. 'Sorry, sorry. I'll stop. But that's probably why you're not making any progress.'

I frown again. 'Because of your teasing? I completely agree.'

'Because this forest is for shadow work.' Mischief huffs and stretches. 'Your feelings for Leverett aren't some dark side of you. They're just feelings. Not something to fix or accept about yourself.'

I'm not so sure. 'Maybe that's the problem. I've been trying to get over it, but maybe I need to accept how I feel about him first.'

And maybe that'll help me accept how he feels, too—or rather, how he doesn't feel. Maybe I can focus more on our friendship, and *maybe*, in time, my feelings for him will vanish.

I hate that there's so much uncertainty, but this is new territory for me. I've always just got over people, and always before they got over me. I'm the one who ended every relationship. There was never anything to work through or accept, but I don't see any of my usual reasons for breaking up in Leverett. He isn't immature. He isn't an arsehole. He doesn't treat me like shit. In fact, he's the very opposite of those things.

I've never felt this safe with anyone, either. I've never felt like I could be myself, talking about paranormal interests and such. Leverett lets me embrace who I am, even encourages me.

I let the ground swallow me up to my ankles. I'm not convinced I'll ever not have feelings for him, but maybe that's okay. I value our friendship, too. Going forward, that's what I'll prioritise, and I'll chase away every vision I have of him being naked or of myself wrapped around him. Or thoughts of how his chest might feel if I ran my hand over it. How he might react if I slowly traced my fingers down towards his trousers...

Damn it.

Mischief sits in front of me. 'It's not too late to summon dream-Leverett.'

'Not happening.'

While I do want to know how all the above would feel, my lucid dreams don't have the answers. As Mischief said, it would be wish fulfilment, not reality. If I can't be with him when I'm awake, being with him in my dreams would be a pale imitation of the real thing. My unconscious would merely fill in the blanks. None of it would be real, and that's not what I want.

Mischief said something else I can use, though. I can be a grown-up and, in this case, get over it. People do it all the time, don't they? I can do it too. I just need to figure out how.

And given that I'm seeing him tomorrow, I hope I'll do it quickly.

CHAPTER FOUR

I haven't even entered Leverett's shop yet, but my legs already feel like rubber. Even my hands are shaking a little. I've never before waited outside someone's home too nervous to knock or ring the doorbell, but here I am, waiting a few steps down from his door on the busy high street so he doesn't know I'm fighting myself.

This is beyond ridiculous. Has he put some kind of vampire spell on me to make me fall for him so hard? That would imply that he has feelings for me, too, so… I think I can easily brush that idea aside. Besides, he'd never do that to me, at least I don't think so. It doesn't seem like him.

Not that I really know the man.

Fuck.

He did mention something like that, though. Something about how vampires used to charm humans into oral sex.

Well, *there's* a thought I don't need as I walk into his shop, but it's too late now.

I'm so relieved he can't read minds.

If I could stop being a hormonal teenager now, that'd be

awesome.

Leverett sits behind the counter with a book. When the bell over the door chimes, he looks up and relief floods his face.

'Esta!' He jumps up and hurries over to me. A few steps away from me, he stops like he isn't quite sure what to do now he's so close. Like his rush to get to me surprised him, too. His voice calmer, he says, 'I'm glad to see you. How are you feeling?'

I swallow and hope it takes the awkwardness away. 'Fine. I can sleep again, which is nice. My dreams are… normal. They are normal.'

I blush at the lie. My dreams are anything but normal right now.

Leverett smiles. 'I'm glad to hear it. Can I interest you in a cup of tea?'

'I don't want to keep you from work.'

It's more an excuse than a reason. His shop is usually empty, he's the only employee so he makes the rules, and he'd know if anyone entered the shop. His vampiric hearing would tell him. But it's one thing being alone with him down here, where the shop windows face the high street. Being alone with him upstairs, in his very private flat, is another challenge. I'm not worried I'll lose my cool and throw myself at him because I'd never, but as for what I might say? How I'll act? There's *awkward* and then there's whatever that would be.

'It's fine,' he says. 'I'll know if I'm needed down here, but we can talk down here if you'd prefer. You've had some time for everything to sink in. I understand if you don't feel comfortable alone with a predator.'

Well, I can't say no now or he'll think I'm scared of him. He said it with a smile and a little glint in his eyes, but that doesn't make it less true.

'It's not that, it's—' And just *where* were we going with that, brain? I *cannot* elaborate. *Please don't ask me to elaborate.* 'Upstairs is fine. I'd love a tea, I mean.'

He smiles again. Hopefully, he won't do too much of that upstairs or I'll have serious logicking issues. That's a word, right? Logi— *Reasoning.* I meant reasoning.

Oh gods.

'If you change your mind, you can leave any time,' he says. 'Please know that I never want to make you uncomfortable.'

I gulp again at the sincerity in his voice.

'I'm not scared of you.'

Something about the words sounds too revealing, like I've said more than I meant to, but they've rushed out of my mouth before I can stop myself. I just need him to know. He possibly should scare me, what with the whole apex predator thing, but he doesn't. I know he'd never hurt me on purpose, and given how long he's been around, I imagine his self-control is more than good enough that he won't hurt me by accident, either.

Leverett pauses. Slowly, he looks back at me with an expression I can't read. 'Thank you.'

How am I supposed to understand that?

He moves towards the back, and I follow him. Into the storage room. Up the stairs.

Into his flat.

I know nothing will happen, but that doesn't help my

nerves. On the plus side, if I can get through this without making a complete idiot of myself, it's proof that I can be friends with him. So this is a good test.

Though when we enter his flat and he nods to the sofa, telling me to get comfortable, it feels more like a final exam that I haven't studied for.

I sit on the sofa, same as the last times I was here. I've been here often enough that it's starting to feel like my seat—the sofa is mine, the armchair is his.

'What tea are you making me today?' I ask, desperate for something other than my thoughts to fill the silence.

I want to join him in his kitchenette and offer my help, but that's too cramped. I can't be that close to him. Nowhere there's a risk we might accidentally touch, gods forbid. I dread to think how I'd react.

'I have refined the cinnamon recipe you liked,' he says. 'I thought I'd make you a cup of that.'

I smile my thanks. Leverett makes delicious tea.

'Sounds great.'

While he's busy in the kitchen, I take a few deep breaths and hope he doesn't notice. I try to come up with a good excuse in case he does and asks. I'm not used to stairs? He knows my bedroom is on the first floor—he bloody carried me there, and I bloody missed it—so he won't believe that. I'm excited for the tea? No one gets *that* excited about a hot drink. Although, his blends really are divine. Maybe that would be a good reason. Or maybe I can blame it on the coming heatwave. It's somewhat muggy outside and he knows I don't cope well in heatwaves because we met during one, so that could be believable.

He hands me a cup before I can decide. It's similar to the one I broke, which reminds me: I must thank Bonnie for repairing it. I found it good as new on the counter this morning.

I wasn't prepared for him to sit next to me. He's on the other side of the sofa, yes, but that's still next to me. Not in his armchair. I suddenly don't know how to position myself. Everything I do feels clumsy, like I've forgotten how to sit.

'You'll have to let me know how it is,' he says with a nod to the tea. 'If the blend is right, I can give you a bag to take home.'

I inhale and let the cinnamon's warmth relax me. It's still too hot to sip, but the smell alone is beautiful: a little spicy and a little sweet. But there's something else in there, too.

'It smells wonderful,' I say. 'What's that beside the cinnamon?'

He chuckles. 'Good sense of smell! Apple, and a touch of vanilla.'

I would happily drown in it. I don't care if I burn my lips; I take a sip.

It's every bit as sweet and spicy as it sounds.

I sigh and have another drink. 'That would be lovely around Christmas, or just going into autumn.'

It tastes too warming for the coming heatwave, but I don't care. I'll drink this every day of the year.

'Would you like to wait to take some home until the weather cools?'

I huff. 'No.'

He chuckles again. It's become my favourite sound without

me even noticing.

'I'll prepare a bag before you go.'

I pull out my notebook and open it on the right page before the silence can get awkward. 'Kate offered to teach me tarot and buy my first deck. She said to order it through you, and she'll pay you when it's here.'

'That's kind of her. May I?' He holds his hand out for my notebook. I pass it over. 'If she hadn't already offered, I would gladly have bought your first deck, but since she's beaten me to it I won't interfere.'

I blush. Now that would have been a treasure.

'I only asked her to teach me yesterday. You couldn't have known.'

'I'll get it ordered today.' He hesitates, and I brace myself for whatever is coming. It's not often that I see him searching for words. 'Say, an old friend of mine has invited me to a social gathering at his place. I wasn't planning on going, but I think you might enjoy it.'

I frown. 'I doubt that. Me and social gatherings don't go well together.'

'You are free to decline, of course, but allow me to elaborate: My friend is a vampire. The one you saw in my shop last week, if you remember? He came by to drop off my invitation. I have little interest in such things, but many of his Veiled friends and acquaintances will be there. I have told him about my human friend and have explained your extraordinary circumstances, and he has extended the invitation to you.' He holds up a hand in apology. 'I didn't tell him any personal details, of course. Just enough so he could judge for himself.'

I nod as this sinks in. Leverett is inviting me to go to a party with him?

It sounds like quite a few Veiled will be there.

And *Leverett invited me to go to a party with him.*

I know it's not a date, but it's close enough to one that I can pretend. Which is a perfectly healthy thing to do. Right?

'How does that work?' I ask. 'I thought the Veiled didn't like humans.'

He inclines his head. 'I'm afraid your introduction to our community was a rather violent one. The Dreamcatcher was told to go on the offensive because someone is scared of what you might do. Clearly this someone has a lot of knowledge over us or she wouldn't know the first thing about your existence. The truth is that you're not the only human to know about the Veiled. It's rare, but not unheard of. Some Veiled have married humans, for instance. Other Veiled have befriended humans and eventually deemed them trustworthy enough to tell them their secrets. We are slow to trust, so most of those cases took years to unfold. Yours is a special case.'

I think for a second. Even apart from me *going to a party with Leverett,* it sounds like a good opportunity to make some Veiled friends. Except I've never been great at making friends, and they may not like me. But at least we'd have the chance to meet. It would also be interesting to meet other humans who know, learn how they navigate it. And if his friend knows how I've come to my... powers, for lack of a better word, and invited me anyway...

'I don't need to dance, do I?'

Leverett laughs. 'No, don't worry. It's not that kind of

gathering. There will be music—nothing unsafe for humans, I assure you—but no one expects anyone to dance. Mostly this is a chance for us to catch up every now and again.'

I raise my eyebrows. 'Nothing unsafe for humans?'

'Fairy music is infamous for enchanting humans to dance until they die of exhaustion… or rather, it is infamous amongst the Veiled.'

I gulp. 'No, I've heard that, too. You're sure it won't be like that?'

It dawns on me how vulnerable I would be at such an event. Amongst so many Veiled, is there anything I—a mere human—can do to protect myself?

'Don't worry,' Leverett says. 'I'll make sure that no harm comes to you. I give you my word.'

I want to melt into his sofa.

Instead, I smile. 'I'd love to go, but I don't even know what to wear. What does one wear to a social gathering?'

'Whatever you like,' he says. 'Some Veiled use the opportunity to dress up, but there's no formal dress code. I for one have never felt like myself in a suit. You could wear pyjamas, if you wanted. Most of the Veiled would likely see it as some human eccentricity.'

I laugh. 'That takes the pressure off.' I'm fairly confident I can pull off pyjamas, but maybe… I imagine Leverett and myself on a balcony, my arm linked through his, and I'm wearing a beautiful fancy evening dress I'd likely never wear again.

'If you're interested, I should warn you,' he says. 'Some of the Veiled who'll be in attendance are ancient, by human standards, and still hold traditional values. You may see a fairy, for example, who's enchanted a human he doesn't know to accompany him simply to show he's still superior to humanity, and the human won't remember it in the morning.' He hesitates again. 'You might also see a vampire or two with human… servants, who attend to the vampires'… drinking needs.'

I nearly choke on my tea. 'I can't decide if that sounds like a pleasant evening or an uncomfortable one.'

Leverett nods. 'It's one of the reasons I don't attend more often. But I thought you might find it a kinder introduction than what the Dreamcatcher was made to do. Does this mean you're interested?'

I nod. Some of it will be uncomfortable, but the rest? I can't pass up the opportunity to meet friendly Veiled who haven't been hired to kill me, or to meet other humans who know.

'Then there's one last thing you should know,' Leverett says. 'Most of the Veiled have adjusted to the modern world, but some… tastes are slower to die out. Some traditions are lingering. I've no doubt that some of the Veiled there still see humans as little more than cattle or possessions.' He gives me a heavy look. 'Or toys.'

His previous remark about vampires spelling humans for sex rushes back into my head.

'I won't let anything happen to you,' he hurries to say. 'Vampires are territorial creatures. The fae are more mischievous by nature, but all Veiled tend to respect another Veiled's choices, at least to a degree. As long as they see us together, none will hurt you, but it is important that you stay with me all evening. Perhaps vitally so.'

My throat has gone dry, but I nod again. He's warning me as a general safety precaution, nothing more. Besides, staying by his side all evening? I suppose I'll manage.

'I'd still like to go,' I say. 'When is it?'

I do want time to prepare myself. While it sounds perfectly acceptable to rock up in my oldest, most tattered pjs, I also want to make a good first impression. These people don't know me and have no reason to like me, but if just some of them know whoever employed the Dreamcatcher, then they might have a reason to dislike me. And from what Leverett said, some will start with dislike just because I'm human. I don't want to come across as clumsy or ignorant or anything negative. They don't need to love me, but I definitely don't want them to hate me. It'd be great if I could leave the evening with a few new friends rather than on several people's shit lists.

'It's next week. Saturday.' Leverett smiles. 'I'm already more looking forward to it. If that's too short notice, though—'

'No, it's fine! It's like a date.'

I.

Hate.

Myself.

Gods. Fuck. On second thought, I think I'll just go throw myself out his window.

But Leverett merely gives me a surprised look for a second, then smiles. And there's a warmth in his eyes that promises to melt me when he says, 'Yes. I suppose it is.'

CHAPTER FIVE

I don't come down from cloud nine the rest of the day, evening, and most of the night. When I told Bonnie, we both got so excited that we shrieked like teenage girls—which seems fitting, given how I and my hormones have been behaving.

I'm going on a date with Leverett.

Deep breaths, Esta.

I am going on a date with *Leverett.*

I try to be calm and not expect anything, but the being calm bit, at least, is really fucking hard. I said it was *like* a date. That's what he agreed to. Neither of us said that it's an actual date. Big difference.

When I finally fall asleep, I'm out of it. For the most part, anyway. The excitement keeps waking me up, and for the first time in… gods, I don't even know how long, I can't tell whether I'm awake or dreaming. Everything kind of blends together. I briefly dream about sitting up in my bed, annoyed that I can't fall asleep—except I definitely am asleep, because the pyjamas I wore in the dream were all black and glitzy and very formal, as far as pyjamas can be dressy. It only occurs to me—hours later, after when caffeine wakes me—that I don't own anything like that and never will, either. They are so far out of my usual style zone that I'm shocked I believed it was real for even a second.

At some point, I wake up and my throat is dry, so I go downstairs to get a glass of water—or I dream I do, anyway. Or I think I dream I do? Either way, Lady is watching me from the sofa, and I startle when I see a guy in my kitchen.

Suddenly I feel very awake—like I did when I wore the fancy pjs, so this means nothing tonight.

'What the fuck?' I gasp. 'Who are you?'

The man startles, too, like I caught him doing something he shouldn't be. I mean, obviously—he doesn't live here, so what's he doing in my house? But dreams are irrational like that when you don't control them, which definitely isn't happening tonight.

I clear my throat, which is still dry as sand paper. 'Who are you? Why are you in my house?'

It's time I remembered that my dreams don't control me. I can take at least some control back by asking him what he signifies.

He has the audacity to look angry with me, like I'm the intruder here.

'You'll regret that!' he says.

I'm about to ask him what he means, if he's a nightmare or maybe a suppressed fear, but I blink and he's gone. The next moments are a blur, too: I drink that glass of water, I slink back into bed, then the sun falling through my curtains wakes me.

That last dream especially left me with a weird feeling in my gut, so the first thing I do is take a cautious walk through the house. None of the locks or windows are broken. That's how I know it was just a dream. That, and I'd like to think I wouldn't just have gone back to bed if there really was a stranger in my house. Come to think of it, Lady was right there and she didn't react. We didn't exactly train her to be a vigilant guard dog, but at the very least she'd have been curious about the new person.

If it still seems important tonight, I'll ask Mischief about it.

Case closed.

I'm sitting on the low wall halfway up our garden, gazing up at the clouds, when Bonnie finds me.

'Hey,' she says. 'What are you doing?' I don't need to see her face to hear the grin in her voice. 'Daydreaming about your date?'

I can't help grinning, too, but I really wish I could. This isn't a date. It can't be. And hoping it is won't make it so; therefore, the mature thing to do is to expect absolutely nothing. Besides, I'll meet more Veiled and other humans in the know at this gathering. I don't need to get anything else out of it.

And date or not, I do get to spend the whole evening with Leverett. If I thought being alone with him in his flat was like a final exam, I don't know what this'll be. My graduation ceremony? If I can't be normal around him then... we'll be surrounded by other Veiled. I was worried before that Leverett could smell it when I'm aroused, but I also think he has the decency to not point it out. What about everyone else? What about those Veiled who see humans as little more than toys? I blush fiercely. If I don't get a hold on myself before then, I'm doomed. Although, I've no idea how to control my body's natural responses to being close to him.

Bonnie giggles and sits next to me. 'I take that as a *yes*. Your face is all red.'

I look at her, my eyes no doubt full of fear or just plain embarrassment. 'What if they'll *know*?'

She gives me an innocent look. 'Know what? Didn't you say Leverett told his friend about you?'

I grit my teeth. I can't believe she's making me spell it out. 'You know what I mean.'

She giggles again. 'Then we'll just have to make sure you'll look so gorgeous that it won't matter.'

I squint at her. 'How does that make sense?'

But I know it's too late. Once my sister has a plan, she gets severe tunnel vision.

'We'll go shopping, I'll do your hair, and you'll look so stunning that he just has to fall in love with you,' she says like it's the easiest thing in the world. 'Ooh, maybe Kate knows a love potion!'

'*No*,' I say, maybe a little too forcefully. I know nothing about it, but it doesn't feel right. Maybe I'm wrong, but in my head, using a love potion would take his decision away from him, and not only could I never do that to anyone, I also want whatever we might have to be real, not the result of magic. And that's saying nothing of the horrible consent issues. 'If he…' I blush again. 'If he falls in love with me…' Fuck, just the words make my heart race. One week isn't enough; I need longer—to get used to this, to know if that's what this is. 'I don't want it to be because of some magic. I want him to love me for me.'

Those last words come out so quietly that I blush deeper. Why do they feel like a confession? I suppose they are, in a way, but it's nothing new to Bonnie or myself.

Her eyes sparkle. 'What if you're destined to be together? Would that be magic?'

I sigh. 'You sound like Mischief, and you read too many fated-mates novels.' I never really cared about the trope, but oddly enough, it seems very romantic lately. Funny, that.

Bonnie clasps her hands before her mouth like she just had the epiphany of the century. 'But what if you *are*? Think about it—he could have moved anywhere in the world. Why here? Why near you?'

'Stars, *just* like Mischief.' I sigh again. 'Because Eastport is unassuming? Out of the way? The perfect place for a vampire to hide for a decade or two?' I whisper the word *vampire* just in case anyone is listening. I think I'm getting the hang of this. 'Besides, a vampire and a human destined to be together? Does that sound likely to you?'

'Buffy and Spike did it.'

I laugh. 'Buffy isn't any ordinary human, though. She's special. Besides, she *should* have been with Angel. Look how that turned out.'

I'd rather not be the reason all hell breaks loose just because Leverett and I slept together once. Although—

Bonnie gives me a stern look. 'She's a vampire *slayer*, and he's a vampire. They made it work. And you're special, too, Miss Super Veiled Vision.'

I snort. I guess I can follow her reasoning, but Buffy is fiction. My life isn't. These stories are fiction because someone wants them to be real. For a moment, I feel kinship towards the writers—what if they were like me? A human in love with a vampire? Or maybe a vampire in love with a human. That seems even more unlikely, though. How could a human possibly be interesting or exciting enough for someone like the Spikes and Leveretts of this world to fall in love with them?

'That's different,' I say. Not a strong reason, I know, but I don't want to keep justifying why Leverett will never feel the same for me.

'Okay,' Bonnie says. 'But we're still going dress shopping, right?'

I smile. 'I do want to make a good first impression. But if we're getting me a dress, we're getting you a new bikini.'

It's Bonnie's turn to blush. 'We'll be underwater for most of the date. It's not like she'll see it.'

I shrug. 'I don't care. If I get to dress up, so do you.' Visions of us going on a double date with Leverett and Sunitha flash through my head. Now that would be interesting—especially because Sunitha has no idea about any of this and I have every intention of keeping her out of it. I haven't forgotten the conundrum the Dreamcatcher gave me. Maybe one day Bonnie will choose to tell Sunitha about the Veiled, but that'll be her call. Right now, it's beyond unnecessary… and unless something happens to change either Bonnie or her date into one of the Veiled, it'll technically never be necessary.

'So, what *were* you doing when I found you?' Bonnie asks. 'Were you actually daydreaming about your date? No judgement from me if you were. Very understandable.'

I wish I'd brought tea with me, but I didn't know I'd be doing anything other than cloud watching when I came out here today.

'I don't even know where we're going,' I say. 'All I know is that this gathering is very laid-back and at his friend's place.'

Did Leverett say something about a mansion or did I invent that part? Perhaps I *was* daydreaming a little.

'And there's no dress code?' Bonnie gazes at the sky. Maybe we'll get lucky and she'll see the kind of house I'm going to. 'You don't want to be the only one who's overdressed, either.'

'He said some of the guests use the opportunity to dress up.' Therefore, it's okay for me to get all dressy. Not that I'm going to buy some expensive ball gown—my gallery job doesn't pay *that* well.

'Hmh.' Bonnie stands. 'Shall we go inside?'

I can see in her eyes that there's something she doesn't want to discuss out here, though I've no idea what it might be. Maybe she's just tired of tip-toeing around words like *vampire* and *Veiled*? Of whispering every other word? Whatever her reason, I nod and follow her into the house.

As soon as we're in and the door is shut, Bonnie hugs me.

'What's wrong?' I ask. The gesture puts me on high alert. It's not like we never hug, but this feels too sudden.

'Be careful, okay?' She pulls away to look into my eyes. 'Your last encounter with the Veiled didn't go so well.'

Bonnie saw some of the nightmares the Dreamcatcher put me through—Kate brewed her a tea that allowed her to join me, and we kicked ass together. We convinced the Dreamcatcher and the Mara to hear us out in our living room, but only after we dodged a small army of zombies and had to knock them out without killing any of them. I'm not surprised she's wary.

'It'll be fine,' I say. 'Leverett will be with me, and I'd say my last encounter went plenty well, all things considered.'

I would probably be dead now if my sister hadn't thrown a shoe at my boobs. Clearly, it wasn't their original plan to let me go, but here I am.

She nods. A small smile creeps onto her lips. 'You'd better tell him how you feel.'

I freeze. 'I don't know. We were joking about the date thing.'

Weren't we?

'Would he have just laughed it off if that's the case? He didn't have to agree with you when you called it a date.'

I swallow. 'I guess I'll see.'

The spark re-enters her eyes, and my shoulders relax. 'Make sure you're home by midnight, and call me if you need backup.'

I roll my eyes. 'Yes, mama.'

But the thought of her, hands on hips and asking Leverett what his intentions for me are, puts a smile in my eyes.

CHAPTER
SIX

I'm excited for Bonnie when she leaves for her date. It's been a couple of days since I ordered the tarot deck from Leverett, too, so hopefully by tonight we'll both have news: Bonnie will officially have a girlfriend, and I will officially have—

A deck of cards.

Very pretty cards, sure, but… I can't help comparing it. I know it's stupid. Who knows? Maybe I'll meet a nice Veiled who's totally into humans; although, would that be… what? Racist? That's not right. Xenoist? Shit, I don't know. Either way, my point is—

I grumble at myself. I don't know what my point is. I'm not jealous that Bonnie has a date and will definitely find her forever partner in Sunitha. I just wish I had more than cards. Like a vampire bookseller who makes me tea and destroys my sanity with a smile.

If I'm perfectly honest, though, I'm excited about my thing, too. And if I'm perfectly, completely, brutally honest, the issue isn't the lack of actual dates with Leverett, it's that the event he's invited me to has got into my head. I'm not nervous as such, I—

Okay, yeah. I'm nervous.

But I'm determined not to let it get to me, at least no more than it already has. Leverett isn't forcing me to go, so I take a deep breath and make plans for my day. Bonnie left early since it's a bit of a drive and the two love birds want to make the most of their day together, so it's only just gone nine a.m.. I'll try a bit of cloud scrying—maybe I'll even be adventurous and try a candle flame—and then I'll head over to Leverett's to ask about my cards and maybe some more questions about the event. Really, though, I just don't want to admit to myself that I need to see him again or that I'm a little freaked out over the event. The cards give me a good excuse to go. Not that he'll believe it—he can hear my heartbeat. But at least I'll have a good excuse for being nervous this time. I can't stop thinking about a small group of vampires isolating me and tearing me apart while Leverett is busy catching up with old friends. What if this is just a trap to get me out of the picture?

I take another deep breath and put the kettle on. Here's another reason to go see him: I forgot to take his tea with me last time. I smile at my favourite mug, all whole again. I forgot again to thank Bonnie for fixing it, too.

Everything that's happened lately has me… not on edge, exactly, but a little scatterbrained. Or more than a little, actually. Maybe I've been lying to everyone. Maybe I'm not as alright as I've made myself out to be.

I make a mental note to ask Kate if she could teach me some nerve-calming tea recipes—or maybe I should ask Leverett, my local DIY tea expert—and pour my water.

The mug breaks into a hundred tiny pieces.

'*Fuck.*'

Boiling water splashes all over the counter and drips to the floor. Some gets my leg, but fortunately it's not enough to leave serious burns. If it were winter, trousers would chafe against it, so I guess the heatwave is a good thing now. Though I imagine I'll really feel the added heat later if it blisters.

'Fuck fuck fuck.'

Lady waddles into the kitchen to chase away my attackers and barks when she doesn't see anyone. Bless her, but I don't want her anywhere near the shards.

'Come on,' I say as I try to move her out of the kitchen. 'Mama needs to make the floor safe again for you.'

The small burns on my legs hurt a little as I move. Damn it. Maybe they're worse than I thought. Or maybe I'm overreacting as the adrenaline from the initial shock wears off. That's more likely.

I get Lady out, grab the hoover, and shut the door behind me. At least I didn't cut myself. At least Lady didn't hurt her paws. At least I didn't slice my hand open enough to drip blood all over my kitchen. I know Leverett said he chooses not to drink blood, but would he struggle if I walked into his shop with a fresh, bleeding wound? I don't want to find out the hard way. I don't want to tease him over his choice. And what if he can't control himself when he smells it? I don't want to die, either.

Although, dying with him pressed to me and his mouth on my neck doesn't sound so bad.

I blush as I soak up the tea. All over my kitchen like this, it cools quickly, and I allow Lady back in the room before we know it. When I grab another mug, I hate how suspicious I am of it. What if this one breaks, too? I don't have the patience to wipe it all up again and make another cup. And what if *that* breaks as well? What if I'm stuck in some never-ending circle of shattered pottery and wasted tea? Maybe the one mug I broke somehow unleashed a curse upon all my other mugs.

Maybe it's me who's cursed.

I sigh and swallow the worry. Of course I'm not actually cursed. I mean, no, I suppose I wouldn't know, but accidents still happen. There've been a few things now, sure, but they were all small things. Hardly on the same scale as what the Dreamcatcher was tasked to do. Whoever is really after me likely won't move from nightmares to spilled tea. Although, isn't there some superstition about breaking glass? Maybe it applies to mugs, too. Maybe it's not just superstition but one of those things the Veiled have hidden in plain sight.

I tell myself again that I'm not cursed but decide against candle scrying, just in case. This doesn't seem like the right time to set anything on fire, even if it's something that's meant to burn. With my luck lately, an ember will spark onto my clothes and burn me alive.

I'm more relieved than I care to admit when my second attempt at tea doesn't break another mug.

I down it quickly, because I've changed my mind: I won't try any kind of scrying right now. I want to see Leverett. I'll be nervous around him, but that's a good kind of nervous, and I know he'll say just the right thing to put me at ease.

'Do you want to go for a walk?' I ask Lady.

She gives me a happy bark and tail wag in response. No matter how I feel, my puppy is happy enough for the two of us.

'Right, let's go. Let's see Leverett.'

As I grab the leash off the wall, I swear my dog throws me a knowing look.

Leverett smiles in surprise when I enter the shop. I've tied Lady up outside with a bowl of water since she's not allowed around all these old books.

Leverett walks around the counter and over to me. 'I didn't expect you back so soon. After what happened, I… I figured you needed more space. Your cards haven't arrived yet, I'm afraid.'

I cock my head. 'Why would you think that?'

I did need space, but not for whatever reason he thinks. At least I hope not. Whatever will I say to him if he says it's because I'm in love with him and needed to sort out my feelings? I guess I'll just shrug and wave it off?

He takes a step away from me, his face unsure. 'Then I must confess something to you. The night you spoke with the Dreamcatcher, I carried you to your bed. I thought Bonnie would have told you by now?'

I blush. I'm still angry at myself for missing it, though if I had been conscious enough to realise, I'd have passed out the moment he took me into his arms.

'She mentioned it, yes.'

'I thought perhaps you needed space because I overstepped. Under ordinary circumstances, I would have asked your permission, but you were already asleep from Kate's tonic. I had no business entering your bedroom uninvited, either. I apologise, and I apologise again because I should have said something last time you were here.'

I swallow at the sincerity in his tone. That's what he thought this whole week?

'Oh, no, not at all,' I hurry to say. 'I'm not angry about that. I had to get into my bed somehow, and I don't think Kate could have carried me. Bonnie is stronger than I am, but I don't think—'

Wait. Could she technically have got me upstairs? I bet it was her who suggested Leverett take me, too. I clear my throat when I get hung up on him taking me. 'It's fine.'

'Good,' he says. 'I'm glad to hear it.'

We fall into an awkward silence. Or maybe it's only awkward because I'm still hung up on him taking m— *the thing*. I glance towards his counter, see myself sitting on it with my legs wrapped around him, his fangs in my neck—

This isn't helping.

'Anyway,' I say and blink to clear my head. 'Could we talk about this social event again?'

'Of course. Do you want to go upstairs?'

I shake my head, perhaps a little too desperately. 'No, down here is fine. You can't always close your shop just because I'm here.'

He pulls up a stool from the storage room for me, and we sit at his counter together. Since there are no customers around, it still feels kinda private, so… my cunning plan didn't quite work.

'What can I tell you?' he offers.

'You said I'll be safe as long as I'm with you'—I ignore the heat that creeps into my cheeks—'but do we have a plan should we get separated?'

His eyes darken like I'm in immediate danger already. Not gonna lie, it does things to me.

'I won't let that happen.'

'You won't be the only vampire there. Isn't it possible that your friend has told some of his other guests about me? Isn't it possible that some of them might want to…' I can't say *kill me*. My bravery is wavering as it is, but I'll need to face the possibility sooner or later. 'Will I still be safe if you lose sight of me for a moment?'

Leverett hesitates. 'No. Which is why I told you to stay with me.' His eyes soften again when no one jumps out of the storage room to kidnap me. 'I understand if you don't want to go. There is a certain risk involved, I won't hide it. Doing so would only put you in more danger.'

'I do want to go.' The last thing I want is for him to think that I don't want to spend all of my time with him. 'But I also think we should have a backup plan. Just in case.'

He nods. 'There are several things I can do should we become separated. I would smell your fear, for one—my friend's estate isn't so large that I would lose all sense of where you are. I will also remain tuned in to your heartbeat. If you call me, I will come. In short, I will know if you're scared. My friend and his husband will also keep an eye on you.'

I blush again. Despite my reason for this visit, I realise I do feel safe with him. Leverett won't let anything happen to me—

I know this beyond a doubt.

I raise an eyebrow. 'That sounds exhausting.'

He chuckles, and my legs go weak. It's a good thing I'm sitting already or I'd be clinging to the counter—or worse, to him. It'd be difficult to explain that away.

'I don't do it all the time. I have more than enough practice to tune it out, but I think on this occasion, I'll feel better knowing exactly where you are.'

My mouth goes dry. Is that a hungry look he gives me or am I going mad? Probably going mad. And anyway, wouldn't it be a thirsty look, since vampires drink blood? Not that he does, and not that—

I make myself take a deep breath. *Get your shit together, Esta.*

I nod slowly, not sure if I want to meet his eyes—which, to me, seem way too intense right now—or if I should look at the floor or what.

'Th-thank you,' I mumble. I'm not convinced it sounds like words. 'Is there anything I can do besides calling your name?'

He thinks for a moment. 'I believe there are various protection spells you can use, though I've never had use for them myself. Vampires don't use magic in the same way other Veiled or witches do.'

I cock my head. 'But you do use magic?'

This seems like a safer subject.

Leverett gives me a grin, vanishes in a cloud of fog… and my heart misses a beat when he reappears right behind me. So close I can feel his warmth on my skin—his *surprising* warmth. Just goes to show how little I know about vampires. If he leans in just a little, I'll feel his breath on me, too, and then this is too close to my dream.

'I imagine some Veiled might consider this magic, don't you?'

But I'm completely lost for words. I don't know how to handle this. Is he flirting with me or is this wishful thinking? No, of course he's not. He's a several-hundred-year-old vampire. He's having fun toying with the naïve human. Sure, he doesn't drink blood and I don't think he'd ever hunt me for that, but his natural instinct is probably still there, isn't it? That's plausible. That's what this is. Didn't he say before that he just wanted to see how I'd react?

'Yes, I… I suppose they might.'

I resist the urge to turn my head. What if I do and it brings my nose within an inch of his? I'm barely breathing as it is.

His presence at my back disappears. I blink, and he's sitting opposite me again. I didn't see him turn into fog again, but I like that I felt the difference. I'm either very good at sensing my surroundings, or I know him well enough now to know when he's there.

Or maybe, says a voice that sounds like a strange combination of Mischief and Bonnie, *maybe it's because you're fated to be together.*

I resist the urge to snort at the idea. I'd shake my head to clear it, but I'm worried I'd pass out.

'I'll ask Kate,' I say. 'Maybe there's something easy she can teach me.'

Although, to be honest, I doubt any novice magic would do anything to impress a centuries-old Veiled, and I bet some of them are older than that. Whatever magic Kate might teach me before the event, it's unlikely to be strong enough. But it might amuse them before they tear me to pieces, so at least one of us would be laughing, I guess.

'Do you feel better now?' he asks. 'Or is there anything else I can do to put your mind at ease? Allow me to repeat again that it's alright if you've changed your mind. We have no obligation to go.'

I start to nod, but…

'Can I think it over a day? It's not that I don't want to go, it's just that…'

I'm not even sure what it is, exactly. I just know I'm hesitant.

'Of course. I understand if this is too much too soon.'

His words hit home. I didn't realise that this is what it is, but hearing it now… It *is* a lot, and very soon. A month ago, I didn't even know about the Veiled, and I've barely had a chance to catch my breath since then. The Dreamcatcher certainly didn't give me any breaks. Everyone else at this event will either be Veiled or have known one or more for years. It hasn't even been four weeks for me. And with everything Leverett told me about some of their behaviours at these events… I'm throwing myself into an ocean to learn how to swim and stupidly hope I won't drown. In a way, it's the void lake all over again, except I know what's on the other side.

I'm not sure if I'm ready to take that step this time.

'Here.' He writes something on a Post-it Note and hands it to me. My heart misses a beat. Is that— 'It's my number. Call me or send me a message if you have any more questions or if you have decided. Saves you having to walk all the way to my shop every time.'

I quickly stuff the paper into my bag, afraid I'll hold it with way too much reverence if I give myself the time to think about this.

Before I have a chance to lose my nerve, I reach over to take another Post-it and write my own number down. 'This is me. I mean, mine.' Smooth. 'Now you won't need to go via Kate just to let me know my cards are here.'

He gives me one of those genuine smiles that melt me to my core. 'Let me get your tea before I forget again.'

He vanishes in a huff of smoke, and I take a moment to breathe. We just exchanged numbers. I feel silly getting excited about this—we're not teenagers, damn it—but we can literally contact each other whenever now. I won't abuse it and message him all the time and I doubt he'll message me just to say good morning every day, either, but my heart races at having this new little connection between us. The general area where the paper must have landed in my bag seems to be glowing at me.

This is a perfectly normal thing for friends to do, I remind myself. And isn't that what I came here to prove? That I can be regular friends with him? Well. Friendship achieved.

Leverett reappears, and I note that I don't startle anymore. Something about him doing his fog thing has become so normal, like this has always been in my life.

He hands me a pack of his home blend. I can smell it even though the wrapping.

'Thank you.' I stand and make towards the door. 'Call me when my cards are here?'

I inwardly cringe. Did that sound as cheesy as it did in my

head? At least I didn't wink. Stars, that would have been bad.

He nods. 'Call me if you have more questions.'

I know he means about the event, but it almost sounds like an open invitation. Like I could call him at three in the morning and ask him about the universe.

My heart takes too long to calm down as I walk home, that spot in my bag slowly but surely burning a hole into my leg. And when I reach my front door, I'm not convinced the breeze has carried my blush away.

My face is still burning when the door opens and shuts downstairs that afternoon. I glance at the clock—it's only just gone three p.m.. Surely Bonnie isn't back already? My heart drops for her. What if her date went badly?

I abandon the books on my bed and hurry downstairs. There's no sign of Bonnie in the corridor and she didn't say anything, but then she might think I'm out. This doesn't have to be a bad sign.

I find her sitting on the sofa, legs pulled up and head down. If she hears me entering the room, she doesn't react. I sit next to her and lean my head against her shoulder. This is so far removed from what I was expecting that everything seems to slow. I was so sure she'd come home beaming and gushing about Sunitha. Seeing her like this, hurt and fragile, colours my earlier joy in dark greys.

'Want to talk about it?'

Bonnie peeks out from under her arms. 'She's a mermaid.' My sister unwraps herself more and leans her head against mine. 'And I didn't react well.'

'Oh.' I want to say something clever or comforting, but I wasn't expecting this. Sunitha is a mermaid—I guess that answers how we'd tell her about the Veiled. 'What happened?'

'We just walked around the beach for a bit, you know? Looked at the arcade, talked about getting ice cream later. I suggested fish and chips, she said great but she might get a sausage instead.' She huffs without any real strength, like she should have known Sunitha was a mermaid from that alone.

It breaks my heart how defeated she sounds. She was so excited about this date, and now she's falling apart on our sofa.

'Everything was going great,' Bonnie says. 'When we waded into the water together, I thought she looked like she was sparkling. Like she was covered in glitter. Then we started swimming and I realised she no longer had legs but a tail, and the sparkle wasn't glitter but tiny scales. And I…'

A sob escapes her, and I put my arms around her. Bonnie holds on to me like I'm the only thing keeping her upright.

After a while, she says, 'And I got way too excited, but I just wanted her to feel safe with me, you know? I was about to say something, tell her that I know about the Veiled and she doesn't need to hide from me, but then she turned around with this huge, happy smile and I forgot how to talk. My eyes must have been huge.' Bonnie looks at me, her eyes red and swollen. 'I stared at her tail for far too long, saw her pale when she realised that I didn't see legs, and then I just… left. I think I mumbled an apology. She didn't come after me.'

'It's okay,' I say, because I've no idea what else to say right now. No one trained me for this situation. If this had been a date with a human, I'd have told her the same thing, so that's all I have.

It's probably for the best Bonnie didn't comment on Sunitha having a tail, though. Granted, her face apparently said everything, but maybe Sunitha thinks Bonnie is one of the Veiled, too? No, that would be worse. If Sunitha thinks Bonnie lied about that—that a human lied to get close to one of the Veiled—then this relationship is definitely over.

'It takes a while to get home, doesn't it?' I ask, hoping the right words will just kind of come to me. 'That's plenty of time for her to try and make sense of what happened. You should message her.'

Bonnie sniffs.

'Need a tissue?' Finally, something I know how to help with.

She nods, so I grab a pack from the kitchen and hand it to her.

Bonnie blows her nose. 'She already messaged me. She asked me what happened, if I saw anything that scared me in the water.'

'But you haven't replied?'

Bonnie wipes her tears away on her sleeve and shakes her head. 'I don't know what to say. Shit, I wasn't prepared for this! I thought we'd just have a nice day together, hopefully plan the next date. I feel terrible about how I reacted. What if she can't trust me now? What if she can't trust me once she learns I'm not one of them?'

'You should talk to her,' I say. 'We fought for this, right? For the freedom to see the Veiled for who they are? This is—'

'We fought for *your* right,' Bonnie says. 'When we made that deal with the Dreamcatcher and the Mara, they had no idea that I'd get your super vision thing, too.'

I shrug, but really I'm hurt. It's not my fault she can see them, too; at least, I don't think so. We don't know why she can, but I doubt it's because of me.

'That doesn't matter,' I say. 'This is the perfect chance to prove that we can stay calm around the Veiled, that we can be around them without exposing them. So what if you didn't expect her to be a mermaid? I didn't expect Leverett to be a vampire when I walked into his bookshop. We didn't expect Kate to practice witchcraft when we moved here. But we're fine.'

Bonnie mumbles something under her breath that sounds a little like, 'That's not the same,' but I don't quite catch it.

'Besides, you should apologise for running away. She probably thinks you thought she looked awful in a bikini or something.'

A small, pained smile creeps onto Bonnie's lips. 'She didn't. She looked beautiful.'

It makes me smile, too. Disaster averted, hopefully… or rectified, anyway. 'Right, you should tell her that. Tell her why you left. This is probably new for her, too—I doubt she's come out of the mermaid closet to many humans by accident.'

Slowly, Bonnie nods. 'You're right. I'll message her.' She leans into me again. 'Thank you.'

'*I* should thank *you*,' I say. 'This actually helped me make a decision, too.'

She blows her nose again and raises an eyebrow with her nose still in the tissue. 'Oh?'

'I had second thoughts about going to the event, but not anymore. I'm going.'

After the speech I just gave Bonnie about not running away and proving that we can stay calm around the Veiled, that we deserve to know or at least aren't a mistake, I can't very well run away from the event and the Veiled. Besides, Leverett will be there. I'll be fine.

I pull out my phone and type, 'Hey, it's me. Esta?' I blush. If he's saved my number into his phone, my name would come up. But what if he hasn't? Shouldn't I explain who I am? But the question mark after my name seems so excessive. He might not recognise the number, but I sure as hell hope he remembers me. I delete it and start again. 'Hey, it's Esta.' Better. 'I'll come with you. Looking forward to it :)' I hit Send before I can regret the smiley.

I do regret it immediately afterwards. Is it too much? Will he think it weird or too straightforward? What if—

'Whoa. Hold on.' Bonnie peeks at my phone. 'You have Leverett's number?'

The blush creeps back onto my face. 'He gave me his so I can call him when I've decided what to do about this party. I gave him mine since, you know.' The blush threatens to burn my skin. 'It would have been weird not to, and now he can call me when my cards are there.' That's totally why. Just being polite.

Her eyes widen, and she looks more like my happy Bonnie again. She takes out her own phone and starts typing.

'I guess if you could do that, I can do *this.*'

We smile at each other like we've been to hell and back.

'I'm proud of us,' I say.

'Me too.'

Then our phones buzz. Bonnie smiles, and I can't keep my own grin off my face.

'Sunitha is asking if she can come over in a day or two. To talk about what happened.'

'Wait, she's coming here?' For some reason I figured they'd only ever meet in Bournemouth. I didn't have a logical reason for this, I just hadn't thought about it, either.

Bonnie nods. 'We said earlier today that we'll meet up at mine next time.' Her lips curl again, more cautious this time. 'I guess this is a good sign. What did Leverett say?'

We squeal like school girls who just caught a glimpse of their crushes without shirts on when I show her his text:

'You won't regret it.'

CHAPTER
SEVEN

Lady is bouncing up and down Kate's path before we even have a chance to knock. Bonnie is coming along, too—I was going to ask Kate about some simple protection magic, and we figured it wouldn't hurt Bonnie to know some as well. We'll both be able to protect ourselves better, even if our initial attempts probably won't amount to much. I still don't think it'll be enough in time for the party, but that's not a reason against starting to learn now.

Kate gives us a radiant smile when she opens her door. Lady shoots straight past her and greets her dogs first, then gives Kate's hand a happy little sniff.

'Are both of you joining me today?' Kate asks. 'It hasn't been a week yet, though I'm happy to see you're eager to learn. How is your homework going?'

I don't want to admit that I let it slide a tiny bit yesterday. There's so much going on right now, but I'm grateful it's all positive.

'It's overwhelming,' I say honestly. 'How do you memorise it all? All those different V—' I catch myself. We're not exactly out of earshot here. 'All the different kinds. Do you know all of them? By heart?'

Kate's smile turns into her patient teacher version I love so much. 'Give yourself time. I find it's more about accepting the variety than trying to memorise every single detail. Much of it is simply common sense, and you don't need to be able to recite the rest without error. That's what your encyclopediae are for. They'll remember if you don't, but I think you'll surprise yourself.' She turns to Bonnie. 'Are you joining our lessons from now?'

Bonnie shakes her head. 'I wish, but my internship starts next week. I wouldn't have the time. No, this was all Esta's idea just for today.'

Which sparks another idea. Maybe we can ask Kate about mermaids—not to go behind Sunitha's back, but just to make sure we're aware of anything we shouldn't say to mermaids. Preferred presents, maybe, so Bonnie can apologise in style. And maybe, if Bonnie doesn't give her any regular flower bouquet anyone might have thought of but a... whatever is special to mermaids, Sunitha will see that Bonnie really just overreacted and can be thoughtful. I smirk in her direction. It's a good thing she can't read my mind or I'd have a bruise forming on my arm right about now.

'Leverett has invited me to this social event this Saturday,' I say. 'Do you know any... *self-defence* I can use to protect myself?' I cringe a little at the over-emphasis. At least I stopped short of wiggling my eyebrows and winking.

Kate ushers our dogs across the road, and we follow like well-trained puppies ourselves. Anywhere Kate goes, we all go.

'Ah, I see. I believe I know the one. I'm invited, too, though I don't intend on going.'

'Why's that?' I ask before I can stop myself. It isn't really any of my business. I don't know if I'd feel even safer with Kate there or if I'd feel awkwardly watched the whole time. And what if Leverett confesses his undying love for me and kisses me? It'd be really weird if she watched from a distance.

'It's not my kind of event,' Kate says, 'and I already have plans for the waning crescent moon that night.'

I almost wish I could join Kate's moon ritual, or whatever she has planned, but I wouldn't give up spending a night with Leverett for anything. I'm starting to look forward to the event, everything he might show me. Everything I might learn.

We enter the park together and begin our slow walk towards the other end. Our dogs shoot down the meadow like they haven't been outside in weeks.

'I take it the guest list is your reason for wanting to learn self-defence?' Kate asks.

I nod. 'But also it'd be nice to know some anyway. Bonnie knows karate, but I've got nothing.'

'Would karate do anything against the Ve—' Her eyes go wide. 'Against one of them?'

I hadn't considered that, but now she's said it I can't imagine her punching a werewolf's lights out. It's nothing against her skill, but in my head all werewolves have jaws of steel.

Kate smiles. 'Only if you take them unaware. It depends on whom you're defending yourself against, of course, and it might still get you out of a pinch, but it'll be better to have more means at your disposal. Although…' She thinks for a moment. 'There isn't enough time to teach you anything truly helpful before the event. There are plenty of easy recipes and spells I might teach you, but don't forget who you'd be fighting. It's nothing they haven't seen before. You might even find that your instincts are a better help.'

As if on cue, I trip and spot some dog shit on my shoe. When did that happen? People here are supposed to pick up after their dogs, but there's always someone who doesn't.

'Are you alright?' Bonnie asks as I straighten.

'Yeah, just fine.' I sigh. 'If people aren't prepared to pick up after their dogs, they shouldn't adopt any.' I sigh again. 'Sorry. I don't know why this annoys me so much.' I'm far from unflappable, but this wouldn't normally bug me. I did mean to wear these shoes into town later, but I have others. This isn't a big deal.

'It's not unusual to think you're okay after trauma when you're anything but,' Kate says. 'Have you given your emotions an outlet since that fateful dream?'

I drag my shoe over the grass to get at least some of the shit off. 'I cried loads during that time.' Sleep deprivation had something to do with that, but I was also genuinely terrified to fall asleep.

'I mean since then,' Kate says. 'If you bottle all your emotions up, they will come out sooner or later.'

'No, I'm fine. Really.' Aren't I? After we had the chat with the Mara and the Dreamcatcher, I just kinda moved on. I *thought* I was alright. It's over, so there's no point dwelling on it, right? But maybe Kate has a point. My being on edge these last few days hasn't come from nothing. Maybe there really is a small storm brewing inside me.

'I'm glad to hear it.' Kate doesn't look convinced, though. I'm no longer so sure myself. 'Shall we go into the forest so we can talk more freely?'

Bonnie nods, excited to see this forest for herself, but I just follow along, still on what Kate asked me. I've been doing shadow work around my feelings for Leverett, but maybe I should explore if I have any lingering anxiety from the nightmares. I haven't seen the Mara or the Dreamcatcher since then, but I didn't expect to. Their job here is done. It's not like we promised to stay in touch, and I'm not sure what we'd talk about if we had. *Hey there. Cause any great nightmares lately?* I'm not sure I'd want to know.

I follow Kate and Bonnie into the forest. I'll ask Kate to teach me some defensive magic anyway, even if it won't do any good for the event. Who knows when I might need it? But she also said my instincts might be more useful. What could I possibly—

Bonnie screams. It's a high-pitched sound that speaks of true panic. Before me, she's running around Kate and waving her arms at her leg. I don't see anything, but our dogs come running and my heart misses a painful beat.

'What's wrong?' She looks unhurt, but her scream said otherwise.

'Stupid wasp!'

Oh.

Not actual true panic then, but they certainly hurt enough

to justify her reaction. Ask four-year-old me who got stung in the knee and never quite recovered psychologically.

'Where did it get you?' I ask.

She takes a few deep breaths and points to her knee. 'I didn't even see the damned thing until it was too close. I wasn't threatening it or anything.'

'Let's get you home,' Kate says. 'I'll have a look if the stinger is still in there.' Bonnie pales. 'I can help the healing along, but I recommend rest for today and likely tomorrow depending on how much it's hurting.'

Bonnie gives me a watery look. 'I guess we won't be going dress shopping after all.'

I wave her off, but I'm not gonna lie to myself: I am a little disappointed. After everything that happened, I was looking forward to something so normal.

'We can still look online,' I offer. 'Wasp stings hurt like a bitch; you're not going anywhere today.'

Fortunately we're not too far away from home, so Bonnie doesn't have to hobble far. But I can't help noticing that's two things that have gone wrong today alone. In total, I've had the mug break on me, twice, and I'm falling over my own feet more often, I literally stepped in shit, and now Bonnie was stung by a wasp. Can all this still be coincidence? Because it's starting to feel like there's a little too much bad luck following me around.

And when we reach our doorstep and Kate excuses herself to grab something for Bonnie, I can't help wondering if I really have been cursed.

CHAPTER
EIGHT

'Mischief?'

'Esta?'

'Am I cursed?'

Mischief stretches, gives me a long, self-indulgent squint, and yawns. 'How would I know if you don't? I'm an extension of you, remember?'

'I know, but…' I'd hoped that my unconscious might have picked up on something the rest of me hasn't, even if it's just a niggle at the back of my mind. But I guess that's not the case. 'So there's nothing at all?'

Mischief yawns again. 'Nope. No blocks or anything. Although…' She sniffs the air like she can smell evil magic on the breeze. 'There is one thing.'

My whole shadow forest stills. The leaves stop rustling as my heart beats faster. If Mischief can detect anything, no matter how small, I can pass it on to Kate. Maybe I won't need to. Maybe I can address it right now.

'What is it?' I whisper as if I'm suddenly afraid of my own unconscious. I'm not. Haven't been for a long time.

Dreamcatcher aside, that is.

Mischief hops into my arms and nuzzles into my neck. 'Esta, I… I think you're in love with Leverett.'

I almost drop her. 'You're lucky I adore you.'

Mischief nuzzles her face into my neck, purrs, and jumps out of my arms again. 'Sorry. I can't stop teasing you if you don't stop teasing yourself.'

I sigh and slide down against a tree. I've been so preoccupied with the possibility of being cursed that I've barely noticed my shadow forest today, but I let the breeze pick up and stroke my skin. I've opted for an almost see-through dress. It flows beautifully in the breeze, like it's made of air currents. I've never found such a dress when awake, but in here I can do anything I want. Flowy air dress it is.

At least I'm not surrounded by half-naked Leveretts. Maybe being preoccupied with something else for a change is a good thing. Huh. Who knew?

'So there's really nothing?' I ask one more time. 'I don't care how small or faint it is.'

Mischief loafs next to me. 'There's really nothing, but I will keep my kitty senses on high alert for you.'

I don't want to correct her and say it's for us, but I can't help thinking it. Can't help remembering that the Dreamcatcher messed with her just fine until I took back control. I know that none of it was real, but who knows what a curse might do? If someone tried to scramble my mind, how would it affect Mischief? She can't really lie to me since she's part of me, but what if that's part of the curse? She could be cursed and not even know it. What do I—

Mischief paws at my leg. 'Esta.' She draws a claw along my knee, and I feel a thin trickle of blood drip towards my ankle.

'Sorry. I know you'd tell me.' There's no point dwelling on what-ifs. It's not healthy. 'Let's talk about something else.'

'Yes,' Mischief purrs. 'Let's talk about Leverett. You know you want to.'

I sigh again. I do and I don't. Although, this could be great practice. I'll have to act normal during the event, too. Maybe I should allow just one shirtless Leverett to join me under this tree… If I can keep my cool with him around, I can definitely pretend during the party.

Next to me, a warm hand takes mine. I make the mistake of looking over and end up with my face mere inches away from Leverett's very naked chest. I look up, and he smiles at me. I blush so severely that the grass and leaves around me turn red. For a moment, my shadow forest experiences its first autumn.

'Nope,' I say. 'Bad idea.'

I will him away and bury my head in my hands. I can only hope that the other Veiled at the party will be so lovely and welcoming—or that I'll be in so much danger—that I'll barely even notice Leverett.

That's probably impossible at this point.

'You should tell him how you feel,' Mischief says. 'He might still reject you, but at least you'll know.'

I groan and sink deeper into my hands. I know she's right. I know it's the grown-up thing to do.

But what if he does reject me and every visit to the bookstore is awkward after that? What if it ruins our still very new friendship, too?

I fight the temptation to summon Leverett again for the rest of the dream, if only to spend more time with him, but I meant what I told Mischief before:

I don't want him like this. I'll either have him for real or not at all. Even just having a conversation with him here feels wrong. The way he took my hand feels like a betrayal.

But Mischief didn't pick up on any bad magic on me, which means I've really just been unlucky. So, there's that.

'Are you ready?'

Bonnie has been pacing all morning. Sunitha will be over any minute now, and from the way Bonnie has tidied the whole house several times, she really likes this woman. Because of the wasp incident, we didn't get around to asking Kate about mermaid present ideas, but my sister made brownies last night, and I know she's about ready to fall to her hands and knees and beg for forgiveness. Not that she's even done anything yet—she overreacted and I won't argue it, but she hasn't told anyone that Sunitha is a mermaid. Well, except me. And no one would have believed her anyway.

'Sit down,' I say when Bonnie doesn't answer. 'You're making *me* nervous now.'

'Sorry.' Bonnie sits on our sofa where Lady is already lounging. She starts tapping her foot instead. 'I should have done more. I could have at least bought her some flowers.'

'Do you even know which ones she likes?'

Bonnie shakes her head too quickly. 'I should have asked her, shouldn't I? A good date would know. I should have—'

I squeeze myself between Bonnie and Lady and make her

look at me. 'You've been on *two* dates. If she expects you to know everything about her after so little time, that's her problem.'

Bonnie nods again, but her eyes have spaced out, like she's trying to remember every single word Sunitha has ever said to her on the off chance that she's mentioned her favourite flower once.

We hear a car pull up, followed by a car door falling shut. Bonnie flies over to the window.

'It's her!'

I hurry over to her and give her a quick hug. 'You need to calm down, Bonita.'

She pouts at me. 'You know I hate it when you call me that.'

I smile, because she's stopped pacing, at least for the moment. 'Shall I wait in here?'

She nods but the movement flows into a head shake, which flows back into another nod. 'Probably best if it's just me? Or I don't know, that might tell her you're not here. Open the door with me? You can always go, but at least Sunitha won't think it's just her and me.'

Bonnie jumps a little when Sunitha knocks.

'Come on.' I open the door before Bonnie can run and hide. 'Sunitha! It's lovely to meet you, come on in. I'm Esta, Bonnie's sister.'

She's a petite woman with warm brown skin and warm brown hair, but her smile is warmer still. If she has any lingering resentment over Bonnie fleeing the beach, I don't see it.

'Hello. Thank you for having me over.' Her timid voice has

a slight Indian accent.

Bonnie scoots in next to me. 'Hey.' She clears her throat; I make a mental note to tease her later about the most put-on, cool-sounding *hey* ever. 'Thank you for coming. I mean, come in.'

Sunitha wrinkles her nose a little when she steps over the threshold. Huh. I make a mental note of that, too, because our interior decor isn't why we're here. Her face relaxes back into her smile a second later, and she follows us into the living room.

Lady trots over. I'm about to ask her to take it easy, but Sunitha is already on her knees and fawning all over our dog.

'You must be Lady!'

Our puppy barks and hops up and down on her front legs. Her tail is going wild. I knew Bonnie liked Sunitha, obviously, but it's reassuring that she gets Lady's seal of approval, too.

I give Bonnie a glance that says *I like her*, and my sister blushes.

Not sure where to go from here, I ask, 'Can I make you a tea or get you anything else to drink?'

Sunitha gives me a shy look. 'A tea would be lovely, if it's not too much trouble?'

'Not at all.' Honestly, I'm glad to leave the room a moment and let Bonnie start this one.

That doesn't mean I don't try to listen in over the kettle, though. I don't hear much since I do need to make the teas, but I hear Bonnie apologising and Sunitha saying that it's okay. When I walk back in with the teas, though, I don't know how far she got. Has anyone said the m-word yet? Or the V-word?

'Here you go.' I give Sunitha her cup first, then Bonnie, and I go back for my own. 'I can come back later or just leave,' I say. 'It's not really my—'

'No, stay,' Bonnie says. 'I think this'll be easier with you here.'

Sunitha understandably looks somewhat confused.

'It will?' She raises an eyebrow, then what she probably thinks is realisation dawns on her. '*Oh.* Are you— I know you said you're sisters, but you're not actually related, right?'

It takes me a moment longer. 'No, we just grew up together.' Next to me, Bonnie looks just as confused, but then it dawns on me, too. 'Oh. *No.* No no no no no. We're not— That's not why she's asking me to stay.'

Sunitha smiles and cocks her head, like this was all just a ploy to get the conversation started. Crafty woman.

'You mean, she's not about to tell me you two are dating? Phew! That's a relief.'

I laugh, but Bonnie looks mortified under her nervous giggle.

'I think you'd better tell her why we're all gathered here today.' I can't help the wedding pun and burst out laughing again when Sunitha laughs, too.

Bonnie, on the other hand, awkwardly clears her throat. 'Oh, erm… When we went into the water…'

I want to help her so badly, but she needs to be able to talk to Sunitha if they're to have any chance of working out. Clear communication is key to any successful relationship.

Awesome. Now go talk to Leverett, a voice at the back of my mind says. I probably imagined Mischief's purr.

I give Bonnie an encouraging nudge. And here I was worried we'd accidentally out the Veiled. Turns out, Bonnie at least is perfectly tongue-tied.

Sunitha is starting to look worried herself now, so I nudge Bonnie again. *Just say it,* I will her.

Bonnie takes a deep breath. 'When we went into the water, I saw your scales and tail.'

Her voice trails off towards the end, but the important bit is out now, so I jump in.

'We know you're a mermaid. And Bonnie has been beside herself trying to figure out a good, personal gift to, erm, give you, to show you that your secret is safe with us, but she didn't want to get it wrong and we didn't know who to ask and—' My turn to take a deep breath. Bonnie may get tongue-tied, but I ramble when I'm nervous. I over-explain. No miracle the Dreamcatcher was completely focussed on me and not even a little bothered about her.

Sunitha pales. 'How do you—' She catches herself. 'I mean, I don't know what—'

'It's my fault. Probably,' I say. 'I unlocked something in my unconscious that lets me see through your magic. Bonnie didn't, but then she entered my dreams to help me talk down the Dreamcatcher and the Mara and—' I throw up my hands to make myself shut up. 'The point is, it was a whole thing, and now we can both see the Veiled.'

Yeah. My rambling is definitely the greater threat. So much for clear communication.

Sunitha sits back. 'Wait, that was you?'

'Huh? You heard about it?'

Sunitha gives a small nervous laugh. 'Yeah. I think the entire Veiled community has heard about it by now, though I've no idea how it spread. I thought it was a hoax, you know?' She blinks like she's really seeing us for the first time. 'That explains what I smelled when I entered.'

I remember her crinkled nose. 'You mean it wasn't the decor?'

I probably shouldn't have said that, but she laughs again.

'No. I think you have a lovely home. No, there was… something else. Something not human.'

Bonnie and I exchange a glance, and I nod. We've come this far now and Sunitha is one of the Veiled herself, so I deem it safe to say a little more.

'The Dreamcatcher and the Mara were in this room,' Bonnie says. 'There was a vampire, too.'

'And a witch,' I add, 'though she probably smells human to you.'

It does make me curious how Bonnie and I smell to her, if anything about our scent changed when we gained our super sight. I don't suppose I'll ever know; I'm a little sad about that.

Sunitha sniffs the air and shakes her head. 'No, it's not that.' She shrugs. 'Anyway, that's why you left?' she asks Bonnie.

My sister nods. 'I didn't— I should have reacted better. We want to help the Veiled, not—' She sighs. 'It was different when I met the others in person. I knew it was coming. Seeing your scales and tail… I had no idea. I'm really sorry I ran.'

Sunitha smiles. 'And here I thought you didn't like me in a bikini.'

I give Bonnie another nudge to say *I told you so.*

'No, that's not…' Bonnie blushes. 'I think you're beautiful.'

I clear my throat and get up. Sounds like it's time I excused myself. I have something to ask Kate, anyway:

Sunitha clearly smelled something in our house, but it's not the Dreamcatcher, the Mara, or Leverett? What the hell is it, then? She expected the smell of humans—whatever that is— so it's not me, my sister, or Kate. She expected Lady, too, so it's not her. A shiver runs over my arms and down my back.

If it's none of us… what is it?

CHAPTER NINE

I feel lighter as soon as I step outside, like a blanket has slipped off my shoulders. I guess I was more awkward with Sunitha in the living room than I thought. It's really Bonnie's conversation to have, so I'm more than happy to clear out. Maybe I'll go for a nice long walk once I've talked to Kate, just in case they get up to anything while I'm out.

I couldn't stop thinking about what Sunitha said when I was still at home, but now that I'm standing in front of Kate's door, I'm ninety-eight percent sure I overreacted. Of course she sensed something that isn't human. She said it's none of the Veiled we listed, but what makes me think she can be so sure? Sunitha is only… well, not human, obviously, but I'm sure mermaids are capable of making mistakes, too. Maybe she hasn't smelled many Dreamcatchers before and got it wrong. In fact, she probably hasn't. How many of them can there be? I shiver at the thought of a whole army's worth. Frankly, two would be too many.

But I'm here now, so I might as well ask Kate. I knock on the door and hear one of her dogs come to a scratchy standstill right behind it seconds later.

Kate opens the door with a smile when she sees me. 'Esta! To what do I owe the pleasure?'

I suddenly feel like I'm intruding. We've always chatted here and there, but lately, I feel like we're around each other all the time. She probably has better things to do than baby me.

'I can come back if this is a bad time,' I say, already taking a step back. 'It's not important. At least, I don't think so.'

'Then you wouldn't have found your way to me. Come in. I can spare a moment.'

I enter and take a look around. I haven't been inside her home before. We've always chatted in the garden or, lately, when walking our dogs together. It's cosy. There are pictures of Keano and Bruin all over the living room wall, and some dogs I don't recognise. It's like a memorial to all the dogs she's loved. The walls are painted a dark grey and the carpet is black, but it's not dark in here, at least not in any negative sense. It feels warm. Like an autumn evening. The window lets in plenty of light, but Kate has lit a few candles anyway. I smell lavender incense. Bushels of the dried plant hang over a fireplace, and I passed a hanging broom as I came in. I feel like the house itself is welcoming me.

'You have a beautiful home,' I say as I'm still looking around. A painting of the moon phases hangs over her sofa, and a small bookcase stands beside it. Huh. I kinda thought she'd have a whole library in here, but then I haven't seen the upstairs.

Bruin is asleep in a large dog bed in the corner. Keano is bouncing around me and begging for ear scratches. I'm happy to oblige, but Kate sits on her sofa and Keano sits next to her, like he's guarding her.

Kate nods to the space beside her. 'Please, join us and tell me what brought you here today.'

'Bonnie is at home right now talking to Sunitha.' I realise I don't remember if we told Kate about her. I definitely didn't mention that she's a mermaid, but I don't know if Bonnie said. I spaced out a little when we all went for our walk together, right up until Bonnie got stung by that wasp. 'They're dating,' I quickly add. It's up to Bonnie how much she wants to say. Really, it's up to Sunitha, but it's definitely not up to me. 'They had a… well, "fight" isn't really the right word, but they're talking it out. I thought I'd leave them to it.'

Kate cocks her head. 'And you came here?'

I guess I'll have to say a little more after all. 'Sunitha is one of the Veiled. When she entered our house, she smelled something not human, but she says it's none of the Veiled we've had over. I was wondering if you might know what it is.'

'Something not human, you say?' Kate thinks for a moment. Next to her, Keano whines until she pets his head. 'I didn't detect anything unusual when I've been in your house. Have you had anyone else over since the last time I was there?'

I shake my head. 'We generally don't have people over a lot.'

We're both way too anti-social for that.

'Don't forget that anyone coming to your door could be Veiled—your postmen, delivery drivers, the people sticking fliers through your door. Some of the Veiled have stronger…

how do I put it? Their energies are stronger. Usually it's older Veiled or those who embrace their magic more. Glamours can also affect it. Even younger Veiled can have a more potent aura, if you will, than their elders depending on what they are going through.'

I remember something Leverett said about younger vampires struggling more with their nature. Perhaps it's something like that.

'Sounds like it could be literally anyone leaving their scent on our doorstep.'

I shiver slightly. When I put it like that, it sounds like our house is marked. Only, who marked it, and why? From what Kate said, it's likely just a coincidence. A Veiled knocked on our door to deliver, I dunno, pizza, we accept it, and the Veiled leaves again with their scent automatically clinging to the doorbell. Nothing sinister about that.

I breathe a sigh of relief when Kate nods.

'I doubt anyone left their scent on purpose,' Kate says. 'These things happen naturally for many Veiled. Humans can't detect it, so there's no danger of anyone finding out that a werewolf, for example, frequents the area.'

I nod, more to myself than to her. 'Like cats spraying their favourite trees.'

Kate gives me a proud teacher smile. 'Exactly like that, except a little more incidental. Cats mark their territories on purpose, but I don't think this is the case here. Did Sunitha sense this inside your house or only as she entered?'

'Just when she first came in, I think. She did sniff when we asked about it, but she let it go.'

Kate nods. 'Then perhaps the sense of someone else was stronger at your door? It doesn't sound like she felt any danger.'

If Sunitha just let it go, it's probably fine. All this confirms that I overreacted. My gut is rarely wrong, and I haven't worried about it since I got to Kate's. If my gut says it's fine, Sunitha says it's fine—or just shrugs it off like it's nothing, anyway—and Kate says it's fine, chances are it actually is fine.

'Thank you,' I say. 'I was so focussed on it when I left the house, but I've felt better since I got here. I feel silly that I came over for this now.'

For a moment, Kate looks surprised, but then she smiles again and I feel better yet. 'Nonsense. I'm glad you feel you can come to me with any magickal concerns. I'm happy to have a look through your house if you like? Perhaps I'll pick up on something I missed before.'

'No, that's alright. As you said, the Veiled sometimes leave their scents by accident. If I find anything, I'll let you know.'

Now if I found a pile of bloody bones on my doorstep, that would worry me. But there hasn't been anything out of the ordinary except for all the Veiled in my life lately—and they've always been there, too, I just didn't know—so I get up from the sofa feeling reassured.

'Will I be able to sense the Veiled like that?'

Kate said other Veiled can sense each other like Sunitha did, but I didn't feel anything. Granted, I'm not Veiled, but since my super sight lets me see through their magic… I thought maybe I'd have this superpower, too. I'm disappointed and glad that I don't—disappointed because it would have been neat, and glad because my sight already invades their privacy too much as it is.

Kate stands with me and slowly walks me to the door. 'Perhaps? Right now, you have barely met anyone. Maybe, as your experiences with different Veiled grow, you'll begin to pick up on subtle signs.'

I'm in absolutely no rush. If this is something that may or may not come with experience, I'm happy to let it surprise me.

Stepping out of her comfy house feels a little like I'm leaving a safe cave, and now the whole world opens up before me. I go home, hoping I've left enough time for Bonnie and Sunitha to talk.

But as soon as I unlock the door and step inside, that heavy feeling is back, and I wish I'd asked Kate to search the house after all.

CHAPTER
TEN

I feel like a goddess in my dress. It arrived the day after I ordered it—I paid extra for next-day delivery because I didn't want to risk it not turning up in time. It's a gorgeous thing made of black lace and tiny glittering gemstones; I feel like I'm wearing the night itself when I put it on. It's too beautiful for me. I've no idea when or if I'll ever wear it again, but tonight, at least, I feel breathtaking.

I can't begin to imagine what Leverett will think when he sees me in this. Possibly nothing, but... Even I can admit I look gorgeous tonight, and I'm not one to care about looks.

I really hope I'm not the only one who dressed up. To be on the safe side, I didn't do anything special with my hair or make-up, so my hair is its usual messy bun—which looks oddly elegant with this dress, like this fabric will make anything look incredible—and my make-up is my usual foundation-and-eyeliner combo, the one I can throw on in roughly ten minutes before I need to go to work. Little effort.

No big deal.

But when there's a knock on the door and I know it's

Leverett, it feels like a bloody massive deal.

He explained to me that many vampires don't have cars since they can turn into fog and fly, so he's taking my and Bonnie's car to drive us to the party. The thought didn't even cross my mind until he brought it up. How long is this drive? How awkward will it be? Me, sitting all made up next to him as he drives, pretending this is normal. Just me going to a Veiled party with a vampire. Nothing to be nervous about.

I wish my racing heart got the memo.

Lady bounces around me with her tail wagging when I open the door. I have to hold her back so she doesn't throw herself at Leverett. What if he's wearing a fancy suit he can't get dirty? As far as I know, my dog's paws are clean, but with the way my luck has been going she'll drag a long smear of dirt down his legs, and then I'll owe him a small fortune in cleaning bills. So I wrestle with my dog with one hand while I open the door with my other.

And that's how I greet Leverett: awkwardly crouched over to keep my dog off him.

'Hello, Es—' I pretend his voice fails him because of how I look and not because he wasn't expecting my dog. But then he chuckles, and the illusion dies. 'And hello, Lady.'

My dog barks in greeting and, happy to have been acknowledged, waddles off into the living room, leaving me just a little bit breathless from the sudden change in energy and very unsure of what to say.

'*Now* she leaves.' It's not elegant, but it buys me precious seconds to get my head on straight. I clear my throat and straighten. 'Hey, Leverett.'

He didn't go to the same effort I did, but somehow he still looks fancier than I do. Must be his hundreds of years of experience shining through. He's dressed in all black—suit trousers, a casual shirt, and a jacket. It's a simple outfit without making me feel overdressed, and he looks incredibly sexy in it.

'Hello.' He smiles, and his eyes darken. I don't know what it means, but I'm getting ready to overanalyse the shit out of it. 'You look…'

I blush. Fiercely. 'This isn't too much, is it? I can still get changed if it's—'

'No, it's— You're—' His shoulders relax, and his smile settles. 'You look beautiful. Shall we?'

My everything does a somersault inside me. He's just being polite, I know, but what if he's not? What if he, a several-hundred-year-old vampire, thinks I'm beautiful? I know how that sounds. He's definitely just being nice.

'And you look handsome, as always,' I say as I pass him the keys. I'm quite proud that came out without a stutter, but I'm overanalysing this, too. What's he going to make of the 'as always' part? That was too much, wasn't it? I was going to say *dashing*, but that didn't feel right so I changed it to the first word that came to mind and now I feel like I went overboard. *Dashing* might have been a lighthearted compliment. *Handsome* feels too… personal. Romantic. Too much like I'm in love with him. Which I am, but—

He takes the keys and spares me further mental torture. Except I now have the car ride to look forward to. That'll go well, I'm sure.

'I've brought your cards, by the way,' he says as we walk to the car. 'They finally arrived yesterday. My apologies for the delay—there was a hold-up with the supplier.'

I smile at him. 'No harm done. Thank you.'

Even if tonight doesn't go well, I'll still have my deck to look forward to.

But first I need to survive this car ride.

'How long will it take to drive there?' I ask.

I hope he didn't already tell me. I don't want him to think that I'm not listening to him when in reality, I remember exactly everything and nothing he's ever said to me.

'About an hour.'

Oh gods. I should have prepared for this better, though I've no idea how. I just know I'm unprepared for being in a car with him for that long.

We both get in, and I'm racking my brain for things to talk about. The moment we sit down—him in the driver's seat and me next to him—my mind goes blank. This feels too personal, too. Or rather, it feels too private. Too familiar. Like we might share a car any day. Like we live together. Like we're—

'My friend got in touch with me this week,' Leverett says as he starts the car and pulls away from the kerb. 'He told me everything about this event, in case you were interested.'

Oh, bless his friend. Something to talk about. Score. Thank you, Mister… I don't know his name. This vampire invited me to his event of old friends, and I never even asked.

I nod, grateful to have something to talk about. 'I am. What's his name? I feel bad that I don't know.'

Leverett gives me a quick smile before he focusses on the road again. 'His full name is Anton Frederik Villum Thagaard, but he won't mind if you call him Anton. All his friends do.'

'But he doesn't even know me.'

'I told him a lot about you, so I think he feels like he does.' Leverett smiles again as he says it. What has he told Anton besides my encounters with the Mara and Dreamcatcher and what led to those?

I return the smile. 'Only good things, I hope?'

He doesn't answer, just smiles more. Damn. I don't know what to make of that—again. I guess I'll have to ask my new bestie Anton.

'So,' I say before we fall into awkward silence again, 'who will be there? Anyone important I should know about?'

I'd hate to step on the wrong toes. I doubt any presidents or big political people will be there, but what about huge business people? For all I know, all the big companies are run by the Veiled. For all I know, my boss is one. Now that would make work interesting—I haven't seen Eloise since I walked into the void lake, and my summer break had already started then. I won't know until I'm back at work, but that's a way off yet.

'Let's see… I've already told you about Anton. It's his event and we'll be on his property, so he's the most important person there. I mentioned his husband, Saif? He'll be around, though you may not see much of him. He's happy for Anton to host these occasional gatherings, but he doesn't love them himself.' Leverett hesitates. 'I should warn you that Chiara will be there. She's been around nearly as long as I and Anton have, and she isn't humanity's biggest supporter.'

My stomach drops a little, though really this was

unavoidable. I remember what he told me, that some Veiled see humanity as little more than cattle.

'How will I know her?' I ask.

'I'll introduce you if we run into her. Do you remember that I asked you to stay close to me?'

I nod. How could I possibly forget? I'll be damned if I leave his side all evening.

'Veiled like her are the reason for my request. Should we get separated for any reason, find Anton or Saif. They'll look after you and guide you back to me.'

I swallow but nod again. I'll be a clingy kitten all night, that's for sure. Except I mustn't let her—or any of them— intimidate me. So many of them are natural predators. Shit, maybe they all are. They'd smell my fear from a mile away, and I'm walking right into their midst. I know they're not mindless animals, but I won't pretend I'm not helpless before their vast amounts of varying powers.

Leverett grips the steering wheel for a second, then relaxes his grasp again.

'I'd have told you sooner,' he says, 'but I only found out shortly before I left. She was one of the first to arrive, so hopefully she'll be too preoccupied with old friends when we get there.'

My stomach twists uncomfortably. 'Were you...'

I don't know how to ask if they were ever a couple. Just the thought of someone else near him makes me angry, and yes, I'm very aware that I have no right to my jealousy. Besides, this could have been hundreds of years before I was ever born. I don't expect him to not have a past; I don't have a right to that, either. We're not together. I need to get over it.

Leverett hesitates a second too long, and my heart drops. 'No.'

I try not to let my relief show, and I hate myself for feeling relieved at all. I'm not a child—I expect he's had partners over the centuries. Probably many of them. That doesn't mean I want details.

'I sense a but,' I say.

'She once pursued me, viciously so. She didn't take my rejection well.'

'How come you weren't interested?'

It's none of my business, but I feel like regular friends would ask. Like it would seem weirder if I didn't show any interest.

'We've never seen eye to eye,' he says. 'I haven't always defended humanity, but we met after I started. As far as I know, she hasn't moved on from what some might call our glory days. If she separates us tonight, if she gets you alone… You'd be in danger, Esta. Don't let her trap you anywhere alone.'

I try to swallow again, but my throat has gone dry.

'What would she do?'

I don't really want details of this, either, but if the worst she'd do is have a go at me for existing, I'll relax.

Leverett hesitates again, and that says enough.

But then he elaborates.

'She wouldn't just kill you. Chiara is someone who plays with her prey. You would suffer before she ended it. And you'll be in more danger for arriving with me.'

Don't leave Leverett's side for anything—noted. I won't even use the loo while we're there. Honestly, I've always struggled to go in public anyway.

'How long ago did she try to… date you?'

I'm not sure it's the right word—do vampires date like humans do?—but it's not so far removed that he won't know what I mean.

'Two centuries ago.'

Damn. Vampires can hold a grudge.

'I haven't kept up with her, but the last I heard, she has never really moved on. She plays with her partners for a while, then discards them.'

The way he says it makes me think that *plays with* means *tortures*, and *discards* means *kills*. I shiver in the warm car. I *want* to meet all the Veiled and other humans at this party, but I'm not convinced I'm ready for this.

'And if we do get separated?' I ask. 'How do I find you?'

'If you can't find Anton or Saif, stay amongst people. There are many others who don't get along with her and will come to your aid, if only to spare you from having to talk to her.'

So, basically, don't be alone at all. For any reason.

No pressure.

'She can't turn invisible, can she?'

Leverett chuckles. 'I'm afraid that's one trick vampires haven't learned, although I suppose it's a good thing tonight.'

We continue to talk about the other Veiled, and he tells me not to consume any food or drink the fae try to give me, not to dance unless he invites me just in case the music is enchanted after all, and some other stuff I barely remember.

My mind is still on Chiara wanting to torture me to death for fun.

And when we drive through an open gate and up the longest driveway I've ever seen, I can't stop my legs from shaking. Relief takes over as we pull up and get out, though. Other guests arrive at the same time we do, so the parking lot is full of people sizing each other up, embracing old friends… or judging one another's outfits. I actually feel underdressed looking at some of them. Apparently no one does fashion like the Veiled.

There's a fairy—judging by her wings, anyway—who wears a dress seemingly made out of leaves and flowers that hug her delicate skin like they want to be there. Her hairdo is the same. It's all so elegant I start calling her Summer in my head. Then there's a couple dressed like actual royalty, minus the crowns; though I believe she's wearing a diadem? I think that's what the sparkly, possibly diamond thing nestled in her hair is. I don't know fashion, but I wish I knew the names for all those layers and ruffles. Veiled aside, I feel woefully out of my depth.

And then I see something that makes my heart stop for a second.

A human on a chain.

Her eyes are glazed, but there are definite puncture wounds on her neck and, I think, on her wrist. I assume the man holding her chain like a leash is a vampire. Despite her glazed eyes, she stands straight and looks at him like he's her entire world. I suppose he is while he holds her in his thrall.

A warm hand lands on my shoulder, and I realise I've been shivering in the mid-July heat.

'Are you ready?' Leverett asks.

I nod. 'Ready as I'll ever be.'

'If you want to leave at any point, tell me. We can go home anytime.'

His words warm me anew, and I feel safer. It sounds like we live together.

I nod again. 'And stay by your side all night. I can do that.'

He smiles at me, and I feel better. This may be unbelievably far out of my comfort zone, but Leverett knows some of these people. He's done this before, and he's one of the Veiled himself. I literally couldn't be in better hands tonight.

I blush at the thought of his hands all over me. His hand *is* still on my shoulder, so that's a start.

'Anton and Saif know that you're with me, but if anyone asks, tell them I drink from you or that we're a couple. Other Veiled will respect those boundaries more than friendship. You'll be safer.'

Can I go all night introducing myself as Leverett's girlfriend and not stumble over every syllable? Seems unlikely.

'Won't they know you don't drink from me?' I instinctively touch my neck. That other vampire clearly isn't trying to hide his bite marks on the chained human. Would it be odd to tell people that we covered them with make-up? I don't know enough to improvise.

'You can give one of two reasons everyone here will accept: You can either say that I heal your puncture wounds, or...' His smile turns into a teasing grin. 'Or you can say that they aren't anywhere visible to them. Up to you where.'

Oh.

Oh.

My mind goes blank for a moment. Now there's an image I didn't need tonight. Of Leverett's head between my legs, biting me too close to my now-too-sensitive clit. I can't say this to anyone here even once. I just can't.

But then again, who knows what situation I'll find myself in? If it saves my life, maybe I can say anything. I guess I'll learn the hard way.

'Okay,' is my lame answer. He must hear my heartbeat and know how much his words have affected me. Is he toying with me, or is this still good-natured teasing between friends? Friends can do this without it meaning anything. Can't they? But friends would have laughed, probably teased back. If I do that now, it'll be far too late to be believable. So, really, there's zero point to playing it cool.

I clear my throat and try to save whatever is happening. 'How would you heal it?'

Now that he's put the image in my head, it's really hard to not picture him between my legs. I really hope he can't smell what it's doing to me, or that he at least has the decency to never bring it up. Ever.

'Saliva.'

I blink. 'What?' If I don't snap out of it, everyone will think he's put his vampire magic on me after all. I should just have nodded and moved on, but it's too late for that now.

'A vampire's saliva has wondrous healing properties. Vampires often lick their bite marks after drinking from their human lovers to help them heal.'

Well, that doesn't help. The last thing I need to add to this delightful mental image is his tongue on my skin.

It's probably for the best if I stop asking questions. I can't fault him for answering honestly; I'm the one who keeps digging herself a deeper hole.

'Alright,' I say. 'I'll just tell them I'm here with you.'

Which is very true and shouldn't lead to anything embarrassing.

Leverett smiles and offers me his arm. I comply because it would be more awkward not to and hook my arm through his.

'Then let's find Anton and introduce you.'

CHAPTER ELEVEN

I feel privileged as I walk towards the house through the gardens beside Leverett. Anton must have a whole team of gardeners on the job—I suppose with a property this size, he needs to. Even the fastest vampire could probably get it all done, but why would they *want* to? Constantly? My and Bonnie's garden is tiny, certainly by comparison, and we can't be arsed to keep up with the weeding. If we could afford a gardener, we would totally hire one.

There are a few shrubs carefully trimmed to look like gargoyles, which is a nice touch, and the lawn was recently cut back because there isn't one blade of grass out of place, but there aren't that many flowers. Just a few bushes here and there, some roses and some... I'm not sure. Like fashion, flora isn't my strong point. Their petals are more intricate than your regular round-ish shapes, though, and the yellows and reds are vibrant, like they've soaked up every single ray of sunshine that's ever kissed them. The whites are almost paradoxically bright, like snow under the summer sun. I barely recognise the herbs Kate has told me about, and I don't see any sage or peppermint. I do see some rather large lavender bushes, though, and smaller patches of what might be rosemary. The bees must love this place.

And, of course, the house itself is massive. I know there are bigger, but to me, this is a palace. How many bedrooms does this place have? Four? Five? More than ten? How many bedrooms does a mansion need? I don't remember if Leverett said if Anton and Saif have a family. For all I know, they do have children but they moved out several hundred years ago. If I had that many spare bedrooms, I'd definitely turn at least one into a library. It'd be a crime not to. Maybe knock down the wall between two bedrooms and turn them into an even bigger library.

A girl can dream.

'What do you think?' Leverett asks with a chuckle. 'You look awestruck.'

'I think this is the biggest place I'll ever visit.' There's a zoo near me that has a mansion on the grounds. This manor reminds me of that, so I can always go there and relive tonight that way—or pretend to, anyway, in a pale comparison of tonight. 'Please tell me there's a library in there and Anton would let me use it?'

Leverett is about to answer when someone else swoops in, clasping Leverett's arm with one hand and giving me a huge grin.

'I most certainly would! Leverett, my old friend, it's good to see you again. And you must be Esta.'

I find myself grinning, too. It's hard not to—Anton's energy is infectious. And he did just say he'd let me use his library.

Leverett clasps Anton's arm in return. 'My friend, it hasn't been that long this time. May I properly introduce you to Esta?'

Anton winks at me and holds out his hand. 'It's a pleasure,' he says even before I take it.

He's not what I expected. He looks younger than Leverett, but didn't Leverett say they're roughly the same age? Or maybe I'm remembering it wrong. It's more likely, though, that Anton drinks blood regularly, while Leverett doesn't. Leverett did say it's slowly kil—

But I don't want to dwell on that. Not when tonight is supposed to be fun.

Anton's light blond hair seems to have trapped some of the sunlight. His blue eyes should be cold but actually make me feel welcome. The sparkle in them puts me at ease. It could be vampire magic, but I don't think that's it. I think it's the combination of his sparkling eyes and the bright blue velvet suit he's wearing. On the off chance that I get separated from Leverett, I'm pretty sure I'll be able to find Anton. The man would stand out anywhere.

'It's nice to meet you,' I say. 'Leverett has told me a lot about you.'

'Not as interesting as what he has told me about you, I'm sure. Come in. Make yourselves at home. I have more guests to greet but will find you both when I can get away.'

And with that, Anton hurries away to greet the next guest.

'He's usually a little more reserved,' Leverett says, 'but he comes alive during his social gatherings. No one adores a catch-up with old friends quite like Anton.'

'He seems nice,' I say. 'I don't see myself getting lost while he's here.'

Anton has walked almost all the way back to the gate—it hasn't been enough time, so I imagine he's flown some of the way—but I can still clearly see him. His guests fade into the background around him. His energy and his suit are like a beacon everyone else gravitates towards.

Leverett laughs. 'He has that effect on people. He's a gifted storyteller, too. I'm sure you'll find that out before long.' Leverett nods towards the house. 'Shall we?'

Reluctantly, I extract myself from his arm. I need to keep some distance between us or I'll never learn how to be just his friend.

There's a coldness where his arm rested against mine.

'Show me around the gardens?' I ask.

Leverett's soft smile sends a tremor through me. 'With pleasure.'

The front doors are wide open. I figure we'll walk through the house, but Leverett leads me around the lefthand side. I'd call this a wrap-around porch, except those are made of wood, aren't they? This is made of concrete, or... some other hard, stony material. Architecture is *also* not my thing. I can appreciate it just fine, I just don't know any of the terms. I can point to the roof on any house, but I've no idea what the difference is between a gable roof and a mansard roof or what they look like. I just remember the terms from something, but not even the source stuck with me. This house has three stories, brick walls, and, as far as I can tell, a regular-ass roof in that terracotta shade every other house in my neighbourhood has. I noticed three chimneys poking out, so there are at least as many fireplaces inside. All the windows are tall and provide a good view at the pompo— *lavish* furnishings inside. Anton and Saif don't do anything by halves, that's for sure. Anyway, details aside, it's a very impressive house.

The gardens opening up before us are breathtaking—I don't need to know technical terms to see that. Paths snake through them, surrounded by flowers, trees, shrubs—all that pretty stuff I don't know the names for. There's a gazebo in the far-right corner and a fountain in the centre. To the left is a small maze with another gazebo in the middle. I picture myself reading there.

'Just how rich is Anton?' I ask.

'He's had a long time to amass his fortune,' Leverett says. 'Saif has also done rather well for himself. I expect you'll meet him when I show you the library.'

We walk down some steps at the back of the house and into the gardens. I've been so distracted by this ridiculous splendour that I didn't even look at the Veiled. Despite what Leverett told me, this feels more like a regular social gathering, at least at first glance. Small groups of people stand together, chatting and laughing like the old friends I expect they all are. I occasionally smell the roses and other sweet fragrances, which I'm not convinced come solely from the flowers around us—it seems stronger around some of the fairies. Are they enhancing the natural scents just by being here? Some of them give me curious looks in passing, but no one looks maliciously towards me. Most of them smile and nod in greeting.

But everything changes when I look closer. Some of these

guests look… tired. Their eyes glazed, their bodies slightly slumped. I spot bite marks on wrists and necks. There aren't many of them, but enough that they make my skin crawl. I want to ask why Anton is okay with this, but I don't know his own preferences, and saying it in front of all these Veiled seems dumb.

'Where are we going?' I ask.

Leverett hasn't approached anyone, and we're still walking down the path.

'I saw you looking at the gazebo at the back of the garden. I thought you might like to see it.'

I beam at him. 'I'd love to!'

We turn a corner, and my eyes widen. I know the two fairies in front of me. One of them turns to look at me as if she felt my eyes on her—probably did; I was staring for a second there—and we just kinda stare at each other in surprise for a moment. Then she smiles and interrupts her partner, who is talking to someone. She nods to me, and I have the same moment with the second fairy.

The couple from the park. The ones who want to get their kids a dog next year.

And here I wondered if I'd ever be able to tell them. I guess they know now. They don't look annoyed with me, though—I think we're all mutually surprised. They excuse themselves and walk over to us.

Leverett gives me a curious look. 'Friends of yours?'

I smile at him, slightly nervous. I hope they won't be angry that I didn't tell them. 'More like casual acquaintances. I've seen them around the park outside my house.'

Leverett straightens as if he senses danger. 'Do you think they're watching you?'

I place my hand on his arm to show him it's okay.

'No, not at all. They—' They reach us. 'Hey!' I almost say *I didn't expect to see you here*, which is true but feels too movie-cliché. 'Erm, I'm Esta. From the park.'

Right. That's way better.

'Hello, Esta from the park,' the lady with the pretty red hair says. 'We didn't realise you were one of us.'

'I'm not, I…'

I don't know how to introduce myself with my power. It hasn't really come up before now, but at this event? Of course I'll have to tell sooner or later.

'She's my plus one,' Leverett says. 'I'm Leverett, a vampire. Esta is human.'

The other fairy—a pretty brown lady with sparkling golden eyes—whistles. 'Now this is unexpected! I'm Poppy, by the way. This is Sorcha, my wife.'

It feels so odd to be introduced as *human*, but I'd better get used to it. I doubt it'll be the last time tonight.

'It's nice to meet you properly, sort of,' I say.

'I expect we'll talk more later,' Sorcha says. She has a lovely, thick Irish accent. 'We have a few more things to discuss with our friend, but let's catch up later?' She glances at my neck. Looking for bite marks? 'We'll look forward to getting to know you more, Esta from the park.' She winks, and they walk back to their friend together.

'That was awkward,' I say to Leverett. 'It feels really weird to be introduced as "the human."'

Leverett chuckles. I want to sink against him for support. I felt alright when we first entered the garden, blissfully distracted by all the pretty, but now I've actually talked to someone—and someone I sort of know, no less—I feel less steady.

'You get used to it. After a century or so, you barely hear yourself telling other Veiled that you're a vampire.'

I give him a look that says *I don't have that kind of time* but don't make an issue of it. His point is that it took him a while, too. I have nothing to worry about. While some Veiled have come embracing their natures—I have to duck more than one pair of wings as Leverett leads me through the garden—others are harder to determine. As far as they're concerned, I could be human… or a werewolf, or a vampire, or something else entirely. I'm wondering if some are keeping their glamours up because it's easier than taking them down and then remembering to put them back up again.

We take five steps before Leverett pauses again.

'Watch out,' he whispers in my ear.

I want to ask what for when a woman steps out in front of us. Her eyes light up when she sees Leverett, but the moment she sees me, with my hand still on his arm, her pretty face turns into an ugly sneer. That must be his stalker. I instinctively start to remove my hand from his arm, but Leverett places his hand over mine and keeps it there. I don't care that he's making the point that he's still not interested in dating her. He can hold my hand for whatever reason he wants; it's his.

I put on my best fake smile and straighten right along with

him. He wants to make a point, and I will help him make it.

Her eyes turn to acid, but then she looks at him and it all melts away. There's no way he didn't see it, though.

'Leverett! How lovely to see you. It has been such a long time.'

Her Italian accent is like honey, except it's too thick and laced with razorblades.

'Has it truly?' he says with a smile. 'I barely noticed.'

I suppress a giggle. That had to hurt. Personally, I'm delighted.

'May I introduce you to Esta Anderson? She is my date.'

My heart flutters. I hold on to him a little tighter. He'll feel the difference, but I don't care. I can always just claim that it took me off guard, which it did. Didn't he say that I'll be a lot safer if people know I'm here with him? If this is what it takes to convince her that she shouldn't rip my throat out, I can pretend to be his girlfriend all evening.

Although, I haven't liked that term for a while, and it seems even weirder for a vampire as old as him. We're not fourteen. There needs to be a grown-up version less vague than *partner* and less serious than *married*.

Not that it matters. She doesn't look at me again.

'How have you been, Lev?' She almost purrs the nickname. I glare daggers at her.

'I've been very well,' he says. 'I've opened a bookshop, and Esta has been with me almost every day since. She's been very open-minded.'

He gives me a wink that could mean anything from 'she's accepted me being a vampire' to 'I've tied her to the bed and blindfolded her every night.'

Two can play this game—or three, I guess.

So, I lean against him and give him the most loved-up smile I can muster. It's not hard.

'I'm so glad we met,' I say. 'There's no one else I would rather spend all my time with.'

I hope she reads the same ambiguity into my words. It seems to be working—she turns to me and would probably spit pure venom into my eyes if she could. Thank fuck that's something vampires can't do or I'm not sure Leverett could protect me.

Leverett puts on a pretty believable loving gaze and pulls me closer.

'Esta, meet Chiara. I'm not sure I've mentioned her?'

I make a big show out of trying to think. He did mention her in the car, but he needs her to think that he forgot all about her, so…

'No, I don't think you have.' I give her my kindest fake smile. 'It's so nice to meet you.'

People who hate you hate the kindness you show them even more. I may be writhing internally to get away from her, but I show her that she doesn't bother me.

'Likewise,' she purrs. 'It's always lovely to meet another of Leverett's temporary playthings. I've known him for many years, and it never gets old. Of course, none of them are alive now, are they?' She gives me a pitying look. 'You poor things. Humans live such short lives. It must be strange to think that Lev and I will still be here long after you're dead.'

'Not at all.' My voice shakes slightly, though.

Confrontations like this are not my natural habitat. 'As a poor human, I'm rather aware I don't have centuries. Is it strange to have so long and yet still only catch up once every few decades?'

I wanted to say something clever and conversation-ending about how she may have all the time but he still isn't spending his with her and me being dead won't change that, but I couldn't think of the words. I never can in the heat of the moment. I think she gets the point, though, because her face grows still as fire blazes in her eyes.

'You are nothing, silly human.'

Leverett tightens his grip on me. I let myself feel every inch where his arm touches me.

'She is *mine*, Chiara,' Leverett growls. I forget how to breathe. 'You will not hurt her. If you can't remember your manners, don't come near her.'

She takes a step back like he slapped her. 'You would choose her over me?' It almost doesn't sound like a question, but her eyes are off me and on Leverett again. I feel like I can breathe more easily again... except for what he just said. Nothing we told her before this was a lie, we just embellished the truths a little by being vague. But what he said just now... If I wasn't flushed before, my whole body is now hot enough to melt.

Leverett relaxes and smiles at me. 'Let's find Anton. He must be done greeting guests by now.'

I completely ignore Chiara when I smile at him and say, 'Yes, let's.'

I'm also more than happy to get away from Chiara, who is

glaring poisoned daggers into my back, neck, and gut. She said all that to get to me. I know that. But it did hurt, even while I know that it shouldn't. Was any of that true? Leverett said she toys with humans by torturing them and killing them slowly. But from what she said… No, he hasn't hurt anyone. He wouldn't do those things. He told me he didn't, and he definitely doesn't now. Unless…

How would I know? My feelings for him could be fabricated. Even the meeting with Chiara could be staged. They could be lovers who destroy their oblivious prey together.

But then Leverett pulls me into him as we walk away from her, and all doubts disappear. I won't let her get to me.

'Are you alright?' he asks.

I nod. 'She seems nice.'

Leverett chuckles and eases away from me a little. I wish he'd stay. I liked his arm around me, and my head is still on how he growled '*She is mine.*' I will never not hear that in those quiet everyday moments.

'You handled her well,' he says. 'I'm afraid she doesn't understand a clear no, which is part of the reason why I stay away from her. Vampires are proud creatures, though. She will hate it, but she will respect that you're here with me, especially now she thinks we're together.' He gives me an apologetic smile. 'Sorry about that. She wouldn't have accepted anything less.'

It didn't look to me like she'll accept anything other than my violent death, but Leverett knows vampires a whole lot better than I do. If he says she'll respect this, albeit very begrudgingly, then I believe him.

'That's alright,' I say. 'I don't mind.'

My voice comes out a little too soft.

Leverett leads me into the mansion. It's a greeting hall, of sorts. A wrap-around staircase leads to the first floor, and the wooden double doors to the left and right are open. There are so many people around that I don't get a good glimpse into either room. I do, however, get a good look at the large painting by the staircase. It's of Anton and a man I assume to be Saif. It looks like a Renaissance painting, and for all I know, that's when it was created.

We hear Anton call Leverett's name before we see him. One glance up the stairs, and I don't know how I missed him in his bright blue suit.

He beckons us up to him. 'Come, my friends! Let us talk in private.'

CHAPTER TWELVE

Anton leads us into a… well, I don't know what to call it. It's a large room with sofas, a few bookcases, a fancy rug, and a fireplace. I guess it's a sitting room? I wonder what it's like to have so many spare rooms that one is just for sitting and talking to guests. But I suppose if Anton and Saif don't have children, they need to do *some*thing with this space.

I feel like we're in a meeting as we sit opposite Anton, who chooses a plush-looking arm chair for himself. I've no idea what this furniture is made of, but it's *soft*. Are velvet sofas a thing? Or satin sofas? It's excessive, luxury for the sake of luxury, but of course a vampire who's been around as long as Anton can afford it just because. The only time I've ever treated myself like that was when I bought a fancy camera… okay, and every time I see a book I want, but even then I still try to restrain myself.

Anton opens his arms wide and grins at us. 'Leverett, my old friend. It's so good to have this chance to catch up.'

Leverett chuckles. 'You know you can come see me anytime.'

Anton waves him off. 'And come see you at work, when you're busy? Much nicer to chat when it's just us, wouldn't you say?' He turns to me, and his smile turns welcoming. 'Esta. Welcome to my humble abode.' He laughs to himself. 'It's a touch more than we need, it's true, but why not spoil yourself a little when you can.'

I don't know what to say to that since I've never quite been in this situation and doubt I ever will be. Fortunately, Anton doesn't wait for an answer.

'Leverett tells me you're the one everybody is talking about. The Dreamer.'

I startle. 'What?'

'It's what the Veiled have started to call you,' Anton says. 'Most of us don't know your name. We just know that the Dreamcatcher and the Mara had a, shall we say, run-in with you, and decided to give you the benefit of the doubt. Some have taken to calling you the Prophesied One, but I much prefer the Dreamer.' He laughs to himself again. 'Either is much shorter and to the point than the-human-who-fought-the-Dreamcatcher-and-the-Mara-and-won, wouldn't you say?'

I nod slowly, a little taken aback. I've never had a title before. It feels weird, like too much responsibility has been placed on me. Although, I suppose all they expect me to do is dream. That's not so bad. But dream of what? The lucid dreams I usually have, or a better tomorrow? I don't see how my regular dreams would be interesting to anyone, least of all benefit them, so…

'No pressure,' I mumble.

Anton winks at me. 'The Veiled are watching, Esta

Anderson. We're excited to see what you'll do next.'

I shiver when his words echo the Mara's.

'You're not worried I'll accidentally doom us all?'

I regret the words as soon as they're out. It sounds too casual, not really fitting the war they are terrified of. But Anton shrugs and winks again.

'Oh, there's always something that might do that. Take it from me—I've lived a long time. We've done rather well hiding our tracks, wouldn't you say? Every hundred years or so there's a human who somehow stumbles upon us and tries to expose us, but no one ever takes them seriously.' He does a fake huff and rolls his eyes. 'Vampires, during the day? Sure. Do tell.'

That does make me feel a little better. Less like I'll start a war by saying the wrong thing at the wrong time.

'Does the Dreamcatcher always deal with it?' I remember him saying that I wasn't the first, but I didn't ask how often this has happened.

'Oh, my dear, I couldn't say. I'm sure he does a lot of the time, but your circumstances were special, weren't they? You lucid dream whenever you wish. You were already on his turf. Most of the time the human makes a ruckus one day and vanishes the next, never to be heard from again. Whoever wants *you* silenced is thorough.'

'So you don't know, either?' Leverett asks.

'Who's behind this, you mean?' Anton asks. Leverett nods. 'Afraid not, my dears. I'd tell you if I could.' He looks at me. 'Most of the Veiled have been around a very long time. So many years where grudges could fester and it wouldn't help anyone. We just stay out of each other's business, see?'

'Like Chiara?' Again, the name is out before I can stop myself, but Anton laughs and Leverett does that chuckle I love so much.

'I like her,' Anton says to Leverett.

It's weird how much I want his approval, but this is the most casual I've been around the Veiled. It feels like we might be friends even, or become friends, anyway. I've been so worried about accidentally outing a Veiled, about angering or upsetting someone, that Anton's easy acceptance is a blessing. I want Leverett to say that he likes me, too, but he doesn't. I suppose that was hoping for a little much.

'Do you have any idea why Esta might be different?' Leverett asks instead.

I give him a questioning look while Anton cocks his head in thought.

'Different?' I ask.

'As Anton said, humans who find out about us aren't usually much of a problem. No one believes them, and they're taken care of silently. But the Dreamcatcher feared that you would start a war, and it took some effort to convince him and the Mara to let you live. You seem to be more of a threat.'

'I'm afraid I don't have answers, old friend,' Anton says. 'I wish I could help. Naturally, you're both welcome to browse my library for anything that might help.'

'I would love to,' I say, maybe a little too quickly.

'Perhaps it's that curiosity your silent assassin is worried about,' Anton says. He winks yet again, but it looks forced and the playful tone in his voice is gone. 'If you won't stop looking into us, befriending us, who knows what you'll uncover? Perhaps whoever is after you is worried you'll find them, specifically.'

'No one has come after Esta since the Dreamcatcher,' Leverett says. 'I had rather hoped that they'd given up.'

'You should know better than that, old friend. We Veiled have time. We don't need to rush from one plan into the next. What's a year to this person, hm? It's only been around two weeks, hasn't it?'

'The Dreamcatcher and the Mara mentioned that she's female,' I say. I definitely remember them referring to this silent assassin as 'she' and 'her.'

'That doesn't narrow it down all that much, I'm afraid.' Anton stares out the window as he sinks into thought. 'I wonder...' He catches himself, blinks, and then his smile is back. 'Never mind me. You seemed interested in my library. Would you like to see it?'

My heart jumps. 'If that's okay?'

Anton stands and waves me along. 'Absolutely. I only ask that you don't disturb Saif, if he's in there. My poor husband has been engrossed in his research lately.'

I'm a little sad that I won't get to meet him, but the plethora of books will make up for that.

Leverett and I follow Anton down the corridor to a surprisingly boring door on the right. I expected ornate double doors for his private collection, but it's a door like all the others—plain and made out of a light wood.

Anton opens it and herds us inside. 'I've lost count of how many books we have, but feel free to browse as much as you like.'

This is something out of a dream. The room is huge, and the bookshelves reach the ceiling. They're stuffed so full I can't help marvelling at the sheer number of tomes. My head is buzzing at the amount of knowledge. No sign of Saif, though. Maybe next time.

'Leverett, old friend, do you mind if I borrow you for a moment?' Anton asks.

Leverett hesitates. 'I'd rather not leave Esta alone.'

'Do your fine senses detect any danger up here?' Anton asks. 'The party is happening outside and downstairs. No one knows she's here. She'll be perfectly hidden as long as she stays away from the balcony.'

'I'll be fine,' I say. 'There's no one here, right?'

I can't wait to read these spines, take in the topics and smell a book or two. I'm very curious about this balcony, too, but I'll heed Anton's advice and not go near it. I don't need to, anyway—I won't exactly get bored in here.

Leverett gives me a worried look but nods. 'We won't be far. If anything at all makes you feel unsafe, call me. I will hear you.'

'We'll be right next door,' Anton says. 'The room to the left of this one. Please, feel free to interrupt us if you as much as get a bad feeling.'

I nod. I was nervous about being left alone when we were still in the car and when we were outside, but I'm a lot calmer now. Nothing bad has happened, and I always feel safer in libraries. Besides, as Anton said, no one even knows we're up here. Sure, someone might have seen us walk upstairs—there *were* people around—but they had no reason to pay any attention to us. I'm a big girl. I can wait on my own for ten minutes.

Anton and Leverett leave me to it, and I have a look around the shelves. If Anton has a classification system, I don't see it, except perhaps a loose organisation by subject. Everything on this shelf and the two next to it seems to be about history. The few books in my gallery's library use the Dewey system, but as far as I can tell, there's nothing on these books that would tell Anton where to shelf them. Maybe he doesn't need it, and I don't suppose it matters. It's his and Saif's private collection after all. There's no need to send panicking students with looming deadlines to the right shelf.

I spy the balcony from the corner of my eye. Its double doors are wide open, and a lazy breeze dances into the room. This is all I need to be happy—wind and books. And time to myself to go through them all. I hope Anton meant it when he said I could come back, because there are too many for just one evening. I expect I won't even have that—as soon as Anton is done discussing whatever he has to share with Leverett, we'll likely go back outside.

So, I decide to make the most out of my time in here.

I wish Anton had at least some kind of hint as to what's on every shelf. How does he find anything in here? He didn't know how many books are in here, but I bet it's several thousand at least. I browse the spines and find heavy tomes on history, an encyclopaedia on the Veiled—I take it off the shelf so I can leaf through it—and...

Huh. A book on scrying techniques.

It's not the thickest book here. Not that I know how many scrying techniques there are, and it wasn't like I was specifically looking for a book on it. Kate mentioned clouds, flames, and mirrors, and I kinda can't think what else there might be. Crystal balls are probably similar to mirrors, so that's not likely to count as its own thing. Or would it? I look at the table of contents first and realise that Kate has been holding out on me. There are so many ways to scry, and most of them never even crossed my mind. Of course, I didn't know cloud scrying was a thing until Kate told me about it, either. I open the book on a random page:

Star scrying.

I have visions of myself and Leverett lying under the stars, enjoying each other's company and seeing the future written in a constellation. I leaf back to the book's introduction and read that scrying isn't about telling the future but about listening to your higher self, spirit guide, unconscious—whatever you want to call it. So there goes that idea. Didn't Kate say something similar about tarot, too?

I go back to the pages on star scrying. It's about observing the night sky. It's about seeing patterns and shapes in the invisible lines between the stars, in the dark void in between. Not like constellations, though—the book specifically states that they are their own thing.

It's a shame I live in an area with so much light pollution. I bet Anton doesn't have to worry about that out here. To me, all this feels massive. All Anton needs to do to see the night sky better is turn off the lights. If I do that and our neighbours keep theirs on, it doesn't make a difference. Maybe I can convince Leverett to take me into the countryside one night, just so I can try this? But I don't have a good enough reason to ask him. Kate's the one who's teaching me Magick 101. It makes more sense to ask her.

I make a note of the book's title on my phone and put it back before I forget where it lived. There's nothing specific I'm looking for in the encyclopaedia, so I'm aimlessly browsing the pages. It's much older than the one I bought. If there's anything in here about who's after me… But it would take forever to find anything useful. I'd need to read every single entry to be sure, and this book is *big*. Over two thousand pages. Unless Anton lets me borrow it, I've no chance in hell of finding the info I want. And it sounded like Anton was already looking into it for us, anyway. He knows where everything is in here—at least I assume he does—so if he didn't find anything… what hope do I have, with all these untitled shelves?

Something rustles behind me.

I turn around. 'Back already?'

But it's not Leverett or Anton. It's Chiara.

And I'm all alone with her.

She gives me a predatory smile. 'Miss me?'

My heart jolts, but I do my best to put a dismissive frown on my face. 'I thought you were someone else.'

I want to ignore her and get back to the book, but something tells me that turning my back on her would be a terrible idea. She won't hurt me, though. Leverett said vampires respect each others'… what, friends at best? Property at worst. Either way, I can only hope that she respects the same rules like he said she does.

The smile leaves her eyes first. Her lips thin soon after. 'Don't pretend I'm not here, human. You think you're so special, don't you?' She takes slow steps towards me. I can't help feeling like a cornered animal. 'Look at you in your pretty dress, with your back straight like you belong with us. But you're a *human*, silly girl. You're nothing more than a temporary toy. You'll die, and he'll forget all about you long before that. Unless…'

Her nails lengthen and sharpen slightly. I try not to gulp. I won't show her that she is, in fact, bloody terrifying.

Leverett said to shout for him, but that would only prove her point that I am nothing. Maybe it's petty of me, but I refuse to let her think she's won anything.

I stand, straighten my back, push out my chest and square my shoulders, and look her straight in the eyes when I say, 'What do you want? Jealous that Leverett is here with a silly little human rather than with you? Because I don't think he likes you.'

Her eyes turn murderous. 'Do you have any idea how easily I could kill you?'

My legs are shaking, but I will them to steady. 'Uh-huh. I'm not strong or fast, certainly not compared to you. You could kill me in any number of ways. But you won't, because your scent is in this room now. If Leverett finds my body and smells you near it, he will hunt you down.'

I don't actually know that he would. It's clear that he doesn't get along with her, but he has known her for a very long time. And she's right: humans die. Our lifespans are nothing next to a vampire, a fairy, or most of the Veiled, in fact. And I really am weak and slow. I give her a sad smile, because I realise all the reasons why Leverett would never be with me. What could I possibly give him?

'He would have to find you first,' Chiara hisses. 'I could cut you up and hide every piece in another room—in another corner of this country, even. I could throw you over the balcony. I could—'

'Hit a nerve, did I? You sure are arguing a lot for someone who's so superior to me. Did you just come here to show off or did you want something?'

I realise I've gone too far when she grows the nails on both her hands into claws. I don't even have time to breathe in once before she throws me onto the table and presses a sharp nail to my neck.

'Not everyone here is delighted to see you, you disgusting waste of flesh. I can mask my scent better than you can imagine.' I want to struggle against her, roll out from under her grip, but I'm not in a position to move. Her nails are a little too stab-happy at my throat. 'If I don't want Leverett to know it was me, he won't even know I was in this house. You—'

'That's quite enough, Chiara,' someone I can't see says. 'We don't tolerate violence against our guests, and this human *is* a guest. Get away from her before I throw you out.'

I don't know the voice. Chiara snarls and gets up. She pulls me after her before shoving me back against the table and disappearing off the balcony in a cloud of fog.

I awkwardly come up onto my elbows. 'Thank you, erm…'

The man before me, half-glaring at the spot where Chiara

disappeared, is easily the most casually dressed person at this party, because he's wearing what might actually be black pyjama trousers which disappear to the knees under a warm-looking grey fleece. I guess the July heat doesn't mean much to a vampire. He doesn't look like he's sweating but like he was incredibly comfy until Chiara interrupted him.

'Saif. And you are Esta Anderson.'

His style is so different to Anton's that I want to see them side by side. Anton's pale skin, light blond hair, and blue suit would be a stark contrast to Saif's dark skin, black hair, and loungewear.

Saif gives me a warm smile that I happily return—he likely did just save my life, after all.

'I am.' I remember what Anton said about Saif researching in the library, and my heart drops. 'I wasn't interrupting you, was I? Anton said I could come in, and I didn't see anyone, so I thought—'

His chuckle is so much calmer than Leverett's—no less full of joy, just more relaxed. Like he has all the time in the world, which I suppose he does. Like he knows exactly that neither I nor Chiara could threaten him. It makes me wonder what makes a vampire powerful. Is it something that comes with age? Experience? Neither Chiara nor Saif look like they've been in any fights, but how would I tell? Vampires heal so quickly. Chiara would probably be too worried about breaking a nail. Saif seems too relaxed to start anything, but that doesn't mean he can't defend himself. Do vampires need to train in, I don't know, martial arts? Wherever his confidence comes from, I doubt it's misplaced.

'I was taking a short break,' Saif says. 'When I came back, Chiara was already here. I'm glad I didn't have a second drink after all, or I would have been too late.'

It's starting to sink in that she might actually have killed me. Sure, I put on a brave face, but now that she's gone the reality of what just happened washes over me. If Saif hadn't arrived when he did...

And there's nothing I could have done about it.

'Thank you,' I say again, less stunned and more honestly this time. Or maybe I'm *more* stunned? I don't know. I don't often have to face my own mortality like this. Or I never had to before I stepped into that void lakc, anyway.

Saif nods. 'What do you think of our library, Esta Anderson?'

I can't tell if he's trying to wind me up.

'Just Esta.' I feel like I'm asking him to drop some fancy honorary title. 'It's... big. How do you find anything in here?'

He smiles patiently. 'After a century or two, you know what's where. Anton and I have added every single book to this collection ourselves. It may not look like it, but we have a system.'

'May I ask what you're researching?' It's none of my business, but my mind lingers on Chiara. What if she sniffs me out? What if she follows me? Next time, I won't have Saif there to step in. Next time, she might find me, Bonnie, and Lady.

Gods help her if she hurts my sister or my dog.

Saif thinks for a second. 'You, to be blunt. Leverett asked Anton and me to look into your very curious circumstances about a week ago.'

I blush. It feels weird knowing they've been looking into me without me knowing; they haven't really been researching *me*, have they? They've been trying to figure out who's after me. Anton said something along those lines earlier, that he doesn't have any answers. What is he discussing with Leverett? If it's about me, shouldn't I be there? Unless they've found something so horrific or so dangerous that they deem it safer if I don't know, but that's probably pushing it. I just can't get myself to believe that anything so powerful would come after *me*. Chiara is right about one thing: I am nothing, at least in the grand scheme of things.

'Find anything juicy?' I ask.

Saif motions at the chairs, and I sit. He joins me. 'Nothing new, I'm afraid. Just repetitions of the recurring hope—or prophecy, if you will—and the fears of our ultimate end.'

I shiver. 'What prophecy?'

Saif cocks his head slightly. 'You really don't know?'

'I know that the Dreamcatcher and the Mara were sent after me to stop me from exposing the Veiled.'

Saif nods. 'That is part of it, but it's also more complicated. As you've seen for yourself tonight, many Veiled live with humans just fine—malicious vampires notwithstanding.' He winks at me, and I feel better. That's all Chiara is—a spoiled brat. A very powerful spoiled brat compared to meek little me, but still just a child annoyed that she didn't get the cookie she wanted. 'Some Veiled keep lifelong friendships with humans—that's one human lifetime, of course. Others even marry. It's rarer, but not unheard of. You're not the first human to know of us, which makes the attempt on your sanity all the more fascinating.' I frown, and he adds, 'No disrespect intended.'

'None taken.' Well, maybe a little. 'Is that what Anton is discussing with Leverett?'

'I believe they may be discussing ways to protect you, but even I can't be sure. It seems to be a new plan. Anton hasn't told me more.' My heart warms a little at that. Still, I feel I should have been included. 'Don't begrudge them their privacy,' Anton adds. 'We Veiled have many terms and customs that are much easier and faster to discuss with other Veiled. It would slow things down considerably if they had to explain every other phrase to you. I believe they will fill you in if they come up with a viable strategy.'

I nod, but I'm unsure how to feel. I get what he's saying, that they'll make more progress faster without me there, but I still wish they'd at least told me. Unless they worry that me knowing might put me in more danger? If that's the case, they didn't tell Saif to keep the secret. I know now, though it's not like I know details. So maybe this isn't enough to put me in more immediate danger.

I see a bright flash of vibrant blue from the corner of my eye. I turn just in time to see Anton enter the room with Leverett right behind him.

'We most certainly will,' Anton says. 'Alas, this is a tricky case. We don't have as many details as we'd like. That makes things harder.' His face softens into a smile. 'We don't mean to worry you. With Leverett watching over you, you're in excellent hands.'

I blush again. I love every part of that sentence except for the real implications.

'I need to be able to look after myself. There must be something I can do.'

Anton sniffs the air. His forehead wrinkles at the same time as Leverett's eyes darken.

'She's gone,' Saif says. 'I chased her off.'

Leverett is next to me in a heartbeat. 'Did she hurt you?'

I shake my head. 'She just needed to shout at me a little, tell me how much she hates me.'

Saif raises an eyebrow but doesn't correct me. Everyone in this room knows how spiteful Chiara is. I don't even have a scratch. As far as I've seen, she's all bark and no bite.

'There are a few simple self-defence moves I can show you that will work against vampires,' Leverett says. 'That's what Anton and I talked about—whether to share our weak points with you.'

Anton nods. 'We don't mean to mislead you, but I'm sure you understand the delicacy of this discussion.'

I nod, too, because I do understand. They talked about whether they can trust me with how to hurt, maybe even kill, one of their own.

'And what have you decided?' I ask. I want to know how I can protect myself against Chiara or any other vampire who might come after me in the future, but I'll also understand if they won't tell me. This is a big secret I don't imagine many humans know.

'I trust you,' Leverett says, 'and Anton trusts me. Neither of us trusts Chiara.'

'Least of all with a human's life,' Anton says. He claps—a loud, dramatic move and sound, like he's making a point more than anything. 'Well, Saif and I will excuse ourselves. This is something Leverett can show you just fine without us here.' Saif doesn't move at first but jumps to his feet and practically flies to Anton's side when he gives Saif a look.

'Yes,' Saif says. 'Please excuse us. No doubt Anton has things to share with me?' He sounds as confused as I feel. Anton ushers him out of the room, gives me a final wave, and then I'm alone with Leverett.

'That was weird,' I say.

Leverett chuckles. 'You've made a good first impression on Anton, and I imagine on Saif as well. We're sorry we kept the nature of our chat from you.'

I shake my head. Part of me wants to be angry, but they're all trying to help me. As neat as it would be if I could simply defend myself against any Veiled, that's not the case. I imagine a simple kick to the kneecaps won't do.

'I'm glad I don't have to do this alone,' I say. Bonnie and Kate are helping me, too, but they're as human as I am. Kate has more knowledge than both of us combined, true, but that doesn't change the fact that she's human. I doubt the Veiled have left clues about how to kill or maim them lying around, so unless any of them have told Kate, she wouldn't know. And if any of them did tell Kate, she's not exactly at liberty to tell me. The betrayal would be unthinkably huge.

Leverett smiles at me and nods to the balcony. 'After you?'

I swear I can feel my eyes sparkling. I've been wanting to check it out ever since I heard it exists. 'I thought it was too risky?'

'On your own, yes. But I'm here now. I'll be with you.'

I couldn't refuse him even if I wanted to.

I give him a sideways smile I hope looks cute and beautiful in equal measures when I walk past him onto the balcony. My face burns when I step outside—I can't believe I just did that. Since when do I have it in me to outright flirt with Leverett?

I briefly close my eyes and inhale when I step through the doors. I've a feeling I'll be grateful for the fresh air before twenty minutes are over.

I feel like some high-born lady as I overlook the gardens from the balcony, one hand on the railing and eyes roaming over the guests. It'd be easy to pretend they're my loyal subjects and I'm their queen, but only because I've read it in so many novels and seen it in so many movies. That's exactly how this feels—like a scene from a film.

Especially when Leverett steps out behind me and stands next to me. My king in all things.

And he has no idea.

Or he does and is gracious enough to not bring it up. If I think about it—and I'd prefer not to—there's no way he doesn't know. He must. There's no way in all hells that his vampiric hearing misses my heartbeat, the slight ways my voice changes, how my breath hitches whenever we accidentally touch. And yes, I must smell different at times, too. I *really* don't want to think about that. He does things to me. I can't help how my treacherous bastard of a body reacts.

'I'm sorry about Chiara,' he says, looking over the gardens.

I shake my head. 'Don't be. You're not responsible for her.'

His shoulders relax. Like my words have lifted a heavy weight off him, though I don't understand why it would have been there in the first place. He didn't invite her. She is her own person, and a grown-up. Nothing she's done or said to me tonight was his fault.

'Are you enjoying the evening otherwise?' He looks at me and smiles. 'Everything you hoped it would be?'

I beam back at him. 'Yes. And more. I can't believe the fairies from my park are here.' I've already forgotten their names. That'll be awkward next time I see them.

Leverett chuckles, and I resist the urge to melt against him. He's just the right height that my head would comfortably snuggle under his chin.

'Anton is a social man, as you can see. He knows people from all over the country, and other countries besides. I've told you that he arranges several events just like this one throughout the year, but I don't think he ever invites everyone he knows.'

Bloody hell. 'I don't know even a tenth as many people.'

'Vampires have a long time to make acquaintances and friends.'

It reminds me of something Saif said. Before tonight, I wouldn't have brought it up, but the encounter with Chiara seems to have made me braver—first my flirty smile and now this.

I hope it sounds more like passing curiosity.

'I'm surprised vampires bother with humans at all. Or any of the fae. I mean, I'm surprised vampires and the fae bother with humans.'

Well, that could have gone smoother.

Leverett leans forwards onto the railing on his forearms. 'Because of your short life spans?'

I nod. 'In part. To you it must feel like you've barely got to know us, and then poof—we're gone again.'

He hesitates for a moment. I brace myself for the indirect rejection.

'It's true that some centuries feel like they've passed in seconds. Not all Veiled are long-lived, though. Werewolves are more likely to reach a hundred, but I don't know of any who've lived beyond 120. That was an outlier. Humans are much the same, aren't they?'

I want to argue that no human I've ever met has lived to 120, but I have seen news articles every now and again of someone living to over one hundred. It's extremely rare, but it happens. Sounds like the werewolf living as long was an exception, too, likely due to diet and exercise just as it would be for a human.

'Yes,' I whisper into the breeze. 'I suppose we are.' I let my eyes wander over all the guests below. How much am I missing? How many Veiled are down there who are indistinguishable from humans at first glance? 'Fairies can fly and have their own magic. Mermaids can breathe and live underwater. You do the turning-into-fog thing, and you could coerce me to say or do anything you want.' Now that it's out I worry it sounds suggestive, but I don't think it does. I'm just thinking aloud here. 'What are humans good at when compared to all of you? War?'

I knew Chiara's words got to me in the library, but it's

starting to sink in how much they hurt. There's absolutely nothing a human like me could ever hope to offer Leverett. What can I possibly do? Die in a mere fifty years or so to save him the discomfort of breaking up with me?

'It's true that, on the whole, humans have a tendency towards conflict,' Leverett says, 'but I think you can give yourself more credit than that.'

I raise an eyebrow at him. 'Oh?'

'As you're well aware, the Veiled fear another war with humanity. It's true that, while both sides picked at each other for a while, you humans were the aggressors last time, and everything points to you being the aggressors in the future, too. But you've never shown me anything but kindness.' Leverett smiles at me. 'You're an outlier, too.' He nods towards the guests below. 'All of them are. You're proof that humans can accept the Veiled without problems. It gives us hope even as we fear being more open with you.'

I don't know what to say to that. This feels like a big conversation that I haven't prepared for. The breeze strokes around my neck, and I let it soothe me. I don't need to overthink this. I just need to be honest, as I've always been with him.

I gather all my courage and say, 'Accepting you wasn't exactly hard.'

His smile grows and—dare I hope?—has a flirty edge to it. If not that, there's a softness in his eyes that's begging me to stay.

Or maybe I'm imagining the begging part, but either way, I'm not going anywhere. Perhaps that's what it means to love someone who doesn't return your feelings—you're there for them anyway. Even though it hurts.

'Is that so?' he says with that handsome smile.

'Yes. You made it easy.'

'And you really don't see how rare that is?'

I blink. 'What do you mean?'

'Do you remember what I told you about the time I lived under a graveyard?'

I do remember, though he didn't share many details at the time. Even so, he said enough. I know it was a hard time to be different, to be anything other than human.

I nod.

'That wasn't the only time I, or any Veiled, had to hide. Only a few years ago I made a human friend. I thought we got on well, and I decided to take the risk. He seemed open-minded, but it turned out that I misjudged him. Complete open-mindedness is easier in theory, it seems.' For a second, Leverett stares into the distance as he remembers something he doesn't share. 'It didn't end well. While I hated the necessity, I made him forget that he ever knew me after I made him tell me his plans.' His face turns pained. 'He wanted to set my home on fire while I slept.'

I swallow but resist the urge to hug him. Leverett doesn't want pity. He wants me to understand his position, and frankly, pity won't change what happened.

'Well,' I say, partially to buy time while I fumble for words, 'if it helps, I like your bookshop way too much to burn it down.'

Leverett laughs. It's such an infectious sound, so

unexpected after what he just told me, that I laugh, too.

'I've told you a lot about myself that I haven't shared with a human in a long time. But you've accepted everything I've given you. Nothing has put you off.' His face clouds over again. 'Although, I haven't told you everything. If I did... maybe you would change your opinion of me after all.'

'Never,' I say before I can help it. 'There's nothing you can say to me that would make me leave.'

'Really?' He turns to me, and his eyes darken. 'What if I told you about all the humans I've killed only a few short centuries ago?' He closes the distance between us, his face so close to mine I don't know where to look. 'What if I told you that I want to bite you, drink enough of you that I never forget how you taste?'

Erm.

I don't—

How do I—

I want to lean against the railing so I have something to hold me up, but I refuse to budge from him. He's trying to prove something, and so am I.

'That was centuries ago,' I stammer. 'I don't know who you were then, but I know who you are now. You're a good man, Leverett. The best man I've ever known.' My voice is a little steadier by the end, but I flail for words again when I address his second point. 'And I guess if you... if you wanted... I would...' I clear my throat. 'I trust you.'

His lips are on mine before I can rationalise what's happening. I melt against him with my sigh on his lips. I let out a whimper in surprise, relief, lust, shock.

Just as I'm about to surrender into him and put my arms around him, Leverett pulls away slightly. His nose still brushes against mine. His eyes are shut, like he's still savouring the moment. My own eyes are too heavy to keep open, but I needed to see the look on his face when he moved away. I needed to know if there's any regret on it.

'I didn't read this incorrectly, did I?' he murmurs against me. It's almost enough to make me lose my sanity.

I slowly shake my head. 'No,' I whisper.

'Good.'

Leverett puts one arm around me and cups my face with his other hand in the same moment that he brings his lips to mine. I throw my arms around him in complete surrender. I can't think, and I don't want to. He is soft, he is warm, and I can't get close enough to him. I need to feel as much of him pressed against me as I can, need to burn it all into memory so I never forget how his lips feel against mine, how his breath feels in my lungs, how his fangs feel when my tongue scrapes against them. How his low moan sounds when it comes. How it sets me on fire and promises to melt me.

He urges me back against the wall, and I throw my legs up around his waist. His length hardens against me. A low gasp escapes me when his fangs scrape along my neck. I will him to bite me, because I can't get the words out.

I'm barely aware of the library doors flying open, but Leverett slows. He doesn't move away from me, though.

'Esta, my dear, how are you fee—' Anton freezes when he spots us. '*Oh.* My apologies. Pretend I was never even here.'

He shuts the door behind him.

My eyes slowly move to Leverett's. He chuckles and, to my disappointment, sets me down.

'Perhaps we shouldn't rush this.' But his eyes are still dark as he says it. I'm about to say that I don't mind, but he adds, 'If we do, we may have an audience.'

My eyes fly to the garden. No one is looking up, but we're not exactly hidden. I *need* him, in every sense of the word, but maybe I don't want to make it a public event.

Leverett kisses me softly and whispers against my lips, 'I want you all to myself.'

Another whimper escapes me. I've no idea what to say to that, so I kiss him again. He closes his arms around me and pulls me to him. My legs are shaking—all of me is shaking, actually—but I could stay here, in his arms, forever.

'Come to mine in a few days,' he says. I feel his chest rumble with every word and treasure being close enough to feel it. 'If you still want me then, I promise you will have my undivided attention.'

I want to object, tell him I don't need time to decide, but I see his point. Everything somewhat escalated tonight. I know how I feel, but I can hardly blame him for giving me time to think it over. As far as he knows, I might just be high on adrenaline after Chiara's threat.

And as I sink more against him, a small, petty part of me hopes that she saw the whole thing.

I tilt my head back to smile at him. 'I'll be there.'

He brings his nose to mine. 'Think carefully about this, Esta. Once we give ourselves to each other, you won't get rid of me. Consider if you're ready to have an utterly devoted vampire partner.'

I nearly whimper again but swallow it. Everything he just said will follow me forever. My core aches for him, but I make myself nod and step away slightly. He needs to be sure that I am sure, and I can give him that peace of mind. Frankly, I'll do anything he wants—a bit of thinking isn't the most he can ask of me. Maybe a cold shower will help that. And who knows? Maybe he'll be the one to change his mind; although, after everything he just said, I wouldn't know how to begin to recover. Does he have any idea just how hard I've fallen for him?

I smile. 'Alright. I will.' Maybe I'll talk it through with Bonnie and Lady, but I know it won't change anything for me. I may as well think it through, though, because I'll be replaying every single word he said to me tonight anyway. Again. And again.

Because I'm so stupidly and utterly besotted with this man.

CHAPTER
THIRTEEN

I know the blue flashing lights are outside our house before Leverett even turns the corner onto our road. Just a gut feeling. We park behind a police car. My throat goes dry. There's no ambulance or anything like that, so I hope that Bonnie is okay. Against the blue light from the police car, the warm living room light looks wrong. I as good as fall out of the car and race to the door. Behind me, Leverett shuts the door and hurries after me. Our door is unlocked, and I brace myself.

Bonnie sits on the sofa with Lady by her feet, eyes flying between Bonnie and the police officer standing before her. When I enter, Lady gets to her paws and struggles to decide whether to stay with Bonnie or run to me. She whines in protest at the hard decision but stays with my sister. Bonnie's eyes are red and puffy, her arms around herself. The police officer gives me a kind smile, though, so I'm guessing no one died? I scold myself. I'll feel terrible if I'm wrong and joked about it.

'You must be Esta,' the officer says. Her voice is warm and

doesn't betray even a hint of disaster, but something must have happened or she wouldn't be in our house.

'Yes.' I sit next to Bonnie and put an arm around her. 'What's wrong?'

Bonnie looks at me with quivering lips. She opens her mouth to talk, but whatever she wants to say dies in her throat.

'There was a break-in,' the officer says. 'Nothing big seems to have gone missing, just a necklace. Bonnie tells me it's of great personal value.'

My stomach dips. She can't mean—

'My grandma's necklace,' Bonnie chokes out. 'It's gone.'

I tighten my hold on her and gently rock her as she cries into me. I want to ask if anything else was taken, but fortunately I know how insensitive that would sound before I open my mouth. If there was anything else, the officer will tell me.

'We will do what we can to track the thief,' the officer says, 'but this person left very few clues. The locks don't look tampered with, and the windows are whole. Frankly, if it weren't for Bonnie's testimony that something was stolen, we'd be struggling to find any evidence.' The officer looks at Bonnie. 'And you're *sure* you didn't just misplace it?' She looks at me. 'Did you borrow it and just forgot to mention it?'

I frown—like I wouldn't tell her—but it's my sister who snaps, 'Yes, I'm sure! I told you before, this necklace means a lot to me. I don't just lose something like that.'

I get the officer is just doing her job, but I'm with Bonnie on this one: there's no way she just forgot where she put her grandma's heirloom necklace.

My stomach sinks further. It doesn't sound like they'll be able to get it back. I'm gutted for Bonnie. Her grandma's death still feels recent, and the necklace was the only thing she cared to keep. And now it's gone. I squeeze Bonnie again.

'Do what you need to,' I say to the police officer, though I'm sure she already thought of that. 'If there's anything else we can tell you, we'll be happy to help.'

She nods. 'May I ask where you were tonight?'

I'm all too aware of Leverett in the room and wonder what he's making of all this. Would he be able to find the thief? The human—I'm assuming—officer didn't find any clues, but maybe his vampire senses could pick up on something subtle they missed.

'I attended a social event with my—' My face burns. What exactly are we to each other now? I decide to play it safe and hope he won't be offended. 'With my friend. He drove. We just got back.'

The officer nods again. 'I will leave you for now, but if we have a lead or find the stolen item, we will be in touch. Likewise, if you find that anything else was taken, please let us know.' She hands me a card. 'My contact details, and the case number. If you call and ask for me or cite this number, you'll be put through.'

The officer sees herself out, and goosebumps race up my arms and back. What are the odds of something like this happening the one night I'm not home? Bonnie prefers quiet nights in with me, too. This was one of the few nights a year where just one of us was home.

I kiss her hair, rub her shoulder, and extract myself to speak with Leverett. I feel bad that I left him as soon as we arrived, but my sister needed me.

'This isn't the end to our evening I was expecting,' I say with a sad smile. Just the thought that some criminal was in our house makes my skin crawl. This is a safe neighbourhood. Sure, you hear things about drug deals or someone being attacked, but those things are rare. Like, once-in-a-year rare, if that. And it's never on our end of the road.

Leverett smiles at me, but there's an uncertain edge to it. 'I'll search the house and the perimeter, if you don't mind. There's a strange smell in here.'

I go cold. Sunitha said something like that, too.

'Any chance it was the officer?'

She could be a werewolf, or some other Veiled I can't identify just by looking. What do I know? Maybe she farted or ate a big curry before coming here. But I can tell by the tone in Leverett's voice that it's nothing so mundane.

He shakes his head. 'No, she's human.' He moves closer and whispers, 'If it were just you, I would ask you to stay with me tonight. Will you two be alright? I can stay if you like.'

As much as I want to take him up on that, I don't want to stress Bonnie out more. What she needs now is a bit of normality. I hate that some asshole stole her grandma's heirloom necklace, but none of the locks were broken. No money or bank cards were taken. My sister is safe and unharmed and never even saw the thief. It could have been worse.

And that's one of the many things about this that doesn't add up. It feels more like someone just wanted to scare us, but who and why? Is it possible that we discussed the Veiled too loudly one day and someone got scared? But then, wouldn't they have left some indication that this is related?

I inwardly sigh. I need sleep. If I'm missing something obvious, hopefully I'll see it in the morning.

'While I really want to accept,' I say, 'I think we'll be fine. Thank you, though.'

Leverett nods. 'I'll search the area just in case. Give me a moment.'

He turns into fog and disappears. I sink back down next to Bonnie.

'They'll find your necklace,' I say, though I have zero business promising that. I just want to give her hope, make her feel better.

She nods, but it lacks energy. 'I shouldn't have gone out tonight. Maybe someone was just waiting for us both to leave.'

I back away a little so I can look at her properly. 'Where were you off to?'

Despite everything, her cheeks colour a little. 'Sunny asked me out for drinks. I told her you had your thing, so she invited me out, too. We could only stay for a few hours because she needs to be up early tomorrow, but yeah.' She gives me a tired smirk. 'I went on a date, too.'

I silence the voice that's wondering if Sunitha is behind this. It seems like an awfully big coincidence, but I won't even entertain the idea. Bonnie is happy dating her. I won't ruin it by accusing her girlfriend of breaking and entering and theft.

Although, Sunitha could have known about the necklace and decided it's worth something. Sunitha knew I'd be out tonight, and apparently she couldn't stay long. Just long enough for this theft to happen? They went out for drinks, but could she have passed our address and the necklace's location to an associate? Bonnie would have no reason to suspect her.

I hate that my head even went there.

So instead, I smile at Bonnie. 'Sunny, huh?'

Some light finds its way back into her eyes. 'Yeah. I guess that means it's going well, hm?'

I snuggle against her, relieved that I found something to cheer her up. 'Good,' I say. 'I like her. You two are sweet together.'

She blushes deeper and gives me a look. 'I couldn't help noticing that Leverett came in with you. Invited him in for "coffee", did you?'

I'm about to sputter a confused mess between a heavy objection and a confession of everything we said and did tonight, but just in this moment, Leverett appears by the fireplace.

He has the nerve to wink at me. 'We saw the police car and were worried. Or are you offering to leave us alone for tonight?'

I'm not sure who blushes harder—me or Bonnie. I'm the first to regain any semblance of coherent thought.

'Find anything?'

He chuckles, probably at my attempt to stay calm when my face says otherwise.

'Unfortunately, no. The smell is strongest inside the house, but that's normal. The breeze could have blown away whatever it was hours ago.'

Bonnie gives him a look. 'Unfortunately? You were *hoping* to find proof of a break-in?'

'Weren't you?' he counters. 'If I had, we'd have a lead. I could have followed it and found who's responsible. Instead, we still don't know anything.'

I think again how suspicious Sunitha's behaviour seems to me, but I won't say it in front of Bonnie. Or maybe that's worse, I don't know. The best thing to do would be to move on, but my mind is in that in-between place where it's tired from the evening while also running wild from the same evening. Since I can't throw myself at Leverett and the police car was an unexpected break to the excitement, all my tired, nervous energy doesn't know what to do.

I peel myself away from Bonnie. 'Thank you for having a look.' I walk over to Leverett and resist the need to kiss him again. He asked me to take a moment to think this through. Kissing him right now would probably go against that promise. 'Erm… I'll come by on Wednesday?'

His eyes darken again. Is he struggling to control himself as much as I am? Slowly, he nods. 'Wednesday.'

Hormone-driven creature that I am, I instinctively lean forwards. I can't help it, I literally gravitate towards him like he's constantly drawing me to his side.

But before I can get much closer, he disappears in a huff of fog, and then he's gone.

Behind me, Bonnie clears her throat. '*Ahem*. Excuse me! What was that?'

I turn around with every intention to look and act normal, but my grin betrays me. 'What was what?'

'You two undressing each other with those heavy looks. He wasn't kidding when he said about me leaving you two alone, was he?'

I sit back down with her and tell her everything, from the two fairies to Anton and Saif, to our kiss. And our promise. I don't mention Chiara; I'm very ready to put that behind me and never think about her again.

When I'm done, Bonnie's eyes are huge and her hands cover her mouth.

'Esta! You might have led with that!'

I giggle. 'Didn't seem right to bring it up in front of the officer. How about your date with *Sunny*? Did you… ?'

She slaps my arm. '*No*. I mean, I think she wanted to, I definitely did, but she also said how tired she was. So no, we haven't kissed.' She gives my arm another playful nudge. 'You totally got there first.'

I laugh. It feels good to see her eyes sparkle again, to talk like everything is fine and we weren't just robbed.

'I didn't know we were competing!'

Bonnie nods to the TV. 'Stay up with me a minute? I don't know, I feel weird going to bed right now. I don't think I can sleep.'

I'm pretty tired since any kind of social event always wears me out, but I know what she means. When I picture myself going to bed, I can't help remembering that someone was in our house. What if they come back while we're sleeping, moving through the rooms with us completely unaware? What if someone sneaks through our bedrooms while we're asleep? The thought creeps me out, so I happily stay up with Bonnie even as my eyes grow heavier. We eventually doze off together on the sofa. Going to bed is a little easier after that, partially because it's starting to get light outside. Bad things don't happen during daylight, as we all know.

I don't know what Bonnie thinks of as she falls asleep—her date with Sunny, her missing necklace, or her internship starting tomorrow—but my thoughts are on Leverett. I can't believe we kissed. I can't believe what we made plans for. That I ever thought I could just be friends with him seems so stupid and naïve now. What I feel for him is much too strong—much too violent, in an exciting way—and I've no idea how I could ever pretend otherwise.

And as I climb into my bed with the memory of his lips on mine, my biggest worry is how badly Mischief will tease me.

CHAPTER FOURTEEN

As Bonnie starts her internship and I'm supposed to study as Kate asked, I try my everything to take my mind off Leverett. I tried to think about it like I promised, but I'm worried I might want him too badly to think clearly. I can't think of anything that would make me like him less, or anything he's said or done that might be a deal-breaker for me. I've never felt this seen or safe with someone. I know I can be unapologetically myself with him. And the way he kissed me… If I felt his lips just that once and never again… Is it possible to be addicted to another person? Every time I close my eyes, I see his face. I keep thinking his name. Just about every rational thought is chased away by him—his smile, the way his arms felt around me, the things he promised. Try as I might, I keep wondering how his arms will feel when we're both naked, how his hands will feel, where else his lips might roam. I am utterly and completely obsessed with him.

Part of me feels stupid, like I'm a teenage girl with her first crush. Some of my logic seems to have survived, though, because I remind myself that this is what early relationships are like. Everything's exciting, and I can't stop thinking about him. Totally normal. It's just that it's been a while since anyone made me feel like this, and— Okay, fine. No one's ever made me feel quite like this. I've been in love before and I've been in relationships before, but I've never lost my mind to someone like I have to Leverett. At this rate, I worry I'll pass out the moment he slides a hand between my legs and inside me. Seems like something I'd do. Just the thought alone is almost too much. How am I supposed to cope with the real thing?

I try to blink the thought away and take a deep breath. Then another. I'm lying on my bed with my pretty new tarot cards, but it's annoyingly hard to focus on them. Kate told me to go through the deck one card at a time, and that's what I'm trying to do. Some I immediately get a feel for, like The Star and The Lovers—it seems impossible not to understand the latter— but others I struggle with, like Temperance. I'm also surprised by how beautiful Death is. I always thought of it as a negative card, but the one in this deck is full of hope instead. It's like a comforting satin blanket that tells me that every end is a new beginning, too. I've stared at it for two minutes now, taking in every detail, and I think I may be a little in love with it. It's one of my favourite cards in the whole deck, which I haven't even seen half of.

That's my brief reprieve from thinking about Leverett. The closer I get to Wednesday, the harder it becomes.

I blush fiercely when a teasing voice in my head wonders if he's getting harder the closer we get, too.

My phone buzzes, and I jump hard enough for the cards to

shift on my duvet. For a second, I worry it's Leverett, because I'm not sure I remember how to talk, but it's Eloise. My manager.

I pick up with confusion crinkling my forehead. 'Hello?'

'Hello, Esta. I hope you're well?'

I tense. Eloise hates small talk, and she never calls me when I'm off.

'Did something happen?' I ask.

She pauses a moment. I picture her taking a deep breath.

'I'm sorry to have to do this on your summer break, but we've had word from management today that there will be redundancies. While it's unlikely this will affect you, I have a duty to inform all staff.'

My mouth goes dry. It's easy to forget in our little gallery that there are managers above Eloise. This'll likely be university-wide. I know she's right—I'm very far down the chain, so making me redundant wouldn't save the university that much; therefore, it's unlikely I'll lose my job. Then again…

What if I lose my job?

I take a deep breath myself and focus on how unlikely that is.

'Esta?'

'Sorry. Still here.' My hand shakes a little when I ask, 'Will you be okay?'

In her role as manager, Eloise is much more at risk. Whoever they'd replace her with, I doubt we'd have the same easy relationship. It's hard to imagine my gallery without her in it.

'I don't know yet. We've been told that we'll be contacted over the coming week. Again, you have nothing to worry about, Esta. I have to tell everyone in the gallery. This doesn't mean you'll lose your job, alright?'

I nod but then remember that she can't see it. I'm more worried about her now than about myself. If someone else came in to take her place… How would that change the whole gallery dynamic?

'I know,' I say. 'Let me know if you hear anything?'

I want to tell her that there's no chance in hell they'll get rid of her, but they never look at people with these things. They look at numbers and potential savings. It never matters if it ruins anyone's life, if the person who's leaving won't be able to get another job because of age or other factors.

It's a cold process, and I hate what it could mean for me and Bonnie.

'I recommend you use a notebook. It will take a while but it works well, and you will have all kinds of personal associations with your deck afterwards. Esta?'

I'm only faintly aware of Kate in my living room. I *know* I don't need to worry, but I can't help thinking about what might happen if I lose my job. Bonnie and I can afford this house, but only just. We both work part-time, and she works fewer hours than I do since she's still a full-time student, too. She's not getting paid for her internship and had to take time off work for it. If one of us loses our job, we'll lose the house—no point in pretending otherwise.

'Esta?'

My parents would love to have me back, but I really don't want to move back in with them, and what about Bonnie? Do my parents have room for both of us? She can't move back in with her mother and brother. They were never really a family; it would be terrible for her. It's too early for her to move in with Sunny—who I'm still half considering to be a thief—and it's too soon for me to move in with Leverett. If we were further into our relationships, it'd be another matter, but neither of us can suggest it. There's still every chance that neither of us will work out, and then we'd be back with the same problem. Maybe we could rent somewhere? It'd be much smaller than this, but we don't need a lot of space. As long as we can bring Lady, we'd be alright. We only need—

'Are you listening?'

My head finally shoots up. 'I'm sorry. I got some bad news earlier.'

Kate's annoyed expression softens. 'I'm sorry to hear that. Do you need to postpone today's lesson?'

I straighten and shake my head. 'I'm good.'

'I'm glad to hear it. Then please tell me: What's the last thing I told you?'

'Erm…' Damn. I have no idea. Something about my cards and notebooks? I sigh and deflate into my sofa. 'Sorry. I don't know.'

The softness leaves Kate's face again. 'I agreed to teach you because I was sure you would enjoy the lessons and pay attention. If you can't do that, I revoke my offer and you can discuss options with the Mara and Dreamcatcher.'

I pale. Even Kate looks caught off guard, like even she isn't sure where her words came from. Not gonna lie, that's a relief. I'm pretty sure the Dreamcatcher is still up for killing me if this doesn't work out.

'I… apologise,' Kate says. 'I don't know what came over me.' Her eyes flit around the room like she's wondering if it might be the wall colour's fault.

'It's okay,' I say. 'I did space out.'

But Kate still looks lost in thought. I've never actually seen her get angry before, and I've never seen her confused about her own reaction. She's always so controlled that part of me didn't think it could happen.

'I asked you to buy a notebook to learn your cards. The box they came in should have a guidebook. I want you to draw one card a day and write down your first impressions, then add the guidebook's interpretation. As you go through your day, remember the card. Write down any similarities. It will take a while, but you'll have a good grasp on every card's meaning when you're done.'

I nod slowly, because Kate spoke slowly, too. It kinda freaks me out a little that she's still so taken aback by something. Sunny and Leverett both mentioned there being a smell in this house. Is that what she's sensing? A shiver runs down my arms and spine. I hated the idea that someone was in our house when we were robbed, but I hate the idea of some invisible force being here at all times even more.

'I actually already have a notebook,' I say. 'I ordered one when I bought the cards.'

'Yes, yes. Of course. Let's move on to something else: some easy cleansing magic. Do you have any dried sage in the house?'

I shake my head.

'No matter. I'll be right back. In the meantime, you get some salt and open the windows.'

I swallow and do as she says. Kate isn't gone for long; I've just opened the last window when she lets herself back in. She looks confused all over again when she re-enters the house, and I remember how I felt lighter when I visited her. Did she feel the same when she left? I shiver again and make a mental note of everything Kate has said so far: salt, dried sage, open windows… easy. I can recreate this without her if necessary.

Kate joins me upstairs. 'We will work our way through the house and finish in your garden. Take this and do as I say.'

She hands me a bundle of dried sage tied together with string.

'It's a smudge stick,' she says. 'I grow and bless all my herbs myself, as you know. This comes from my garden, too.'

Then she lights a match I didn't see in her hand and sets the sage on fire. In my hand.

I give her a nervous look. 'Won't this, you know, burn me?'

'No,' she says, her patient teacher smile back on her face. 'These burn for a long time and can be used more than once. You will be fine.'

I nod. 'Now what?'

'Blow the flame out so you only have embers.'

I do it.

'Now draw a pentagram before you, starting with air. Do you remember where that is?'

I think for a second. I know a pentagram just fine, but

where the different elements are…

'Top left?'

'Very good. Draw it from there to banish.'

So Kate felt it, too. There's something in my house. I resist the need to hug myself, at least while I'm still holding the burning smudge stick.

I do as she says but look back at her when I'm done. 'What exactly are we banishing?'

She opens her mouth to explain, but then she catches herself and says, 'It's a good idea to cleanse your space and yourself like this every now and again. The dark moon or waning moon is a good time for this, but you don't need to wait if you feel it's necessary now.'

I want to ask again, but I can't really argue with anything she said. It *is* a good reason, and I think she'd tell me more if she knew for sure, so I let it go and follow her instructions. Despite the reason we're doing this, I'm enjoying it. This is the most hands-on lesson I've had so far.

Kate walks me through every room like this until we've even cleansed the stairs and doors. Some of the burnt sage falls to the floor; she tells me to step on it so our carpet doesn't catch fire from the remaining embers. After we've saged the back door, she tells me to go outside to extinguish it.

'Snuff it out in the soil,' Kate says. 'Never use water or it won't light as easily next time, possibly not at all.'

I nod again. I actually think I'll remember all of this, and I already feel better. Maybe it's my imagination or I'm biased right now, but when we go back inside, I don't feel like a heavy blanket weighs me down.

'You can keep this smudge stick,' Kate says. 'Repeat what we just did if you feel it's needed.'

'What did I need the salt for?'

'We'll do that next. I've left a fireproof dish on your mantle. You can leave the sage on there to make sure all the embers are out.'

I follow her into the living room and do just that. Then she hands me the salt.

'I want you to draw a small banishing pentagram in every corner of this house and on your outside thresholds. You don't need to use a lot of salt. It's a purifying mineral by nature.'

Again, I do as she says. Kate leaves me to it this time. She's waiting on my sofa with Lady by her feet when I'm done.

'You did well today,' she says, and my heart swells with pride. 'And now you know how to cleanse your space. You can move the smudge stick down your body to cleanse yourself, starting at your head and ending at your toes, but we should have done enough for today. Do you think you'll remember the steps?'

'Yes, ma'am. It wasn't too complicated.'

She smiles. 'Good. Then I will leave you for now. We will return to your Veiled education next week.'

I give myself a mental kick to get back into that. With everything else going on, I've neglected it a little. I feel energised, though, like the sage's smoke hasn't cleansed just the house but me, too.

Kate goes home, and I go back to my bedroom. My cards are still spread over the duvet. I gather them all into a pile, shuffle them, and grab my notebook—may as well start going through them now.

I draw the first one: The Moon.

It's such a stunning, dreamy card. In my deck, the bright moon takes up most of the background. A woman dances in front of it, her hair and dress long and flowing with her movements. A cute little bunny accompanies her, and there are two pagodas in the background. It's got a Japanese vibe to it. I love how carefree it looks and how it reminds me of my own dreamscape, if only because I have my own animal companion in there. Maybe next time I'll make a moon fill most of the sky, too… Although, that actually sounds a little creepy. I'll see when I get there.

I write down all these positive first impressions like Kate told me to do, then open the book.

It warns me to not fall for illusions, to not confuse reality with wishful thinking.

This isn't a daily drawing. I'm going through the deck one card at a time like Kate asked me to do—I didn't draw this card looking for advice. It could mean any number of things. Mischief has been teasing me to just sleep with dream-Leverett, which would definitely blur the line between reality and dreams in ways I'm still not comfortable with. It's easy to think of that with the little rabbit in the picture.

But as I rephrase the guide's definition for my own notes, I keep thinking about something else. Kate showing me how to cleanse my house made me feel better again, like we've smoked out whatever has taken up residence in here. What if that feeling is an illusion?

What if that bad energy invading my home hasn't gone anywhere after all?

CHAPTER
FIFTEEN

That evening—Monday, so two days away from seeing Leverett, but who's counting—Bonnie and I have a movie night. It feels like it's been ages, and with us both sort-of dating, the break-in, everything we're learning about the Veiled, and her starting her internship today, a night in with a good movie and some popcorn feels like the most normal thing we can do. We put on *Mean Girls*, and the moment the film starts and I sink into the sofa, I relax. We both need this. Lady is asleep on my bed. It's an unusual spot for her, especially when both her humans are down here, but who am I to tell my dog where she can sleep? In that regard, she's much like a cat, and we never tried to train it out of her.

Bonnie hasn't heard from the police or from Sunny, but it's only been a day, so that's fair. The police need time to investigate, and Bonnie said that Sunny had a busy day, so this movie is also good for distracting her.

And me. I definitely wouldn't mind if it distracted me. Leverett messaged me to ask if Bonnie and I are okay, but he didn't mention Wednesday again, so I didn't, either.

Bonnie and I get into the movie, and for a couple of hours everything feels like the good old days when we'd watch this same movie together: laughing at all the same jokes like we're hearing them for the first time, quoting every single quotable line, and generally not thinking about the outside world for a bit. It's nice to not think about anything. Now she's started her internship, she may be too tired most evenings, so it's a movie with popcorn first and then a catch-up with cocktails. We'd have done it yesterday, but she was busy all day preparing for today. They sent her a very detailed Getting Started package, so she spent yesterday reading through that and no doubt worrying about her necklace. Really, we both just want one evening of being teenage girls and gushing over our crushes.

Her phone rings.

Bonnie glances at the screen and sits up. 'It's Sunny.'

I get up and walk to the kitchen. 'You chat, I make cocktails.'

The movie is nearly over anyway. Bonnie nods and picks up, so I busy myself in the kitchen. I've felt lighter since cleansing the house with Kate, so we can celebrate that, too—that things are looking up. Everything was a bit unsure since the Dreamcatcher, but I think we're both finally finding our feet in this Veiled world. Bonnie is dating a mermaid, Leverett and I kissed and will see each other again on Wednesday, and Bonnie is interning at her dream job. I'm learning magic from Kate, and I'm definitely not losing my job to these redundancies. I feel like I've cleansed whatever curse this was right out of the house. That's what I tell myself as I mix our drinks: good things are coming; the bad is over. So what if I drew The Moon earlier? Perhaps it meant the illusion of being under a curse in the first place.

I walk back into the living room with our cocktails. Bonnie is quietly crying on the sofa. I put the drinks down, sit next to her, and pull her into my arms.

'What's wrong?'

Bonnie takes a few deep breaths to steady her voice. It takes her a moment to actually speak. 'Sunitha broke up with me. She said she doesn't feel safe with a human.'

'Oh, no, Bonnie. I'm sorry.'

I don't say what's really on my mind: This is awfully soon after Bonnie's necklace got taken. I know I should mention the possibility, but this isn't the time. Not when my sister is so newly heartbroken. I have no proof, anyway, and she doesn't need an accusation from me right now.

'I just don't know why,' Bonnie says. Her tears are gently rolling down her cheeks and her chin quivers slightly, but mostly she just sounds dejected. 'We talked about it. She said she didn't mind. She said she trusted me.'

Bonnie glances at me with a brief frown. Sunitha may have trusted *her*, but I know she's a mermaid, too. My heart drops.

'Is it because of me?' I ask. 'Maybe I shouldn't have been here when she came over. If she didn't know that I know, she might have—'

But Bonnie shakes her head. 'No.' She rests her head on my shoulder. 'No, she liked you.' Bonnie huffs. 'Though I thought she liked me more, to be honest. I thought she—'

One sob escapes her, so I hold her until she stops crying.

When she pulls away from me, I reach for a tissue next to the sofa and hand it to her. Neither of us makes for pretty criers, so there's snot on her lip and on my sleeve.

'Maybe she just needs a moment to think,' I say. 'Maybe she had a bad day at work and let the pressure get the better of her. And if not, you'll find someone better. You deserve someone better.'

Like someone who doesn't get close to you to steal your heirloom necklace and then breaks up with you right after.

Bonnie blows her nose and nods. She glances at my sleeve. 'Sorry about your shirt.'

I shrug. 'It'll wash out.'

She leans in again. I wait for her to speak.

'Tonight was supposed to be about happy things,' she says. 'You have a date with Leverett?' She cranes her neck to look into my eyes. 'In his flat?'

I'm surprised that I don't even blush. I was excited to talk about it, but it doesn't feel right to discuss my joy right after her breakup.

'We can do this some other time,' I say. 'Maybe after said date?'

But Bonnie shakes her head. 'No, please. Let me live through you.' She nudges me. It feels sharper than intended as her elbow stabs into my side while also lacking all energy because she's been crying. 'I'm happy for you.'

I nod. 'Thank you.'

I'm not feeling it, at least not right now.

'What do you think will happen during this date?' Bonnie asks. 'Tell me again what happened at that party, too. I think

I missed a few details before. There was so much.'

'We kissed.' I swallow a rather heavy lump in my throat. 'He said some things about wanting me to himself, about giving me his undivided attention if I still want him on Wednesday…'

This is beyond not the right time for this conversation. I feel guilty telling her about my success when Sunitha just dumped her over the phone. To make matters worse, just the memory of everything he said, how his eyes darkened, how he sounded… I feel like the worst friend ever, getting aroused right now.

'So on Wednesday, you'll…?'

I struggle for words. I believe his were, *Once we give ourselves to each other, you won't get rid of me. Consider if you're ready to have an utterly devoted vampire partner.*

But telling her that when she's hurting isn't fair. Fortunately, I don't have to.

Bonnie sighs. 'Never mind. Maybe I don't want to know right now. Sorry.'

I hug her again. 'It's okay. Honestly, we don't need to discuss details at all.'

'We'll see, but… Maybe on Thursday, or this weekend?'

I nod.

Bonnie sighs again. 'Sorry, Esta. I think I'll go to bed.'

'No problem,' I say. 'Get some rest.'

That she doesn't want to get drunk with cocktails and talk about how much better off she is without Sunitha tells me that she *really* liked her. I know they weren't dating that long, but sometimes you just know. I really hope for my sister's sake that Sunitha isn't behind the missing necklace; it would break her heart all over again.

And as I sit alone, I think back to the card I pulled. If this curse isn't actually gone...

Could it have spread to Bonnie?

CHAPTER SIXTEEN

'Mischief.'

'Not this again.'

'What in all the hells is that?'

Since I'm convinced all over again that I'm cursed, I thought I'd have another rummage through my dreamscape, see if Mischief has noticed anything since the last time we talked about it.

I wasn't expecting a bloody massive black wall moving towards… me? The centre, if my dreamscape even has one? It's like a gigantic rain cloud of vibrant black, if that's a thing. There's no thunder or lightning, but that might be because I love a good thunderstorm—it wouldn't intimidate me, it just feels like the usual sound effects should be there. Whatever it is, I'm not getting good vibes from that thing. It looks incredibly at odds with the night sky I kept from last time—I have a big, shiny moon and bright stars everywhere on one side, and an ominous-as-fuck death cloud on the other. I'm being unfair, though. This might not be a death cloud at all. It could be an ominous-as-fuck cuddle cloud. Seems unlikely, but it's not like it introduced itself.

Mischief brushes around my legs. I get the sense that it's more to comfort her than to be cute. 'You mean, you don't know?'

I frown at the cloud. 'I've never seen that thing before in my life.'

We stand by my usual purple-leafed tree. I came here to do some shadow work, feel my dreamscape from my shadow forest to sense any sign of corruption at all—which, if I'm honest, I wasn't sure would work; it's not like I've done this before—but the corruption was here first and ready to greet me. The cloud doesn't do anything except move closer to me; at least, that's what I think it's doing. If it moves, it's so slow that I don't actually see it rolling closer. It's more like the sense of approaching doom and the dream-certainty that it's coming for me. I don't know what will happen when it reaches me and I don't want to know.

Still, at least I'm not considering throwing myself into a body of water this time. What's the worst a cloud can do? I can't swim, so I had every right to be afraid that I'd drown, but I've always imagined clouds to feel like cotton candy. Not that this one looks like it'll be all soft and snuggly. It'll probably freeze me to death if it doesn't find a way to stab me first.

This is the second time now that something I can't explain or control has happened in my dreamscape since I stepped into the void lake. I don't like it.

'There isn't another Dreamcatcher in here, is there?'

Mischief paces around my legs, her tail lowered and slightly puffy. 'I don't think so.' She pauses. Her whiskers and ears twitch. Despite the approaching cloud, I can't help smiling—this cat is incredibly cute. And anyway, this is a dream and I refuse to forget it. I can always just wake up. The Dreamcatcher made that impossible for a hot moment there, but if that's not what's happening—

'No,' Mischief finally says. 'It's just us.'

I breathe a sigh of relief. The Dreamcatcher could have killed me. I'm still recovering from the last nightmares he threw at me. As a being that works directly from my deepest fears, he was extremely good at it. I don't fancy that again. I may eat my words in a day or two, but I'd much rather take on a cloud.

I pick up Mischief, and she cuddles into my neck. 'Shall we investigate?'

She squints at me. 'Go to that thing? Are you sure?'

I don't know what'll happen if I touch it or it starts to roil around me. Maybe nothing. Maybe it'll suffocate me. But what's the worst thing that can happen? I mean, really? I'll just wake myself up if necessary. And something tells me I'll find some answers there.

'If this thing can tell me who cursed me or why, I need to know.'

I doubt it'll whisper a name at me, but any hint would be helpful. Between me, my sister, Lady, Kate, and Leverett, surely we can figure this out? If I miss anything, Mischief will point me in the right direction. That's what dream guides do.

'Alright,' she purrs. 'Shall we fly?'

I'm already in the air before she finishes her question. 'Let's approach carefully, though, alright?'

While I can't die in a dream—unless the Dreamcatcher or the Mara kill me, as it turns out—I can feel pain. I'm unsure if Mischief feels any real pain, though, or how this might feel to her. She's a figment of my imagination—a very real dream guide, but her shape and attitude and whole consciousness comes from me.

I freeze.

Glance at her.

A very real dream guide? Does that mean…

'Mischief.'

'Seriously?'

'Are you one of the Veiled?'

It's never even occurred to me. Mischief has always been here. I always understood her as just part of my dreamscape, but now the thought is there I can't shake it. She's so tightly bound to my unconscious that I never thought she might be her own being.

She squints at me again. 'Are spirit guides of the Veiled?'

'That doesn't answer anything.'

'Doesn't it?'

I want to keep asking until she reveals something, but I bite my lip. I promised that I wouldn't hassle the Veiled, and as her words start to sink in, I realise that Mischief *has* answered my question. If she weren't one of the Veiled, wouldn't she simply have said no? That she's dancing around it must mean she can't tell me the truth outright, which means that I need to uncover the truth myself, which means that there's a truth to uncover in the first place.

Goosebumps shoot up my arms. For as long as I've lucid-dreamed, I had no idea she was more than just part of my mind.

She glides in place next to me in the shape of a raven. I've seen this form before—she can technically take on any shape she wants—but I feel like I'm seeing *her* for the first time. I'm dumbstruck. *Mischief is one of the Veiled.* How is that even possible? Why wouldn't it be? I have so many new questions, but Mischief caws at the advancing black cloud, and I make myself fly towards it. Slowly. With all the caution I can muster right after my curiosity was poked with the sharpest stick ever.

'Can we talk about this later?' I ask as we fly towards the cloud.

'You can ask,' she says. 'I may not be able to answer.'

I bite my lip again. I always thought that Mischief simply knows everything I know since she has anytime access to my unconscious, but if she's one of the Veiled… What does that mean for us? *Does* it mean anything?

I let a breeze stroke around my head to clear it. This isn't the time.

We reach the Wall of Doom much faster than I'd hoped. It looked far away, but we arrive in under two minutes. Of course, this being a dream, it's possible that time isn't doing its usual thing here. Maybe it's actually years away and we just reached it quickly because dream logic. Either way, I'm no longer too sure about this as we come to a hovering stop right before it.

The cloud moves like mist over water, except it's black and I'm scared to touch it.

'What are you?' I whisper.

I don't expect an answer, but from inside it comes a deep rumbling. Could this thing be alive? What if this is one of the Veiled, too? I shake my head. *Not everyone is one of the Veiled, Esta. Get a grip.*

'Are you getting anything from it?' I ask Mischief.

'You mean other than the sense of sinister foreboding?'

I float to the ground and stand before it. Mischief follows and turns into a cat again.

This cloud is *big*. I wasn't wrong before when I called it a wall. Standing right at its feet, I almost don't see the top end. The sides seem to extend forever. Black fog gently roils off it and dissipates. I'm surprised I don't feel more. I thought I'd be terrified once I got this close, but there's nothing except some dark curiosity and the sense I shouldn't touch it. What would happen if I did?

I reach out with one hand.

'Esta.'

I pause at the caution in Mischief's voice, just as my fingers are about to touch a wisp of fog. There's a reason this cloud is here or it simply wouldn't be here. There's no perfectly useless information in the unconscious. It all means something. It may not all be big, life-changing information, but the unconscious doesn't waste time on pointless stuff. That more than anything makes me reach out again.

There's no resistance when my fingers stroke the cloud. I swallow and reach farther until my hand disappears to my wrist. Nothing hurts. There's a light softness, kinda like how I imagined clouds would feel but so faint I'm wondering if I'm imagining it after all. It's kinda comforting. I pull my hand out again, and it's unharmed; I don't see any damage, anyway.

'What are you?' I whisper again. It's rare that I find new stuff in my dreamscape. Of course, our unconscious develops all the time just as we do, since all the new experiences need to go somewhere, but I've done this all my life and am used to how new things are represented here. It fascinates me that I've no idea what this cloud is. Unless…

'Could this cloud represent my worry that I'm cursed?'

There's a chance the curse isn't real, but it's increasingly looking like it is. Maybe this cloud is that fear but in dream form. Is this how I might have imagined a curse on me? I didn't really think about it, but once a thought exists, the unconscious gives it shape. I suppose, looking at this ominous dark cloud-wall thing, it's possible that's what it is.

'It could,' Mischief says. I don't like her pause. 'Or it could be the curse itself.'

I back away a few steps. 'You say this now that I touched it?'

Mischief huffs and shakes her head once—her kitty version of a shrug. 'You didn't die, did you?'

'No, but…' There's no point arguing about this. I'm okay and she makes a good point. 'Is this how curses work? If it's just something in my mind…'

Does that mean I can dispel it by deciding it no longer works?

'I don't know,' Mischief says. 'I didn't think so, but what do we know?'

'Nothing about curses.'

I've a feeling Kate wouldn't teach me, at least nothing more than theory and how to undo a curse. And she isn't here right now, anyway. I scan the cloud for answers, but nothing presents itself.

I decide to try another tactic. 'Did someone put you here?' I ask the cloud. 'What do you want?'

A wisp of fog puffs out towards me, slowly and delicately like a, well, cloud. It almost looks like it's reaching for me, so I carefully return the gesture.

'I don't like this,' Mischief says. 'Be careful, Esta.'

I nod and touch my hand to the wisp. It folds another hand against mine, this one made of the same black stuff as the cloud itself. Slowly, a form emerges from the wall, all of it made of the cloud's softness. The form emerges up to her waist before she stops… and I say 'she' because, while she lacks all details and features, she looks like me. Roughly the same size. Hair that falls to the same length. The hand that's the exact shape of mine.

Like it copied me.

A shiver runs up my back and legs. I take a step back, but the cloud-hand grabs my wrist. The other me pulls me towards her with so much force that I lose my balance. Her hand around my wrist is too firm to shake off. Her other hand grabs my head, fingers splayed across my scalp.

Mischief hisses at it. 'Esta!'

I try to wriggle out of it, will myself away from this creature, but nothing's happening. I'm having flashbacks to the Dreamcatcher impaling my limbs on sharp twigs. What if this is him after all? If it is, unless I get super lucky and Bonnie throws another shoe at my boobs, I'm probably as good as dead.

But she has my voice, if more husky and ethereal, when she says, 'Estelle Anderson, you are cursed.'

I mean, how dare she use my full name. No unconscious of mine would forget how much I hate that.

I'm still trying to wriggle out of her vice-like grip, but she's too strong. The other me pulls me into the cloud. The last thing I hear is Mischief's hiss, and then everything goes silent. And dark.

I keep telling myself that this is my dream and nothing else can control it, but clearly that's not the case. I force myself to breathe evenly, but my heart beats faster with every second that I don't see a way out. I will a door to appear—nothing happens. I will myself to fly so I can survey the area better— nothing. I even will myself back to Mischief outside this wall, but that doesn't work, either. I think I could still make myself wake up, but now that I'm here, I want to look around. This *is* why I came here.

I make out a shape not far from me. I walk over to it and realise it's Bonnie, or at least something my dream-instinct recognises as Bonnie. She's made of the same black fog as my double. Bonnie is packing her suitcase. I'm there, too, gesturing wildly, but I don't hear any words. This version of me is either speechless or Bonnie isn't listening.

'I'll be back to get the rest when you're at work,' Bonnie spits as she closes the suitcase. She hauls it off the bed and leaves the room. 'Well done. You've got your wish.'

And then Bonnie is gone. The representation of me sags to

the floor.

I don't know what this is, but it's not something I recognise so it's not a memory, and Bonnie would never leave. I can't imagine this much venom in her voice when talking to me—we rarely even argue. So this must be a regular fear.

The fog-version of me dissipates, and a shadow of Leverett appears. I'm there again, too, looking just as defeated as I did with Bonnie.

'I'm sorry,' he says. 'I can't love a human.'

Despite knowing that this isn't real, hearing those words with his voice makes my heart hurt. He wouldn't. Would he? He told me to take some time to think, but couldn't he change his mind, too?

I'm alone again. Somewhere, a phone rings, and I'm surprised to look down and find my mobile in my hand. I answer, because what else am I supposed to do?

'Hey Esta, it's Eloise. I'm sorry. You've been made redundant. Can you come in to look at the paperwork? HR want to talk to you, too.'

I hang up before I drop the phone. This *is* just a fear, right? Eloise said herself that I'm not at risk. Why would I be? I don't earn enough to save them much.

The scene changes again and again after that. My shadow is at the vet—no sign of Bonnie—and Lady lies in my arms as they inject her with something. I don't need anyone to say what this is to know what they're doing. Shadow-me is shaking enough as she pets Lady's head that there's no other option. Real tears shoot into my eyes, because Lady hasn't been quite herself lately. We thought she was just tired from playing with

Kate's dogs, but what if it's not that? What if my dog is sick?

Shadow-me stands outside our house. Black fog licks towards the sky, and my dream-certainty tells me our house is on fire. Bonnie and I are standing in front of it, holding each other and crying.

I shake my head. None of this is real. For some reason, my unconscious has decided to scare me, that's all. Frankly, the Dreamcatcher did a better job. His nightmares were much more violent and graphic. Everyone's been telling me that it's normal to need time to recover after what I've been through. Maybe this is the last remnants of the fear he made me experience. That would make a lot of sense, actually.

I shake my head again and will myself awake. I've had enough of being scared. The others are right: I need to give myself more time. I'll ask Leverett for a soothing tea, Kate for meditations to relax, and I'll schedule a day out with Bonnie so we can have a real change of scenery.

When I wake up seconds later, I don't feel triumphant. I feel too much like the dream let me go. Instead of leaning into the part of me that just now thought I need to give myself grace, an old fear resurfaces:

What if this was just another beginning, and every new dream will morph into a worse nightmare again?

CHAPTER
SEVENTEEN

After last night's dream, I'm more excited than ever to see Leverett today. He didn't say what time I should come over, but to my own surprise, I don't run to him as soon as I'm awake. I remember Kate's instructions for cleansing our house well enough. After the dream and the lingering fear that I'm cursed, I don't think it's a bad idea. Maybe, if there are any bad influences on this house or me, I can smoke them out. Kate did say to repeat it as needed. Maybe her one cleansing wasn't enough? Maybe something stayed behind when the Dreamcatcher left.

I shiver when I light the sage in Bonnie's room first. The thought that something invisible and evil has been squatting in our shadows is… unsettling, to put it mildly. But I remind myself that this is why I'm smudging everything again, and as I work my way through the house, I imagine warm light filling every room through the open windows. If this doesn't do it, maybe I can ask Kate to do another one together. Maybe two smudge sticks are better than one? I don't know.

I finish as Kate taught me: by snuffing out the gentle embers in the soil outside.

'Please, let this be it,' I whisper as I make sure that every last spark is out. Bonnie left for her internship before I got up since it's a long drive, so the last thing I want is a stray spark setting the house on fire while I'm making out with Leverett.

A breeze brushes over me, and I spread my arms in greeting.

'Please, blow the rest of whatever curse is on me away.'

I don't know if it works like that, but I figure it can't hurt. It does make me feel better, but then the wind has always done that.

I take a deep breath, which I hope is cleansing for my mind and soul, and slowly let it out. I don't know where or how this curse has bitten into me, but I'm trying to cover all the bases. I put the smudge stick away again and seriously hope this is it now. I throw some more salt into every corner for good measure and draw a banishing pentagram on the doors with my finger and salt water. I'm not sure what else to do now except hope it's done and ask Kate for help if it's not.

Lady is still asleep when I prepare to leave or I'd go for a walk with her. Poor puppy has been sleeping more than usual. I remember what the dream showed me, that she's sick, but I refuse to fall into its trap. The Dreamcatcher had me scared to fall asleep. I won't be afraid to be awake now. Our dog is fine. Everyone gets tired, and she's had some exciting adventures with Kate's dogs lately—not for a few days, sure, but I know what I'm like when I get a muscle ache. Maybe she's still recovering, too. Or maybe she's down from the bad energy in this house? I wonder if she can smell it, if she knows what it is and just can't tell me. Generally speaking, I can communicate with our dog just fine—animals are really fairly easy to understand if you're willing to listen and learn their language—but this is beyond my abilities.

When I leave the house, I'm somewhere between more relaxed because I cleansed the house and a nervous mess because of where I'm going. I overthought everything this morning, from how to brush my hair to what underwear to put on. Will he even care when he's busy ripping it off me? I blush. Maybe he won't do that. He's always been so kind and considerate, so he's probably the same in bed. That I'm about to find out has me all kinds of nervous and excited and—

I remind myself to breathe. Every step towards his shop feels heavy, like part of my brain hasn't accepted that this is really happening. It's honestly weird how weird it feels. After the last few days, this seems too good to be true. I shake off the doubt. Leverett invited me over. He knows I'm on my way.

So why is this heavy feeling in my gut there? Maybe because we arranged it in advance. It's not quite the spontaneous passionate moment I imagined, but more like an appointment. It's not how I thought we'd do this, and I had *many* ideas about that. This wasn't on the list.

I'm shaking when I reach his shop. Maybe we should wait, go on another date first or something. As much as I want him and to be his, I'm not sure I want it like this.

As usual, Leverett is reading behind the counter when I enter. He smiles when he sees me and stands, but he looks reserved, too. So at least I won't be destroying his expectations.

'Hey.'

'I was wondering when you'd be here,' he says. 'Shall we talk upstairs?'

Now that I'm here and talking to him, I feel differently again. Maybe I'd be okay if he dragged me to his bed as soon as we're upstairs.

I nod and follow him upstairs. Change my mind yet again. This feels too much like a meeting. He didn't even turn the sign over in the door, so he's not expecting to be away for long.

'Please, have a seat,' Leverett says.

I sit on my usual sofa. He doesn't sit next to me but in his arm chair. Every second I'm here, this feels more like a scheduled business meeting. Colder.

'Have you considered what we talked about?' Something about him doesn't sound quite right, like he's choosing his words too carefully. It puts me more on edge than the dream did. I mentally prepare myself for what's coming.

'I did,' I say. 'Nothing's changed.'

I try a light smile. He does return it, but there's something else in his eyes, too. They still darken when he looks at me, but there's also… regret, maybe?

I want to tell him that I want to be his, that I want to be with him and make him happy every day of my life, but I don't know how to put any of that into words. I've never been great with emotional talk like that. What if I say it and it all sounds stupid or cheesy or cliché? I don't know how to make it sound good.

'I see,' he finally says.

Not the reaction I was hoping for.

'Did I tell you how old I am?'

I blink. Also not what I was expecting. I nearly asked him his age when he first introduced himself as a vampire, but I remembered my manners in time. Leverett didn't bring it up himself, though he mentioned the witch hunt.

'I didn't want to ask,' I say. 'It seemed rude.'

'I'm 419 years old. I've seen a lot of people come and go in that time. Most of the Veiled are still around, some visit from time to time, but we aren't eternal, even if it may seem that way to you humans. The longer you live, the more you lose.

'Young Veiled are taught to not get attached to humans. Sometimes we kill you by accident because we don't yet realise how fragile you are. Most of the time, we simply outlive you, and your children, and your children's children. We don't always succeed in not getting emotionally attached. Most of us take a rather philosophical stance and appreciate the time we have together, but that doesn't mean…' His eyes stare into the distance for a second before he focusses on me again. 'That doesn't mean it doesn't hurt. Just being friends with a human is painful, all the more so when you spend their whole life without them knowing what you really are. You know some of it, and you're still here. I'm grateful for that. But loving a human…'

I want to step in and say something, whatever it takes to comfort him and tell him I'm not going anywhere, but that would be a lie, wouldn't it? I will go somewhere eventually. I'll die.

And when I do, I'll leave him with the heartbreak.

Chiara's words echo in my head: *You're a human, silly girl.*

You're nothing more than a temporary toy. It doesn't matter that she spoke out of jealousy or hatred for all humanity, because that doesn't change that she was right. Would that be enough? To just be a short-loved plaything he amuses himself with for a decade or two before moving on to someone else? I don't think he'd actually see me like that, but… Would it be kinder? I could be with him, albeit shortly, and he might move on without the pain.

But even as I think it, I know it's not enough. It's incredibly selfish of me, but wouldn't that kind of heartbreak be a good thing? I don't want to die knowing that he's already forgotten about me, like I was nothing. I want to die knowing that our years together meant something to him, too. If I can't have that…

The first tears shoot into my eyes, but I blink them away. I will not cry. Not in front of him.

'I understand,' I say. And really, I should have seen this coming, too. At the very least I should have prepared for the possibility better.

'I'm sorry,' Leverett says. 'I can't love a human.'

His words are like ice on my soul. That's exactly what he said in the dream. What if this isn't just a spooky coincidence? What if the other things come true, too? I'm half-ready to bury myself in that obsession if it means I don't have to feel his rejection.

I nod, my head heavy on my sagging shoulders. I want to keep a straight back, but it seems my body has other ideas.

'Where does that, erm… Can I still…'

'Use the bookshop?'

I nod.

He twitches towards me a little like he wants to reach out to comfort me, but he catches himself in the last second. That's okay. I don't know that him holding my hand right now would help, anyway.

'Of course. We can still be friends. Eventually, I'll move away or you'll meet someone, and we'll naturally part ways.'

His voice catches a little, like he doesn't really want to say the words. I expect he doesn't—the way he kissed me and shoved me against the wall was real. He wanted to be with me, too. Everything he said… I can't convince myself that any of it was a lie. He isn't doing this because he doesn't want to love me. He's doing this to protect himself.

And if that's the case, then me still coming here would be unfair. Kinder to cut myself out of his life now than to keep the pretence up.

I don't tell him that I don't think I can be friends. Not now I know how his lips feel on mine, how he feels against me when my legs are wrapped around him. How am I supposed to move on like none of that happened? How am I supposed to look into his eyes again and not break? Being just friends with him is asking too much. I can't do it.

If he can be strong, though, then I can at least try.

'I don't think that's a good idea,' I make myself say. Before he can say anything else, I stand. 'I should go. I…' My nose burns. I don't care if I start crying once I'm outside, but right now I'd quite like to hold it together. I turn around to him one more time and almost fall apart when he looks as broken as I feel. 'Thank you.'

I leave before he can respond. If he wanted to, he could easily catch up with me, but he doesn't. I imagine he's still sitting in his armchair when I leave the shop and close the door behind me. I have this vision of myself walking past his shop every day on my walk to work, sitting on the bus on a rainy day and glancing at his door through the running raindrops and reflected lights on the bus window, and wondering if he's looking at me, too. Of his shop, boarded up years from now because he moved away. Will he still think of me then? Will either of us still wonder what might have been if we hadn't been so afraid of getting hurt?

Because, as I'm walking through the crowds without really seeing anyone, I'm hurting anyway, and I can't help wondering:

What's the point of protecting yourself when you have to break yourself to do it?

Part of me wants to turn around and throw myself at his feet, beg him to reconsider, but I make myself walk onwards. My feet are like lead on the ground, and every muscle in my body pulls me back towards his shop. But I walk on, because it's the mature thing to do. Because it'll be kinder in the long term.

I have to believe that or I'll break down by the main road.

And so, because I don't want to address this pain while I'm out, I focus on the other meaning behind his words. The ones that matched my dream perfectly.

Was that a coincidence, or am I about to lose everything else, too?

CHAPTER
EIGHTEEN

I decide to take a detour when I'm about ten minutes away from home. I know where the path into the forest is now, and I think I've earned a moment of soothing nature. The brook flowing alongside the path will help, and maybe, by the time I get home, I'll magically be over it.

Leverett doesn't want to be with me because I'm human, so there's nothing I can do about it. Tears burn my eyes. Such a stupid thing to cry about. I mean, really. I barely know the man. His rejection shouldn't hurt so much.

But I know enough about him to understand that I really like him, so I think it's fair that his rejection stings at least a little. I get why he said no. It still hurts, or maybe it hurts more because I understand? Maybe I'd have decided the same if our roles were reversed. I don't know. How would I? I'm just a dumb little human.

I sniff against the coming tears and decide to take a detour home. If I'm going to the forest, I'm sure Lady wants to come. I could do with burying my face in her neck. I take a somewhat overgrown, easy-to-miss path to get back to the park, and the moment I enter the meadow, I see it.

Smoke.

How didn't I smell it? Now that I see it, the stench of something burning fills my nostrils and tries to choke my throat. I must have been so absorbed in Leverett's rejection that I—

That's my house.

The smoke. It's coming from my house.

My body doesn't react the way I always hoped it would when faced with tragedy. I always thought I'd run, stay calm, and do something useful, but I go numb instead. My feet keep moving towards home, but I don't feel anything. It's like the emotional part of my brain or my heart has shut down because it doesn't know how to rationalise that my home is burning down. Or maybe it's just one thing too many and I'd already checked out.

Bonnie. I need to call her, and—

Is Lady still inside?

Something snaps back into place, and I start running. There's already a fire engine, and Kate stands on the opposite side of the road with my pup by her feet. Lady whines and trots towards me when she sees me. Kate hurries after her.

'I tried to call you,' Kate says, 'but I didn't get through. We haven't heard anything from Bonnie.'

I start to shake my head, though I'm not sure why. I'm not sure anything else feels appropriate. 'She's at her internship.' I look towards my house. Maybe it's not that bad—it hasn't crumbled in on itself, and I don't see any flames licking out of the windows. It actually looks mostly undamaged from the outside. There's a bit of char around the door, but nothing's collapsed that I can see. 'How bad is it?'

'They're still assessing the damage,' Kate says. 'I was on my way home with my dogs when I heard the fire alarm from your open window. I didn't see any smoke, so the fire brigade got here quickly. Once I knew they were on their way, I opened the door to get Lady out.'

One glance at the door leaning against the house tells me she didn't exactly have a spare key I didn't know about. It looks like an axe went through.

So if nothing else, we'll need to replace that. I'll cope if that's the worst of the damage.

'How did you know Lady was in there?' I ask.

Kate smiles, and oddly enough, it still puts me at ease despite the situation. 'I didn't, but I also didn't want to take the risk. As I said, I tried to call you but you didn't answer. I'll replace the door, of course.'

I nod, but tears burn my eyes again. 'Thank you. For getting her out and calling the fire brigade. What happened? Do they know?'

Kate shakes her head. 'No, and they may not find out. Whatever caused the fire has likely burnt up with it.'

A chill goes through me. What if someone just waited for me to leave and— I can't go getting paranoid at every little thing or I'll never sleep peacefully again. First I suspect Sunitha of stealing Bonnie's necklace, now I think someone torched our house on purpose? It's more likely that—

The chill turns into a shiver up my back.

'What if it's the curse?' I whisper to Kate.

Her smile turns sympathetic… or pitiful. I'm not sure which. Do I sound that paranoid that she pities me?

'I doubt it, Esta. But I'll look into it if you like.'

I nod. 'I need to call Bonnie. We… we need to figure out where to stay.' Even if the fire damage isn't that bad, we're still missing a front door. What happens now? Is there such a thing as temporary emergency doors?

'Nonsense,' Kate says. 'You can both stay with me until your house is sorted. I don't have an empty room, but I can make you two comfortable on the sofas. I've already called a friend to replace your door; he assured me that he'll treat it as his priority. You'll have a new door before the end of tomorrow. They'll board up the opening in the meantime.'

Lady shoves her head into my palm and whines up at me. I go to my knees and hug her. I'm so glad she's okay.

I peek up at Kate. 'I can't ask you to do that.'

'It's no trouble.' Her smile turns inquisitive—not something I've seen often on her. It's like we're about to share a secret. I like it, or I do until she says, 'Or do you have somewhere else to stay? Perhaps with Leverett?'

My heart drops, and I hide my face in Lady's ruff. 'Seems unlikely,' I mumble. 'We…' I almost say we broke up, but we weren't dating, so that doesn't work.

'Oh, Esta, I'm sorry. Is that where you were?'

I want to resist the urge to nod again, but the familiar motion feels safe. I may be lost for words, but this movement is easy enough that I can manage it without needing to think, and there's some comfort in the repetition.

'Yeah. Anyway, thanks for letting us stay. Hopefully we

won't take up your living room for long.'

Kate holds out her hand. 'Unlock your phone. I'll inform Bonnie.'

'You don't need to do that.' But I've already swiped it unlocked before I finish the sentence.

'Again, it's no problem. You've been through a lot this morning. Cuddle your dog while I call your sister.'

New tears burn my eyes again, but I blink them away and do as she says.

'What on Earth caused that fire?' I mumble to myself. 'Did you see anything?'

Lady whines again, and I throw my arms around her neck. I'll never not be grateful that Kate got my dog out. Just the thought of her being trapped inside while the flames are closing in around her while she's frantically scratching at the door for help is enough to make me cry into her.

I sit down next to her on the kerb, and Lady falls against me. I'm still stroking her neck, hoping it'll calm us both, when a firefighter crosses the road to me.

'Are you the owner of this house?'

'One of them. My neighbour called you here. She's just calling my sister. Did you find what caused this?'

He shakes his head. 'No, ma'am, which tells me it was something small. Accidents like this happen all the time. Did you leave a candle burning, by chance?'

I start to shake my head but freeze mid-movement. He sees it as admittance.

'Be more careful in the future. You got lucky this time. If your neighbour hadn't called us when she did, you could have lost everything. Come talk to us when you're ready to hear about the damage and what you can do next.'

Call my insurance, I imagine, but that's not where my head is as he walks away and joins his colleagues. I didn't leave a candle burning—I never do—but I did smudge the house this morning. Kate told me to always pay attention to any falling ashes in case there are embers inside. Did I do that? I don't remember watching the carpet. Did some ashes fall onto the fabric? Is this fire my fault?

Kate returns and hands me the phone.

'Bonnie didn't pick up. I tried a few times, so she must be busy. Her phone is probably in a locker. I left her a message to call you, but if you to give me your phone when she calls back, I'll handle it.'

I frown. 'Then what am I supposed to do?'

'You need time to process all this. Between your conversation with Leverett and now this, you need a moment to yourself. I can make you a relaxing tea, if you like. We can meditate together.'

'I appreciate it,' I say, 'but I need to call our house insurance, I really should be the one to talk to Bonnie, and I need to not think about Leverett for a moment. I need—' I breathe a shaky sigh and make myself take deep breaths until my voice feels even again. 'Fine. You're right, I need a moment. But I need to talk to those guys first. I'll sit after that.'

My instinct is to wander over to Leverett's and talk to him to feel better, but I guess that's not an option anymore.

I feel drained when I approach the firefighters. Kate is right, it's been a lot for one morning.

The firefighter I already spoke to tells me something about how obviously the door needs to be replaced, the carpet on the stairs will need replacing, someone will need to come out to make sure the stairs are still safe to use, that the ceiling directly above them isn't about to crumble… Lots of things like that. I mostly take it all in while being very numb at the same time. I just hope my insurance can take care of it; I don't think I have the energy to tackle much more.

Heh. Maybe it took an actual fire to smoke out the curse? I feel just defeated enough to joke about that.

The firefighter joins his colleagues in the truck, and I sink back down to the kerb. Lady trots up next to me and looks at me with big eyes.

'I guess we'll be staying with Aunty Kate for a few days, hm?'

She seemed positive that the door, at least, would be replaced quickly, but it sounds like everything else will take longer. I don't know what we'd do without her. I could have stayed with Leverett, but, well…

I sigh and put my head into my hands. It seems like everything's gone up in smoke, literally, but at least things aren't as bad as my dream made them out to be. Our house is still… liveable? We can go back once some official person says it's safe. Fuck. I don't want to think about it. I don't want to put in the effort to think of all the right words. I want to curl up under a thick blanket and shut out the world for a bit.

I feel a hand on my shoulder and look up. Kate smiles at me.

'Come on,' she says. 'Sitting out here and dwelling on what

went wrong won't fix it. Let's get inside, hm? I know a tea that'll help.'

I scoff and immediately feel bad about it. Then again, if she really does have a tea that'll somehow make all this better, she should be selling it. She'd make a killing.

Lady nudges my leg, moves between me and Kate, and her wagging tail hits me in the thigh. I guess if she's ready to move on, I can follow her.

We enter Kate's house, and she points to the sofa. 'Sit. I'll make you that tea, and then I'll make a few calls. I know people who can help.'

I raise an eyebrow as I sit down. 'You know people who can, what, magically fix the house?'

I realise how ridiculous that sounds as I'm saying it—ridiculous because she probably does, in fact, know people who can fix it. I wouldn't be surprised if there are Veiled who are good with this kind of stuff, though I'm too mentally drained to think of specifics.

'Sit,' she says again, even though I'm already sitting. I can take a hint, though—a breather first, a talk about options later.

So, I sink back into her sofa while Kate busies herself in the kitchen. Keano and Bruin join me on the sofa, and Lady lies down by my feet. Circumstances aside, I guess there are worse outcomes than being surrounded by dogs for a while.

My phone buzzes. The screen announces Bonnie, so I pick up.

'What's wrong?' she says. 'Kate said to call you back as soon as I could. Why was she using your phone? Are you okay?'

I hate that we worried her, but I don't suppose there's a

non-worrying way to say 'our house made a good go of burning down, but it's okay, Kate is taking us in while the damage gets fixed by her Veiled friends.'

'I'm fine. Sort of. But—'

Kate swoops into the room and holds out her hand. She gives me a stern look that's chiding me for not relaxing harder, and I hand her my phone. I'm glad. I don't want to have this chat, any chat, right now. Kate talks to Bonnie from the kitchen while she makes the tea. I can't quite make out what she's saying because she closed the door on me—on her, whatever—and because I'm surprisingly comfy surrounded by all these dogs. I didn't see Kate light any incense, but there's a lingering scent of lavender. I'm starting to associate it with her house. Bruin spreads himself over my lap and heaves a deep, contented sigh. I close my eyes to soak it all up, and when the door opens to let Kate back in the room, I jump awake. I can't believe I dozed off.

She gives me her usual patient teacher smile. 'Here you go. It'll help calm you down, and you should enjoy a dreamless sleep, too. We can talk when you're feeling better, or we can go over options now?'

I hide a yawn in the cup as I take a deep sip. 'I'll have a quick version?'

She nods and sits next to me and her dogs. 'We'll have the door fixed in no time, as I said outside. I know Veiled who can easily take care of any fire damage, but we'll need to get the carpet replaced by traditional human means. We can visit a carpet shop later, or tomorrow.'

I think she smiles again, but I'm already dozing off.

'I quite like the one you have here, but I'll discuss it with Bonnie later.' I feel heavy from the tea's drowsy effect, but I also feel a little better already. I know I can tackle this when I wake up.

Honestly, all I hear is that Kate is taking care of it. She talks more, I feel myself nod where I agree with her, and then I drift off completely as I finish my tea and Keano snuggles into my side.

And then I have the best, most relaxing sleep I've had in weeks.

CHAPTER NINETEEN

Bonnie wasn't impressed when she arrived at Kate's. I don't think she blamed me but rather was disgruntled with the situation itself. No one wants to come home to find out they've been moved while they were out. I haven't told her that the fire was probably my fault. It's not that I'm trying to keep information from her, it's just that she's already so annoyed with it and I don't want to make it worse. I'll definitely tell her if an opportunity presents itself.

I really hope that's not tonight. It's Friday evening so it's only been two days, but the tension between us, my anger with myself, and my pain over losing Leverett has made them the longest days I've ever experienced. Kate's friend needs a little longer to come out and fix our door, too, so that probably doesn't help her mood.

Kate has gone out to meet her friends, so it's me, Bonnie, and our three dogs. Since Kate's friends have so kindly agreed to help with so much of the damage and refuse to take a lot of money for it, we're not quite as badly off as we first thought. The fire did a number on the stairs, but we got lucky and the ceiling above it wasn't too affected. There are some char marks, but it's not unstable or unsafe. The carpet is too burnt to keep, of course, and it looks like that's what caught fire, which just about confirms my theory: the fire was my fault. How could I be so stupid? Fortunately, my pride took the worst hit. Every update Kate gave us of her friends offering to help made me realise how lucky we are. We are paying her friends, but we know we're getting discounts, or at least it feels that way. Maybe it's more that our local chain businesses are overpriced. Either way, I feel like we got off lightly.

Bonnie's been annoyed with me this whole time. She blames it on her internship being demanding and exhausting, but I know it's because of me. We haven't really talked about it, but I know the fire is my fault, and clearly, she knows it too. So, tonight, we're ordering in with a movie. Our last movie night didn't count since Sunitha chose that time to break up with Bonnie, so we both need the casual evening. It won't fix what I did, but hopefully it'll smooth over this unpleasant mood at least a little.

Except the tension throughout the movie is killing me. Bonnie isn't laughing at anything, and where we normally chat throughout, she's quiet and short with me. We've barely talked about her internship or what happened with Leverett, either. I don't particularly want to revisit the latter, but it isn't like her to not be interested and supportive. She asked me once how it went, I told her, and she said 'Oh. Sorry' before shutting herself in the bathroom for a while. I hope I'm wrong and it really is just that her internship is being a bitch, because I'm getting tired of it. I know I deserve some kind of punishment for my stupidity, but this feels too harsh. I need my sister. Her own breakup with Sunitha wasn't that long ago, so I'd have thought that she needs me, too.

'Pause?'

I blink and do as she says. 'What is it?' The movie isn't at an exciting moment, but I'm happy that she wants to talk about it. Maybe I misread the tension and she really is just tired.

Bonnie gives me a look like I'm dumb. 'It's your turn to feed the dogs tonight?'

I glance at my phone. Damn, it's feeding time.

'So it is.' I sigh and get up. The moment I twitch one toe, all three dogs swarm around me, tails wagging and eyes hopeful. 'Come on, then.'

I hate that I feel more drained from watching the movie. Even the pizza I ordered barely tasted of anything. Our movie nights aren't supposed to be like this. They aren't supposed to make things worse.

I feed the dogs, who waddle around me so closely that I can barely move. Bonnie is gone when I re-enter the room. We're both sleeping in Kate's living room, so it's not like she's gone upstairs to sleep. I sit on the sofa and wait. When I hear the toilet flush upstairs, I quickly grab my phone and swipe through the news—don't want it to look like I was staring at the wall without her.

'Shall we finish the movie?' she asks, but there's no energy in her voice.

'We don't have to,' I say. 'If you're not enjoying it, I mean.'

She shrugs.

I swallow a sigh as I sink back into the sofa. I don't want it to sound like I'm tired of her attitude, but I am. 'What's going on with you? You've been quiet lately. If anything's worrying you—'

'I told you, it's the internship. It's exhausting.'

It hurts that she cut me off. It hurts that it sounds like an excuse.

So I do something I've only ever done a small handful of times. I push.

'And you're being short with me because of it? How is it my fault?'

'You can't be—' Bonnie sighs and stands. 'I'm getting ready for bed. I need sleep.'

I resist the urge to jump to my feet and hurry after her. 'I can't be what? Did I do something?'

Bonnie rounds on me. 'I'm just so tired of your attitude! All you've done since Leverett left you is mope through the house! You're not the only one who just lost a partner, you know? It's not all about you!'

I'm too stunned to reply. Bonnie takes a step back, like she isn't sure where that came from, either. She doesn't correct herself or apologise, though. Shocked as I am, I'm not entirely sure if she should take it back. Do I deserve this? Have I been inconsiderate?

Slowly, I shake my head like I'm trying to shake myself out of a bad dream. 'I was there when Sunitha called you, wasn't I? We sat together. You cried against me. I comforted you.' Or am I remembering that wrong? 'All you've done since I told you about Leverett is say "Oh. Sorry." Which sounded super sincere, by the way.'

Bonnie huffs. 'Please, do you really think you had a chance with him? Where did you see this going, exactly? I'm not surprised he doesn't want to be with a human, or are you actually upset that he's looking after his mental health?'

'I—'

I have no idea where any of this is coming from or how to react to it. Is she right? Have I been that selfish? It's not like I haven't told myself the same thing. I can't blame Leverett for not wanting to enter a relationship when he knows that I'll die relatively soon. Compared to him, I mean. Distancing ourselves like this is kinder for both of us. But I never expected to hear Bonnie say it, or with so much spite.

'How can you say that?' I ask her. It hurts more than when Leverett said pretty much the same thing. I thought my sister and I would always have each other's backs.

Bonnie glares at me with one hand on the stairs' handrail. 'You know it wouldn't have made any sense.'

'Oh?' I cross my arms, more to hug myself and stop myself from shaking. 'And you and Sunitha would have? She's a mermaid, she probably lives in the ocean. You're a good swimmer, Bonnie, but you can't possibly have thought that would have worked out.'

'She has a house in Bournemouth, actually.' She looks ready to run upstairs, but then she spits out, 'It's more likely than a vampire falling in love with you.'

'At least he isn't a thief!'

Bonnie freezes halfway up the stairs. She turns around slowly, with too much anger in her eyes.

And I know I fucked up.

'What do you mean?'

I flap, lost for words, but I finally sigh. It's too late to take it back now.

'Don't you think it's suspicious that your necklace went missing the same night Sunitha asked to meet up? And then the day after that, she just breaks up with you? Over the phone? Out of nowhere? All I'm saying is maybe—'

Her glare cuts me off. 'She didn't even know I had the thing. It's not like I bring people to my room and show them around my priceless jewellery. Fuck, Esta, she's never even been in my room. How would she have known about it?'

My throat went very dry at some point while she was talking. I deflate and give her what I hope is a deeply apologetic look, but she shakes her head and runs upstairs.

'I'm sorry,' I call after her. 'I didn't—'

She slams the bathroom door shut. I sink onto the sofa and lean against Keano, who's comfy on the sofa and very unbothered by our fight.

Why did I think Sunitha would know? It made so much sense at the time. I always meant to bring up the possibility eventually, but not like this. I just thought... Or maybe I didn't. If I had, I would never have gone that far. I might have let Bonnie go to bed without saying anything, and then we might have talked about the growing rift between us in the morning, refreshed and over tea, like adults.

I don't know how to fix this. I want my dog. I want this half-eaten pizza to go away on its own. It feels too much like a reminder of everything that's gone wrong lately. Bonnie and

I have never had this many leftovers—she barely touched hers, and most of mine is still in the box. I look around for my dog, and my eyes fall on the three food bowls. At least they enjoyed their food. Most of it is gone.

Most.

Lady is lying next to hers looking miserable. She hasn't touched her food.

CHAPTER TWENTY

I don't sleep well that night, or at all, come to think of it. I want to hug Mischief and talk it out with her, see if I've missed anything, but every time I think I'm about to drift off, I remember something I said that I shouldn't have or something someone else said that I wish they hadn't. I remember the ominous death cloud in my dreamscape. It seems to be closing in on me even when I'm awake. Was Anton's party really only a week ago? It feels like way more time has passed, and I feel like I've aged just as much.

Between bouts of nearly falling asleep but not quite, I keep an eye on Lady. My puppy still isn't eating. I try to think when this started, but I can't remember. She was eating fine yesterday, wasn't she? Or was she already eating less then and we just didn't think anything of it because she *was* eating? Now that I think about it, she's been sleeping an awful lot lately. Lack of energy, lack of appetite… I slink off the sofa and curl up on the floor next to her. I'll be damned if I let this curse take my girl, but I don't know how to stop this. This is so much worse than anything the Dreamcatcher did. He was exceptional at nightmares, but they were still just dreams, warnings. Nothing he showed me was real. At least the Dreamcatcher showed himself to me, too. I could talk to him, try to reason with him, but I've no idea who cursed me or how to undo it. Kate gave it her best shot, and it hasn't changed anything. Maybe I'm missing something, but I can't begin to guess at what that might be.

About an hour later, I hear the bathroom door open. Was Bonnie crying or just angrily pacing this whole time? I no longer feel like I have the right to ask. I want to get up, throw myself into her arms, and apologise over and over until we're okay again, but we both need time to cool off. We've both said things we shouldn't have. A few minutes later, Bonnie sneaks down the stairs. If she sees me on the floor with Lady, she doesn't say anything. She leaves, and I don't try to stop her. I'm glad she's got somewhere to go, though I've no idea where.

To think, only a few short days ago my biggest worry was that I might be made redundant. Now I feel like life is making me redundant, and I don't even have the energy to acknowledge the terrible pun. I've lost Leverett, and I know I could just try to be an adult and use his shop as always, but I'm not that deluded. Even if seeing him happy without me wouldn't hurt too much, it would be so fucking awkward. Bonnie and I have handled every breakup together, but this is the worst one and Bonnie isn't here for it. Worse, she said I deserve it. That there's no chance in hell he and I might have worked out. Did she think so from the first time I told her how I felt? She isn't normally a good liar, and neither am I.

Her excitement must have been real, at least in the beginning. Neither of us handles arguments well: Bonnie doesn't address problems; she storms away from them and slams every door along the way. I, on the other hand, get too overwhelmed with emotions, which is why I couldn't keep my stupid mouth shut. Why I said all the wrong things. We both hide from our problems in our own ways.

Maybe that's a sign that our friendship can't last. We've been friends our whole lives, but we've never really fought. Not like tonight. Maybe that's the only reason we've been friends this long—we'd rather pretend everything's fine than confront each other.

And what if I do lose my job? I'd be jobless, best-friend-less, and Leverett-less. I can't stay with Kate forever, but without a job I'll have no money, so where would I go? I'd look for a new job, of course, but it's not like they grow on trees. It could be months or years before I even get an interview.

If this is the universe's way of throwing me into my photography career, it's got a cruel sense of irony. I've just made peace with not doing the Veiled project. I know there are other things—loads of other things—I could do, but I can't think of any of them right now. All I know is the warm dog beside me and the uncertainty around her life. And what if Lady really is sick? What if I take her to the vet, and there's nothing they can do? I hug her tighter. She whines a complaint but doesn't move. Her whining has always broken my heart a little, but I don't think it's ever sounded so weak before. I nudge the untouched food bowl towards her. She ignores it.

Tears burn my eyes. I cry into her neck as I decide to take her to the vet tomorrow. I stay in that position until my tears have dried in her fur, until I don't feel my limbs anymore, until a key turns in the door.

Without saying anything, Kate helps me sit, then move to the sofa where she wraps a blanket around me. I hate that she found me like this. I mumble something about how Bonnie and I fought, that Bonnie left. It sounds pathetic. How did this happen? How could I let it?

'Here.' Kate hands me a steaming cup of tea. It looks like one of those old Victorian tea sets, only this one is black with the moon phases around it. If I were in a better mood, I'd ask her where she got it from. The steam smells vaguely of chamomile and lavender. 'It'll help you think clearly and calm down. I can make you another cup of the one that helped you sleep, too.'

I nod, but even that feels like too much effort. 'Thank you.'

'Do you have any idea where Bonnie might be?'

I shake my head.

'I'm sure she'll come home. Bonnie is a grown-up; she knows what she's doing.'

I really hope Kate is right.

'I didn't mean to come home so late,' she says, 'but I forgot the time talking to my friend. He apologises for the slight delay, but he'll replace the door tomorrow—I think you'll like the one he's chosen.'

I'm amazed I have the energy to raise an eyebrow, but something about Kate being here makes me feel better.

She smiles. 'You'll see. There's something else we discussed, too. If you're up for it, I'd like to ask you a few questions.'

I'm not convinced I'm up for much of anything, but her tea is soothing and I do owe her. A lot.

'Ask away.'

'My friend who is replacing your door is very in tune with nature and its spirits. He noticed something odd about your house when he came to measure the door frame.'

A shiver runs up my arms. This again?

'The smell, you mean?'

Kate nods. 'It reminded me of the time you came by and felt better as soon as you left your home. Since you're awake, I'd like to ask you about it now. It's important.'

I straighten a little. 'And your friend doesn't mind you talking about... you know?'

Kate smiles again. 'Not at all. We talked about you tonight, in fact. The Veiled community is abuzz with the news that someone talked it out with the Dreamcatcher. Depending on who you ask, you're the woman of a long-awaited prophecy.'

I blush. Anton and Saif said something like that, but I don't know how much of it to believe. Seems ridiculous that someone like me might have something as grand as that attached to them.

'I don't even know this prophecy. What exactly is it saying about me?'

Kate waves me off. 'Oh, it's not about you in the sense you think. It doesn't name you. But for centuries the Veiled have dreamed of the day that they and humanity might get along, of the day they no longer need to hide and can be themselves without fear. Somewhere down the line, their wish turned into a kind of prophecy by default.'

'So it's not something an ancient warlock has seen in a dream or anything?'

Kate laughs. 'No. Nothing so dramatic. Be that as it may, many Veiled believe in this vision and hope for it. Some actively pray for it. Your small victory with the Dreamcatcher and why he sought you out in the first place is enough to kindle their hopes.'

I don't know how to feel about that. As Kate said, it's not really a prophecy, more like a shared hope. Much has gone wrong lately, but with this, at least, I can do the right thing and ignore it.

'That's a relief,' I say. 'I wouldn't know how to live up to more than that. Frankly, I don't know what to do as it is.'

Kate takes my hand. More and more, I feel like she's adopting me.

'You don't need to do anything except be yourself.' She winks. 'It's not a real prophecy, remember?'

I'm surprised to feel a small smile tug at my lips.

'The point is, my friend and I discussed you a lot tonight, and what the future might hold for the Veiled. Since I told him so much about you—and he, in fact, already knows quite a bit about you—we thought it only fair to be open with you, too.'

I frown. 'Just how does he know so much about me, anyway?'

'I expect the Mara and Dreamcatcher told some of their friends about you, who in turn spread the word. Whether this was intentional, I can't say.'

I try to picture the Mara and Dreamcatcher around a table

with lots of other Maras and Dreamcatchers while drinking tea with their pinkies out. It's too ridiculous; my smile widens and I let out a huff.

'Beyond this,' Kate says, 'you also attended Anton's party. Many Veiled saw you there and talked to you. You may not be aware that many were watching you very closely and looked for you just to get a glimpse. Gossip is not a solely human privilege. Some of them would have told their friends and families about you.'

'It sounds like I'm some celebrity to them.'

'In a sense, you are. I'm sure you remember how skilled the Dreamcatcher is at his job? The Mara has a reputation, too. Both have lived much longer than most other Veiled alive today. Some say they have always existed, before things had names. Many consider them to be all-powerful, so it has made an impression that they have taken exception to you.'

I blush. I did want to meet more Veiled and make friends— I suppose this might make it easier. I was so worried about how I might approach them, but it seems like they'll start recognising me in the street soon. The very idea makes me pause. It's fine if people just want to chat, but I bet there are plenty like Chiara who hate me on principle or who don't want anything to change.

'Can you teach me some protection magic?'

Kate nods. 'Of course. I already made a note the last time you asked. We didn't have enough time before Anton's party, but I can teach you a few things going forward.'

'Thank you.' I take a few sips of my tea, which has slowly gone cold while we talked. 'How is that relevant to what your friend sensed in my house?'

Kate straightens like she's about to share something super secret…

Or like she's about to deliver terrible news.

'As you know, I sensed something off in your house. I kept thinking about it, and my friend echoed what's been playing on my mind. I would still prefer to ask another friend who's a greater authority on the subject, but I'm certain enough.'

I brace myself. 'Someone who's a bigger authority than you?'

Kate chuckles. 'Hard to imagine, isn't it? This must seem so strange to you. Not that long ago, I was the only witch you knew, but your world has opened up since then. The friend I want to ask is a witch, too, though he is an elemental witch. Do you remember when we first met, I told you that I can't conjure fire or anything like what you see in the movies?'

I nod.

'My friend can. He is over a hundred years old and the leader of his coven. Fortunately, he is also very progressive, and doesn't look down on mere human witches like myself.'

I sense a whole thing there, but I also sense that this isn't the time.

Kate cocks her head to the side, not unlike her dogs. 'Perhaps I'll introduce you some time. For now, answer me this: Have you noticed anything odd around your house? Something that doesn't belong, perhaps?'

I immediately jump to the cloud-wall in my dreamscape, and tell Kate as much. 'I felt like it was closing in on me. When I touched it, a mirror-image of me grabbed my arm and told me I'm cursed.' I shiver at the memory. 'I haven't noticed anything around the house, though. But the other me was right, wasn't she?' I gulp. 'Someone really has cursed me.'

To my surprise, Kate shakes her head. 'I understand why it seems that way, but I don't believe this is the case. Think back a little. Has anything out of the ordinary happened since the Dreamcatcher left?'

'Like what?'

I get that Kate doesn't want to put any ideas into my head— she needs me to really remember something, not think that I do because she suggested I should remember this or that— but I've literally got no clue what we're looking for here.

Kate thinks for a second. 'Have you had any, shall we say, unexpected visitors, perhaps?'

Well, there was Sunitha that one day after my sister fled the beach, but Bonnie told me she was coming over, so that probably doesn't count. While surprise pizza sounds great, we ordered all of ours on purpose, and I knew Leverett would pick me up for the party, too.

'No,' I say. 'I can't think of—'

I freeze. I *can* think of something, but I didn't... I thought it was a dream. It certainly didn't feel real at the time, but if that's what Kate means, then someone was in my house at night while we were sleeping, and that makes freaked-out shivers run all over me.

'There was a man.' I consider how to phrase it as I speak, so the words come out slowly. 'I got up late one night because I was thirsty, and there was a man in my kitchen. I was, like, eighty percent asleep at the time. I didn't think it was really happening. Lady didn't exactly panic at the stranger in the house, either, so I thought it was a dream. Is that it?'

There's an odd mixture of relief and worry on Kate's face. 'Yes, I believe that's it, but since you were so sure it was a dream, allow me to confirm a few things. As a lucid dreamer, how experienced would you say you are at telling the difference between your dreamscape and the waking world?'

I pout. I happen to know the difference very well… when I'm actually in a lucid dream. Even for me, not all dreams are lucid. I do still have the regular variety.

'Pretty good,' I say. 'Normal dreams still happen, though. I can lucid dream at will, but that doesn't mean I do it every night.' Sometimes, I just need sleep without Mischief throwing shade at me over something. Sometimes it's nicer to wake up and not remember any dreams, or to not have worked through this problem or explored that idea while I was sleeping. It's a great ability to have, but I like baking, too, and I don't do that every day just because I can. Some days—okay, most days—I prefer to buy my cakes ready-made.

'So it's possible that you wandered through the house half-asleep and mistook something out of place for a dream?'

I nod. 'Yes. I don't think it's ever happened before, but I don't see why not.' Our minds explain away things we don't understand all the time. The guy in my kitchen didn't make any sense, so I just assumed he wasn't really there. I hug myself. 'Who was he?'

'In a moment. Did you say anything to him?'

I try to remember, but it's like forcing yourself to remember a dream as soon as you wake up—the harder you try, the faster it fades.

'I think I asked him what he wanted, who he was, if he represented any fears…' Standard lucid dream protocol, basically.

But Kate looks increasingly worried. 'Before you saw this man, did you notice anything else? A streak of good luck around the house, maybe, or broken objects that were miraculously fixed over night?'

I shiver. 'There was a cup. I dropped it one morning and didn't have glue to fix it, but it was repaired the next day. I figured Bonnie found some glue and did it.' But I never asked her about it or thanked her. There were other things going on. I completely glossed over it. If I had, could I have avoided this whole thing? If I had thanked her for repairing the mug, she would have told me that she didn't touch it, and I might have found that a little suspicious.

'I take it all this bad luck started after you saw the man?' Kate asks.

I try to think if there was anything before then, but I can't think of anything out of the ordinary. There were a few small things, sure, but it definitely got a lot worse after that.

I nod in response.

Kate sighs in relief. 'You're not cursed, Esta. You've got a boggart.'

I blink at her. 'A what now?'

She frowns. 'A boggart. We briefly talked about brownies and boggarts when we went for a walk through the forest. Don't you remember?'

I remember her mentioning household spirits, different

types of elementals… and being surprised to find out that brownie isn't pronounced like the chocolate cake but as broo-nie. Kate must have mentioned boggarts right after that, when I was too busy being overwhelmed with all the information.

So, really, this is Kate's fault. She over-taught me.

'I… remember something, but no details,' I admit. 'I'm sorry.'

Kate sighs again. 'Don't be. It was a lot to take in, and since it was our first lesson together, I didn't go into much detail. It was merely part of the overview I gave you. I'm glad we have solved this mystery.'

Hearing her say those words is like cooling balm on a scorching blister. We've solved the mystery. Everything can go back to normal now.

'What do I do? Is there any way to turn a boggart back into a brownie?'

Kate nods. 'I know of a way. Do you want to do it now, or would you like to sleep first? You look like you haven't slept all night.'

I glance towards the windows. More light than I expected streams in through the curtains. I really did spend all night feeling sorry for myself.

'No, let's do it now,' I say. 'I want this over with.'

'If you'll allow it, I will call Leverett and Bonnie later. I think they'll be interested to know that all your disagreements were likely due to a wronged household spirit twisting their emotions.' Her eyes turn stormy, and I'm suddenly very grateful that we're on the same side. Under her breath, she says, 'I can't believe a boggart tried to manipulate *me.*'

At first I'm not sure what she means, but then I remember that one chat we had where she snapped at me, once. It's not like her to lose her patience, and Kate looked confused about it at the time. Hardly a crime, all else considered, but I can see why she's annoyed.

'Why do you need my permission?' I ask.

Kate cocks her head again. 'Because I thought you might prefer to explain the situation yourself, at least as far as we have discussed it. I would like to invite them to your home to explain everything fully. I thought that better than repeating myself.'

I shake my head. 'No, that's okay. You call them.'

Understanding why our arguments happened doesn't mean I can just talk to them like nothing happened. It's too recent.

'Go next door and get changed, if you like. I'll make some preparations and then I'll join you.'

I nod and stand, but stop myself before I can leave the room. 'Isn't it… I don't know. Dangerous? To be alone?'

I hate how childish that sounds, but Kate gives me a sympathetic smile.

'Not at all. Boggarts delight in ruining lives, but they don't kill, at least not directly. You might find your shower water's temperature fluctuating or that all your clothes smell of sweat, but you'll be safe from any real harm. Besides, I won't be long. I'll be right over.'

I glance at Lady. 'Can she stay here for now?' I really hope her feeling off is just the boggart's influence. If it is, she'll be back to her old self by the end of today. I'll go home, put on some clothes I left on the rack in the kitchen, and put the kettle on while we have yet another crisis meeting.

And before the day is done, everything will be alright again.

Kate gives my dog a reassuring ear scratch. 'Of course.'

'Thank you,' I say. 'Just let yourself in.'

I feel hopeful as I leave Kate's. I won't go upstairs because I don't fully trust the stairs after the fire—is that something else the boggart did?—but it's nice to be in my house again, to make tea in my own kitchen. If everything bad that happened recently is just down to the boggart messing with me, and Kate believes he can be reasoned with… there's hope for me and Bonnie, me and Leverett, me and my job, Lady.

But before I've even shut the front door, I see a dark figure from the corner of my eyes. I turn my head and see Chiara leaning against the fireplace. A dark smile spreads on her lips when our eyes meet.

'Welcome home, my toy.'

The last thing I see before I lose consciousness is her smile twisting into a grin.

CHAPTER TWENTY ONE

My head is pounding when I come to. The rest of me feels alright, just a bit stiff. I'm a little scared to open my eyes in case Chiara is right in front of me, but I don't hear anything, so I risk a peek.

I'm alone and lying on concrete. That explains why my head is hurting so much. I get up, eyes still half-shut against the pain in my head, and am surprised that nothing is stopping me— no chains or ropes around my wrists, nothing tied around my ankles. I blink and take in the room. It's a basement—a *large* basement, but there's nothing special about it except for the floor. The bit I woke up on is concrete, but there's a hardwood floor in front of me. From my position, it almost looks like a stage. It's just missing the chairs.

Blood rushes into my head so fast I feel faint. What if it *is* a stage? Leverett said Chiara toys with her victims, tortures them before she finally kills them.

And now, she has me.

My eyes dart around the room searching for an escape route, but I don't see anything that would help me. Stairs along the left wall lead up to, I'm guessing, the rest of the house, but I doubt they're unlocked and waiting for me to go home. There's only one small window, and it's too tiny to light the whole room properly, let alone for me to squeeze through. The smallest strip of sunlight filters in and throws thin shadows around everything. Not that there is much that could throw a shadow: There's just a workbench along the left wall and a few gardening tools like a bucket, a spade…

My heart skips a painful beat. Is Chiara going to bury me in her garden? It's hard to imagine her trimming the roses. I walk up to the workbench. The surface is stained a dark reddish brown. There are all kinds of mean-looking tools on there. I don't recognise any of them, though they all look like torture tools to me. Best I can do is name a few as knives.

My knees go weak, and I fall back against the wall. Was this always her plan? Maybe I shouldn't have talked back at her during the party, but I wasn't just going to stand there and let her insult me. I hold my hand out in front of me. It's shaking. My whole body feels too weak to do anything, let alone get up, dash upstairs, and run. I don't even know where I am. The small window doesn't give much away, and I don't know how long I was out. Could Chiara have used vampire magic to keep me passed out? For all I know it's been days.

But it couldn't be. Kate was about to come over. She'll have noticed I'm gone, and she'll have called Bonnie and Leverett by now. Bonnie might not have picked up if she was too angry with me, but Leverett would have come. Not wanting to be in a relationship with me doesn't mean he won't help when I've been kidnapped. Maybe Kate saw Chiara carry me out of the house? I've seen Leverett turn into fog and fly through a room several times, and I bet Chiara can do the same thing. Would she be able to carry me like that, though? I could be miles away from home, and it might only have taken her a few minutes to get here. She probably hasn't left a note, so…

I gulp. I can't count on Kate or L—

My phone. I frantically search my pockets for it, my heart missing another beat out of relief this time. But I panic again when I don't find it. Chiara must have taken it off me. Damn it! There goes that idea.

I walk around the room, inspecting every wall for a secret tunnel or something equally helpful, but of course, I find fuck all. There's no way I'm getting out of this basement unless Chiara lets me out or someone rescues me.

I sigh in temporary defeat and look around again. The walls may not have turned up anything useful, but there must be something in here I can use. There are all those tools on the table. They must be good for more than removing fingernails or— Fuck, I don't want to think about it. Not when there's a chance Chiara will use them on me in a minute. She's faster than I am, and stronger. I can't convince her to let me go. Not sure what options that leaves me.

I shrink back when a key turns in the door. There's nowhere to hide. My survival instinct tells me to fight back and/or grovel for my life, but I've already established that the former is highly unlikely, and I refuse to beg Chiara for anything, least of all to not hurt me. If she was a reasonable woman, she probably wouldn't have kidnapped me.

Is it possible that the boggart influenced her actions, too?

Maybe, but even if it did, Leverett said she's kept humans as playthings for centuries. Her hatred for us far outlives anything the boggart has been up to in my house; though if its influence did somehow find her, I doubt she was difficult to convince. She was already halfway there when she threatened me in Anton's private library. Unless that was the boggart, too? But I'd only just met her, and from everything I've heard, it was right in character for her, so probably not. Some people are just assholes.

Since there's no way for me to fight back and no chance in hell I'll plead with her, I straighten my back and square my shoulders. If this bitch wants to break me, she can take her best stab at me.

Though I won't tell her that.

The door opens. I stare Chiara down with an inner strength I don't actually have but fake well, or so I hope. She smiles with every step she takes down. She locked the door behind her again—so she's happy for me to move freely down here, but she won't give me any false hopes in case I reach the door. Does that mean I could actually reach it? I can't deny what seeing the door shut again does to me, though. Chiara didn't have to say anything for my heart to drop. That door is my only way out of here, and she won't even let me try.

My eyes sting, but I blink the tears away and straighten my back again—it had slumped sometime after I made eye contact with her. It's too early for a mental breakdown. I'm worried that if I start crying now, I won't be able to stop, because it dawns on me how hopeless this situation is. Chiara herself reminded me during Anton's party how pathetic we humans are compared to vampires. Even if I did manage to get out of this basement, she'd catch me long before I reached the front door. I can kick and scratch at her all I want, but I bet she kicks harder, and I know her claws are an awful lot sharper than my trimmed nails. Whatever happens next, I'm entirely at her mercy, and I hate how little I can do about that. I don't want to give up, definitely not so soon after waking up, but I'm not deluded. I don't have a chance.

Unless…

Would a hit to her head do anything? Maybe, if she gets close enough…

And then she's right in front of me. I see her eyes and grin for only a second, nose so close it's almost touching mine, before she slams me into the wall. It knocks the air out of me. One arm got trapped behind me, and while I didn't hear or feel a crack, it *hurts*. Chiara holds me up by my neck with one hand, my feet just slightly dangling off the ground. Her free hand strokes my cheek as she makes soft cooing noises. It's disturbing as fuck.

'Did that hurt, little human?' she purrs.

Who knew a voice could be so smooth yet so cold at the same time? I won't tell her that she scares the life out of me, but I probably don't need to. She can smell it.

I put all my anger into my glare. At least, I hope my fear looks like anger. I'd rather surrender to hating her and putting every ounce of that hatred into every word than break down and start crying in front of her.

Chiara chuckles. 'So headstrong! I will enjoy breaking you.'

I freeze when one nail traces my neck.

I've never even been in a normal fight before—the kind where people throw insults around, maybe fists or kicks or whatever—and if I had, I wouldn't have known what to do. I doubt insults will do the trick, and I can't get a punch in, being pinned to the wall as I am, but I try to kick out. I get her a few times, too, but she seems perfectly unbothered. I didn't think it would do anything. I just know I need to hurt her before she hurts me.

Her nail slowly cuts into my neck. All of me goes still, too afraid that I'll bleed out if I wriggle even a fraction. How deep is it? It doesn't hurt much. Because my body hasn't quite registered it yet, because it's going into shock, or because it's not actually that deep? I doubt it's the last one.

And then the pain does hit me. A hot, searing sensation just below my ear. Warm blood trickles down my neck, weirdly soft against the pain. It doesn't feel like much, but the violation of it, the wrongness of my blood on my neck, has me unable to move. If Chiara wanted to kill me right now, there'd be nothing I could do about it. Fortunately, I don't think she'll kill me yet, not until she's tortured me for a while.

Chiara brings her face to my neck. I tense when her tongue touches my skin to lick it up.

She chuckles against me. 'Did he ever tell you how delicious you are? Surprisingly sweet. And here I thought a pathetic thing like you would be bitter.'

She pulls away just enough to look me in the eyes. Her lips are stained red.

Then her smile vanishes in half a second, and she slams me against the wall again.

'I asked you a question! Did he ever tell you how delicious you are?'

I just about manage to shake my head. My insides constrict when I do what she says, but I don't see any other option.

She laughs and lets go. I fall to the floor and don't try to get up again—I've a feeling she won't take well to me doing anything she hasn't told me to do. My hands fly to my neck, my heart racing at the thought that they'll come away slick with blood, but there's only a tiny amount. Her saliva must have sealed the wound. Which means she could literally keep me alive and hurting for... well, I don't know. Whatever her plans are, she can and will make it work.

There has got to be a way out of here, besides the door she came through. If there isn't, maybe I'll find something to...

I swallow. No. I'll fight until she kills me or someone finds me. The longer I keep going, the more chance there is of Kate or Leverett tracking me down. I want to say *the longer I resist*, but I'm not sure that applies. If Chiara wants information from me, she can use her vampire magic to make me tell her anything. If I resist too much, she'll simply kill me since there isn't really anything in this for her. There's a very thin line I need to walk, except it's dark and I can't see a thing.

'He didn't bite you?' Chiara asks. 'Not once?' I shake my head again. She scoffs. 'He really has grown pathetic.' Her lips curl into a smile I'm quickly starting to hate. If I get out of here, I'll be seeing this in my nightmares for the rest of my life. 'So, am I the first to taste you?'

I glare at her. How many vampires does she think I know? What does she think my friends do—pass me around so they can each have a bite? I shiver. That's probably exactly what she'd do, actually.

She genuinely looks surprised that Leverett hasn't bitten me. Not sure if this gives me an advantage somehow, but I'm sure she'll spin it against me.

'Perhaps he doesn't like you all that much after all, then,' she says. For a second, she looks like she's considering options I'm not aware of.

Then she disappears in a huff of fog, reappears right in front of me, and shoves me into the floor. One hand grabs my hair and pulls my head back. It's all happening too fast for me to make sense of. One second, she's over there, the next she's pinning me down—

Chiara rams her teeth into my neck. A strangled scream escapes me, but it flexes my neck muscles against her fangs, and it hurts.

I imagined this many times, with Leverett. It was nothing like this. Chiara doesn't try to make it hurt less—if anything, I'm pretty sure she's making it hurt more just because she can. The sudden brutality of it has me frozen in terror. My whole body goes limp. All I can feel is a searing pain where her mouth is, where it feels like she's tearing a gaping hole into my neck. In one swift strike, Chiara has drained all strength from me, and all I can do is let it happen.

A tear runs down my cheek. I hate myself for it.

Finally, Chiara sits up. She looks down at me, lips and chin smeared with my blood. One finger strokes away the tear.

'Don't cry, Estelle. I can't have broken you already, can I? I wonder how few days you will last as my plaything. Or will it be mere hours before your weak little mortal heart gives out?' She lowers herself back down. For a second, I'm afraid she'll bite me again, but she merely whispers, 'Or might it be that you weren't all that brave to begin with? Here I thought you had to be something special for him to care about you, but we've already established that he doesn't like you all that much, haven't we? You're nothing, just as I said.'

She vanishes in a sigh of fog again. I don't see her reappear because I can't turn my head, but I barely make out a shadow from the corner of my eyes.

'You are *nothing*,' she hisses.

Then the door slams shut, and I'm lying alone with my head in a pool of my blood.

CHAPTER TWENTY TWO

My whole neck feels hot and mangled. I tried to get up once my legs felt up to it, but it hurts so much that I can't even sit, let alone stand and move around the room.

If Chiara has been back, she hasn't said anything, and she hasn't bitten me again. I think she has been in the room, though—I've felt her glare on me a couple of times, though I couldn't turn my head to check. I want to ignore the pain and do something, but I'm terrified the slightest movement will open the wound. I can't afford to lose any more blood than Chiara has already taken, or so I assume, anyway. I can't risk it.

Is Kate looking for me? Has Leverett picked up my scent? I don't see Chiara being so careless as to leave my scent, erm… lying around? I'm not sure Leverett will be able to find her unless she allows it—at least that was her threat back at Anton's party—and if even Leverett can't find me… No offense to Kate, but what's she supposed to do? When I first came to, I'd wondered if Bonnie might forgive me long enough to answer Kate and come looking for me. Now I hope she doesn't. Leverett would have a chance against Chiara, but I don't think Kate and Bonnie would fare any better than I have.

Besides Chiara, I haven't seen or heard anyone else. The basement seems to be soundproof. That, or Chiara makes zero sound as she moves, which is possible—I haven't heard one floorboard creak. Does she live alone? Is there a whole group of human-hating Veiled in this house? But they'd have come to check out the stupid, defenceless human. Wouldn't they? If nothing else, I'm three hundred percent sure Chiara would have brought them down here to gloat. Unless she's brought them down here while I was out cold, but where's the fun in that for them? So I'm fairly sure she's alone up there.

Which doesn't help my chances of running away any. Neither does the lightheadedness.

I don't know how much blood Chiara has taken, but I think I'd be able to stand and walk around if it weren't for the angry throbbing in my neck. The only real assurance I have that Chiara hasn't taken a dangerous amount of blood is that she wants to keep me around for a while. If I die on Day 1, I imagine she'd see it as a waste of a perfectly good toy— although, from what she said, she doesn't expect me to last very long at all. *Hours*, she said. Does that mean it hasn't even been a day yet? All of this is degrading and humiliating, and I want to throw all the threats and dark promises at her if only I could make myself believe them. *I'll make you pay*. Would I, though? *You will regret this*. Oh? What am I going to do? Die faster? Right. That'll show her.

The longer I lie here, the more the dizziness fades. It's

probably a safe assumption that the blood loss was only part of what caused it. The shock and panic made up the rest. If only I could get up, I could test how well I can move. I don't know what I'd do with that knowledge since my chances of running away from the pissed-off vampire are non-existent, but there must be something I can do.

The door opens, and I go rigid. I kept my eyes shut this whole time since I couldn't turn my head to look around anyway and because the dark is oddly comforting, so hopefully, Chiara won't know I'm awake.

I sense her coming down the stairs more than I hear her. Something about the way the air shifts and flows around her.

'Wake up, Estelle,' she coos right into my ear.

I jump. I didn't realise she was this close, and now my sleep cover is blown, too.

'Oh, poor thing,' she purrs. 'Did I scare you?'

She strokes my face with one finger and turns my head to the side. My whole neck screams; the pain flares into my shoulder and scalp. I hate that I gasp. I hate that I give her exactly what she wants, that I can't even keep such a small sound to myself.

Chiara tuts. 'Oh, my. That looks bad, doesn't it? Have you seen it?' She laughs. 'Of course you haven't. Hang on, my sweet, foolish human.'

She sits next to me and pulls me up until I lie against her. She eases my head back against her chest with one hand while fumbling in her pocket with the other. I'm not sure what she's up to until she holds up a small mirror. I instinctively close my eyes. It's not much, but I will defy her in every way I can.

'Look at your neck, Estelle. Look at what I did to you.'

She wants me to cry when I see the wound. She wants me to beg.

I brace myself, determined to give her neither, and open my eyes.

My neck looks like a mess at first glance. Most of it is dried blood smears, though. The actual wound is just two small points—not the wide-open gash the pain is pretending to be. That's a relief. But I still pale at the sight of it.

'Do you see now how pretty you are with some blood on you?' A strand of hair falls in front of my face. Chiara strokes it away. 'Just think how much prettier you'll look when your whole body is red.'

I smirk and confuse defiance with stupidity.

'Leverett thought I was pretty without it.'

Chiara's eyes darken. Her arms around me stiffen, and she rams her fangs into my neck, only slightly off where she bit me before. The pain is so intense I can't even gasp. Whatever strength I had left drains right out of me and down her throat. She didn't take too much before, but she's angry this time.

My vision darkens around the edges. A tear runs down my chin; I hope it mingles with my blood and ruins it for her. Although, she probably likes the taste of human tears.

Damn it, I can't even die right.

But at least I'm going out having made her feel like shit, if only for a moment.

I slowly blink myself awake, surprised that I get to wake up at all. I was so sure Chiara was killing me, but I suppose there's no fun in that for her. I have zero delusions about her ever letting me go, but now that I've taunted her? She'll really draw this out.

It begins to sink in that this room is the last thing I'll see. I'll never see Bonnie again, or Kate, Lady. Leverett. Everything we said to each other seems so stupid now. Did I really think I'd be better off never seeing him again if I couldn't love him? The fuck am I, fourteen? And Bonnie… I can't believe we fought. The boggart twisted our feelings until we said those things, but we still said them. It only brought out what was already there, didn't it? Bonnie and I should have talked it out long before now. When we were kids, we made a pinkie promise to always be honest with each other. Turns out that's a lot harder in reality when you have to take the other person's feelings into account. And did I really suspect Sunitha, who seemed so lovely when she came over?

I'm such an idiot. Even if Kate deals with the boggart somehow, there's no guarantee that Bonnie will forgive me. I might still lose my job. Leverett might still decide that loving a human is too painful.

And I have no right to argue with any of it. They're all grown-ups. They can make their own decisions. And I will respect them, no matter what they are.

But all that is pointless, really, because I'm never getting out of here. I can't fight Chiara, at least I don't see how. I'm losing everything—*have* lost everything, since I'm somewhat trapped—and it's all my fault. If I'd just talked to Bonnie and Leverett, if I'd just taken Lady to the vet instead of being afraid of what her diagnosis might be… I could have saved every single relationship. That option is gone now.

Fresh tears roll down my cheeks. While Chiara has kept me alive for now, I don't think I can move. Everything either hurts or I don't feel it at all. I never really imagined how I might die, but I wouldn't have pictured this—slowly bleeding out at the whim of a mad vampire.

The Esta before this mess was so, so, *so* stupid. If I had any hope of getting out of here, I'd do better. I'd be a better friend. I'd be a better student. I'd be a better dog mum. I'd stop focussing on the things I can't control and focus on the ones I can. I hate that it's taken dying for me to realise how much choice I've had in everything. Losing Bonnie would hurt. Accepting Leverett's rejection breaks my heart. Hearing bad news about my dog's health would make me sob violently in the vet's office. But we all die eventually. Bonnie and I have given Lady the best life a dog could possibly have. That's all we could do.

I don't want to lose any of them, but I realise now that it isn't my decision alone, and some things are simply outside of my control. I can hate it all I want; it won't change anything.

And as the truth of that sinks in, I lose whatever strength I had left as I grow impossibly light…

And float away.

Once again, I'm surprised to wake up, only this time I wake to the purple-leafed tree in my dreamscape and a paw on my face.

'Oh good,' Mischief purrs. 'You're up.'

Her paw slides to my nostrils. She puts so much pressure behind it that it's actually difficult to breathe.

I jolt upright, and Mischief falls away from me with a disgruntled chirp. My hand flies to my neck. No injury. No blood. No pain. My heart is racing, so I make myself take deep breaths to get my thoughts in order. I'm not dead. At least, not yet.

It's still night in my dreamscape, so I make the stars twinkle even brighter than usual. The moon is so large and bright that it illuminates everything. It may be night, but it isn't dark, at least not in here. That's if I ignore the ominous shadow wall. I'm not sure how far away it is exactly, but it's much closer to my tree than it was last time I was here. I can't see anything behind it, so I don't know if the dreamscape it's rolled across is still there or dead or perfectly unchanged. Looking at it, I feel like I should hear a distant rumbling like a coming thunderstorm, but the wall is completely silent. Probably because that's more terrifying. After all, if Chiara had announced herself, I wouldn't have gone home. She only ambushed me because I had no idea she'd be there; although, if I'm honest, she could have overpowered me either way and kidnapped me right out from under Kate's glare. Now that I know about the boggart, I imagine it's got something to do with this wall, too, though I can't address the boggart personally right now.

'Warn a cat before you sit up, will you?'

I shoot her a look. 'I couldn't breathe with your paw on my nose.'

Mischief jumps onto my legs and paws at my face again. I feel like she slapped me. 'What's it matter if you suffocate here or bleed out there? You've given up, haven't you?'

I shake my head. 'I haven't. I just…' I swallow and reach out to pet her. 'I didn't think there was anything I could do.'

'There's always something you can do,' she says. 'Getting up might hurt, but dying isn't ideal, either, now is it?'

I pull Mischief into my arms and let a few indulgent tears fall into her fur. She's so soft, and she's so right. I was too busy feeling sorry for myself to even try. Yes, moving any number of neck muscles would have been excruciating, but am I really going to stay down until I'm dead? Am I really going to let Chiara mutilate me again and again?

I don't bloody think so—pun intended.

Mischief rolls her eyes at me.

'I'm so glad I get to hug you.' I inhale her kitty smell. Since I never had a cat, I made her smell similar to my dog but softer. They both smell of love and home and snuggles.

Mischief licks at my tears as if to wash them away. 'I missed you, too. Now get out there and fight that bitch.'

A half sob, half laugh escapes me. I swear a lot, but for some reason Mischief doesn't, at least not usually. You'd think she'd get that from me, too, but no.

'Hang on.' I let go so Mischief can move freely. 'I still don't know what to do. Waking up wanting to get out won't help me much. The door is locked, and Chiara is probably camped behind it.'

Mischief yawns. 'That *is* a problem. What are you going to do about it?'

I frown at her. 'I don't know. You mean you have no ideas?'

So much for discussing it with my unconscious.

'Neither of us knows what's behind the door or how to

open it, do we? I don't have any more information than you do.'

There goes my hope again. I didn't think she'd have some magical answer that'll get me home in an instant, but I had hoped for better advice than this.

'You just said there's always something.'

Mischief stretches and looks at me. 'Have you tried magic?'

I fall back onto the red grass with a grunt. 'No, I haven't tried magic, Mischief. I don't know any magic.'

I feel her jumping onto my chest, apparently still determined to make breathing difficult for me. 'Don't you?'

'Of course I don't. Wouldn't I know if—'

I stare straight up. I might not know if I can do magic, but… my unconscious would know, wouldn't it? My parents didn't raise me to fling spells around or do the less flashy variety that Kate practices, but if I did have that kind of magic, if I was one of the Veiled…

My unconscious would know.

'What can I do? No one taught me any spells.'

Mischief does her kitty equivalent of a shrug. 'I don't know.'

Thank the stars she's here.

'No time to learn like the present, though, right?' she purrs.

Mischief begins to fade, and for a moment I'm worried the wall is doing something to her, but everything else is fading, too.

I'm waking up.

'Fuck. Quick, Mischief! Is there anything you can tell me?'

She reaches for me, but her paw goes straight through my leg. 'I'm sorry, Esta. The information is hidden even from me.

You'll have to find your own answers.'

I swear again.

And then my heavy eyes open to Chiara's basement ceiling.

CHAPTER TWENTY THREE

It's a blessing that Chiara isn't here when I wake up. A part of me—okay, many parts of me—were worried I'd awaken to her teeth in my neck again, but the room is empty except for me and my blood. I'm amazed I can't smell it, but I've probably got used to it now. Which isn't great in itself.

I don't know how long I have. Chiara could be on her way to me right now, and I've no guarantee that she won't just kill me then. Maybe she's found another plaything and needs the basement. I doubt she'll get rid of me that quickly, but who knows what she's thinking? I'm not taking the chance.

I gingerly turn my head to the left, away from the bite. The small movement sets my whole neck on fire. How am I supposed to get up and walk around, maybe run for my life? I'm more likely to pass out before I reach the top of the stairs.

But I can't stay down here. Mischief is right, there's always something I can do, even if I don't know yet what that is. I just know I'm done feeling sorry for myself. Right now, I'm going to get out of here. I can acknowledge all the fire in my neck once someone finds me and takes me to the hospital.

And if I bleed out before then…

Well, then I guess I'd be dead either way, so I may as well take the risk.

Carefully, I sit up. The strain on my neck makes me dizzy, but I take a moment to breathe once I'm upright, and the pain fades. I close my eyes a second and focus on the tender skin around the wound. It hurts like nothing else ever has, but I don't feel a trickle or a flood. That's something.

I wish I could at least open that tiny window. The breeze always makes me feel better. I can reason through anything when I stand in the wind. No luck with that down here, but I can pretend there's a breeze on my skin.

I cross my legs and pray that Chiara doesn't return now. As much as she loves to play with my life, there must be other things she does. I don't exactly see her having a regular job, but surely she has some form of routine? The painful truth is that I've no idea whether she'll be back in ten seconds or ten hours. I could have loads of time, or she could be moving the key towards the lock right now. My heart races faster at the thought, but I will myself to calm down. I won't do myself any favours if I panic. This might be my only chance, so I need to make it count.

But first, I need to be calm enough to approach this logically, so I keep my eyes closed and consider everything I know about this room. The tiny window is shut tight, and even if it weren't, it'd be too small for me to fit through. Maybe I could punch a hole in it with one of Chiara's tools? Maybe if I ram the spade's hilt into the glass… That would take a lot of strength, though, and I don't have much of that at the best of times. Would I manage to destroy the window or would I just make a racket and tell Chiara that her newest toy is being uppity? I need her to be unaware of what I'm doing, whatever that'll be, for as long as possible.

There isn't an awful lot else in the room I could use, though. If there are any secret passages, I don't see them; though I suppose that's the point of a secret passage.

The way I see it, I have two options: I can either spend my time looking for a hidden tunnel that may not exist, or I can try my luck with the door, which definitely exists but which is also definitely locked, and there's a good chance that Chiara is home. I don't fancy either option, but there isn't a third except waiting for Kate and Leverett to arrive, but I don't know that they'll find me. I can't rely on them for this.

I rack my brain for any weakness Chiara might have shown me, anything Leverett might have said that would help me fight her, but I don't remember anything. Didn't he say that only a vampire can really kill another vampire? That doesn't help me. Add to that my current state, and I'd have exactly zero chance to take Chiara in a fight… and that's with accepting that I wouldn't have had a chance in hell even if I trained for a year and put on some muscle. Besides, as much as I hate her, I'm not a murderer. Could I kill her in self-defense? Maybe, if I got lucky and she slipped up. Adrenaline and survival instinct would drive much of that. But could I challenge her to a fight with the intention of killing her? No. I can't see that. It's not me.

The door lock catches, and my heart misses a beat. Chiara can't be back so soon—I'm not ready. But, of course, Chiara couldn't care less about what I want. The door opens, and she strides onto the stairs with a smug smile.

I'm dying to know what exactly Mischief figures I can do here.

'If you've got any smart ideas, now's the time,' I mumble under my breath.

To no one's surprise, Mischief doesn't answer. Although… she isn't technically part of my dreamscape; she's part of my unconscious. Do I need to be asleep to access that or could I talk this through with her right now? My unconscious doesn't go anywhere when I'm awake. It's easier to access when I'm asleep, but it's not like it's on holiday to Bali right now.

'Took you long enough,' a voice that sounds suspiciously like Mischief says.

Chiara reaches the bottom of the stairs and gives me a crooked smile. 'What's that? Do speak up, human. Was that a last wish I heard? Something about smart ideas?'

I glare back at her, but my mind is working overtime. She didn't comment on what Mischief said—or on what sounded like something Mischief said. Does that mean she didn't hear it? Does that mean it really was Mischief, just in my head?

Maybe I can do something with this. I just don't know what.

'I said it's not a very smart idea, keeping me locked up here.' Fuck knows why I keep taunting her. She's going to kill me anyway, right? I can and will make myself as annoying as I can before she gets fed up. That doesn't mean I'm unaware of the stupidity, though. Chiara has all kinds of torture methods at her disposal, and I keep telling her to do her worst. I'm not prepared to die pleading for mercy, but that doesn't mean I have to go out screaming in agony, either. 'Kate and Leverett will find me. They'll tear you apart.'

Okay, so, I don't know if Kate could tear her apart or if Leverett would do it for a dead human, but it gives me some comfort to picture it. Maybe my ghost can hang around long enough to watch. That would almost make dying worth it. Given what Leverett told me, though, maybe he wouldn't hurt another vampire over an already dead human. What will my memory be worth to him in a hundred years or so, when Chiara, Anton, and Saif are still around and looking dashing at their parties?

'Or better yet,' Mischief purrs, 'you stay alive and tear Chiara apart together.'

I swallow. I've no idea what the limitations of this are or if there's a chance it's not her at all and I'm just going crazy from bloodloss, but that'll be something to consider when I'm home and hugging my dog.

'What do I do?' I say under my breath, hoping that Mischief can hear me and Chiara can't.

Chiara appears right in front of me, her eyes dark with blood lust. 'What else? You can bleed for me, silly human.'

'*Run*,' Mischief hisses.

So I do.

Chiara doesn't expect it, so I'm proud to say that I manage five full feet before she laughs and grabs my wrist.

Good one, Mischief.

'Don't blame me if you're slow,' Mischief purrs. I picture her yawning with a big stretch. 'If you were a cat or a bird, you could have done it.'

I scowl my response at Chiara. Unhelpful as Mischief is being, I feel less alone with her in my head. I don't massively care if it is just a form of insanity right now—I feel like we're a tiny, sarcastic team. I let Mischief down once with the Dreamcatcher. I won't let her down now. If she tells me to run again, I will try again. It's not like I have a better plan.

'Where do you think you're going?' Chiara laughs. 'You don't really think you could outrun me, do you?'

She lets go, vanishes in a huff of smoke, and reappears at the top of the stairs. 'You must know it's hopeless.' She reappears in another corner. 'You humans have such desperate fighting spirit, even when faced with a superior predator.'

She vanishes again, and for a moment I don't know where she's gone. I do notice something, though: Chiara didn't close the door behind her this time. If I can somehow outwit her… I'd still need to actually get out of the house, leave the property—which is no doubt locked behind a huge gate—and flag down someone on the road before she catches up with me, but it'd be nice to make progress.

'Now's the time if you've got any ideas, Mischief,' I hiss.

'Wait for it—'

I sense Chiara behind me before I feel her breath on my hair. Her hand closes over my mouth and pulls my head back. My heart races as she exposes my neck. I can't have her biting me again. I don't think I can endure it.

'Wait for it—'

I don't know what the fuck Mischief wants me to wait for, but what else have I got? I bide my time, as she says.

Chiara's other hand strokes my hair. It's such a gentle movement that it catches me off guard.

'Why do you struggle?' Chiara whispers in my ear. 'You're only making it harder on yours—'

An image of myself ramming my head back into Chiara flashes through my head.

'Now!'

I do what the kitty says and slam my head back as hard as I can. Chiara never saw it coming. I think I hear a crack.

She sucks air in through her teeth in a shocked gasp.

'Run, Esta!' Mischief screams.

I hurry up the stairs as fast as I can. The sudden head movement made me dizzy, so everything is spinning as I dash up the stairs. I feel a trickle of blood run down my neck—the jolt opened the wound again.

'You will regret that,' Chiara growls behind me.

I don't turn around, I don't reply, just three more steps and I'll be at the—

Chiara reaches me just before I would have reached the door. She slams me into the wall and turns me around, one hand on my wrist and the other pushing into my shoulder.

'Silly girl! My nose will heal before ten minutes have passed.' The anger leaves her eyes, and a mad twinkle replaces it. 'Your blood will help me heal the small damage you just dealt. Look.'

And I do look, because there's a thin trail of blood running out of her nose. Did I break it? I can't believe I managed to draw blood. I doubt I have the strength to knock her out completely, but I did that. I managed to hurt a vampire. Only by chance, yes, but that doesn't matter. I did it once, and I can do it again. I've just proven to myself that it's possible.

'You're welcome,' Mischief purrs in my head.

Now what? I think at her, hoping she can hear me. I don't see why she wouldn't, but I don't want to make assumptions.

Mischief has my back, though. 'Give me a moment, I want to try something.'

I seriously hope I have that long. The thirst in Chiara's eyes says otherwise. I beg Mischief to hurry and do the only thing I can to buy time:

I piss off Chiara some more.

'How did it feel when my head hurt your nose? A human, hurting you!' Against my better judgement, which I seem to have left at Kate's, I lean my head towards her as far as I can. 'How did that feel?' I whisper.

Chiara's hand flies around my neck and chokes me. The wound sears to life again. My vision flashes white as the fire returns to my neck.

'And how did it feel,' Chiara hisses, 'when my fangs punctured your weak flesh? You think you've suffered, human? I can bite you anywhere and prolong the pain—your neck is just the easiest place. You don't know agony, you stupid child, but you will when I'm done with you. You will beg me for death long before that.'

My mouth goes dry, because I believe it. If I don't get out now, I'll never get a second chance.

Whatever you're doing, do it faster, I silently beg Mischief.

'Nearly there,' she replies.

It's a good thing Chiara is more sadistic than she is smart. Someone else would simply have killed me, but no, *some*one has to make it last. I thank every god in all the universes that she is that kind of person.

'Where shall I bite you next, hm?' Chiara's hand runs from the wound to the front of my neck. 'Sadly, a bite to your throat would kill you too fast, and you don't deserve a quick death.' Her hand gently glides down my neck to my breasts, my sides, my belly, my inner thighs. Her eyes meet mine, and her lips curl into a smile. 'I know.' She grabs my wrist and brings it up so it's between our faces. 'Watch me drain the life from your veins, you sad creature.'

My legs go weak when her fangs extend.

Mischief—

But my spirit kitty doesn't respond. I hope it's because she's busy helping me.

Chiara brings her mouth to my wrist and licks the skin. My whole body goes rigid. I can't let her bite me again, I just can't. I try to wriggle my hand free, but her grip is too strong.

She laughs, her breath warm against my skin. One fang grazes my veins. Everything around me blurs. My heart beats too fast. No no no no n—

Chiara pierces the skin.

I scream.

I shove at Chiara with my arm still attached to her.

And a burst of bright, green-yellow energy slams into her face. The force of it rips her fangs out of me and shoves me back against the wall at the same time that Chiara stumbles backwards down the stairs, her eyes wide with shock. Mine mirror hers. I've no idea how deep the puncture wounds are. Not very, I don't think. I don't know how badly she's hurt, or how quickly she might catch herself. All I know is that she loses her footing as her heel slides off the step, and then she's falling.

I don't stay to check her pulse. I turn around and run.

CHAPTER TWENTY FOUR

I stumble out of the basement, nearly falling over my own feet in my panic to get away from Chiara.

'The fuck did I just do?' I ask Mischief as I run into the first room I find.

'More running, less complaining!' Mischief shoots back. 'We can talk later!'

I sense through our connection that she isn't sure, either. She clearly did something that allowed me to push Chiara away from me, but that's all I know. It almost looked like magic, but that can't be right. Learning from Kate is one thing—that's magick anyone can do. This, though… My stomach turns when I remember how Chiara lost her footing and fell backwards down the stairs. She was a horrible person and I defended myself, but…

'Esta!' Mischief hisses at me. 'Focus!'

I swallow every question and worry I have and make a mad dash through the house. The basement opened into a corridor. The first room I try is a bathroom, the next looks like a laundry room. I'm silently amazed that Chiara has need for either, but

I suppose she'd have a lot of bloodstains to wash out—and that'll be me all across the floor tiles if I don't hurry. I can't decide if I want her to be dead and therefore incapable of coming after me, or if I want her to be okay because I can't rationalise having killed someone—either way, she might catch up with me any second now.

'*Oh, thank fuck,*' I sigh when I find the front door. I all but throw myself at it and push down the handle.

It doesn't budge. The door is locked.

'*Fuck!*'

Everything around me grows woozy. I was so close to getting out. What if there is no other door? What if there are several but they are all locked? I'm using so much energy and leaving a handy trail of blood drips all over Chiara's house, and it could all be for nothing. For all I know, this is part of her game—a bit of hope, right before I never see sunlight again.

Something tickles my neck. A breeze. I whirl around and try to figure out where it's coming from. I don't think I saw any open windows in the rooms I've already been in, so that must mean it's in the other direction. I hurry away from the front door and try to follow the breeze, but it's intermittent.

Find me, I silently beg it. *Guide me out of here.*

There it is again, and it's getting stronger. I follow it through a dining room—there's a table, some chairs, and cabinets full of wine bottles that I imagine are full of blood—and into an adjacent room. It's an open floor plan with only a handful of doors closed, so I can zap around fairly easily.

I know it's stupid—my speciality lately—but I hesitate when it occurs to me how unlike Chiara this house seems. Not that I really know her or like I've spent a lot of time visualising Chiara's dream home, but something about this just doesn't feel like it's hers. Everything is so… bright. The floors are a light wood, the walls have this odd dark-red wallpaper with gold highlights which does not go with the floors, and the ceiling above the dining room is reflective. Not a mirror, exactly, but I can see my blurry reflection above me as I hurry through the house. I don't know, it just doesn't feel like it would be her style.

But then I see the family photos on the wall. None of them have her in them. The children get gradually older, so I can only hope they'd moved out by the time Chiara, what, stole this place? I bet she saw killing the owners as free and easy blood. But why? Did she do this on the off-chance that she might kidnap me one day? I can't exactly ask her. This whole situation is so baffling to me, I kind of don't want to know. I just want to get out of here and whatever fucked-up thing she's created for herself.

I'm so relieved there's no one else here. I barely escaped Chiara; I can't imagine having to fight off anyone else.

I turn my head towards the breeze to my right and see it: wide-open double doors, leading into a garden.

I hear something from downstairs, but I'm not sure what. Like someone's shuffling something? The angry scream that follows is easier to understand. I pale and freeze on the spot.

'Not the time, Esta! Run!'

Mischief's panicked voice knocks the fear out of me—or rather, it sets it aside and gives me an adrenaline burst.

I run for the open doors, not turning around once, and then

I'm outside. My eyes water when I feel the wind brush around me like it's urging me onwards, like it's as relieved to see me as I am to feel it. I take a sharp right away from the doors and windows, and throw myself towards the bushes along the high walls surrounding the property. Out here, my blood trail isn't as obvious, but I doubt Chiara needs visual clues to find me. I'm effectively leaving little scent markers for her to follow.

I feel safer hidden in the bushes, so I stick to their cover and follow them along the wall. I don't know what I'll do if the front gate is locked, too. I've never been a good climber—not that I've had many opportunities to try—and I've never had great upper-arm strength. Now that the blood loss and pain is leaving me weaker still, I'm not sure there's enough adrenaline in the world to push me over tall gates.

But I've made it this far. Just a bit farther.

I don't dare turn around. It wouldn't do any good, anyway. Chances are, Chiara is following me in fog-form. I could be watching the doors while she's closing in on me without me realising it, and besides, keeping an eye on those doors won't get me out of here.

From somewhere to my left, I hear a metallic rattle. The front gates are opening.

I crawl through the shrubs as fast as I can. Did Chiara invite friends over? Whoever this is, the gates were closed, and they'll likely shut again once whoever's arriving is on the property. If I'm going to get out, this is my only shot.

I follow the row of bushes as close to the gates as I dare. I brace myself. Once the car is through, I will run for it.

But no car appears.

I hold my breath, waiting for someone to show, but nothing happens. So I decide to take my chances.

I run for it.

Turn the corner and bump into someone.

My heart misses a beat. It's Chiara. She didn't follow me out the back doors, she opened this gate and then waited behind it and I fell right into her trap.

I scream and shove myself away. Arms close around me. I try to wriggle free, but it's no use.

'Ssh, Esta. Look at me. It's me.'

My heart in my throat, my eyes fly up before I can make the conscious decision to do so. My heart is still racing from my escape, but the voice slowly calms it down. It's uncomfortable to feel so much at once.

The arms around me aren't Chiara's, they are Kate's. She's here. She came for me.

A sob escapes me as I fall into Kate's hug. I hate that I fall apart the moment I see a friendly face, but it's all the relief I didn't dare hope for. It's over. I thought I was going to die, but I'm alive. I think I'm allowed a few messy tears.

'It's alright,' Kate coos. She turns her head away from me and shouts, 'Leverett! She's here!'

The air shifts next to me, and I turn my head away from Kate. Leverett looks distraught as he takes in my wounds.

'Esta—' He reaches out for me but stops himself and takes a step away. I will him to hold me, but he doesn't come closer. His eyes are dark storms. 'Are you alright?'

Kate gives him a look that says I'm obviously not, but I nod and throw myself into his arms. I thought I was dead. He will hug me, damn it.

He doesn't exactly recoil from me, but he doesn't instantly hug me back like I need him to, either. Then, slowly, his grip around my middle and shoulders tightens until he seems to be holding on to me for dear life.

'Where is she?' He growls into my ear. 'I will tear her apart for this.'

My eyes burn at the raw emotion in his voice. He may not love me, but he cares about me. Thanks to everything Chiara did to me, I now know that it can be enough.

I shake my head but hiss when the wound stings.

'Is Bonnie…?'

Kate shakes her head, but her smile gives me hope. 'She was on her way when we left to get you. I asked her to stay at home and wait for us to return. It would have taken her time Leverett and I didn't want to waste to get back, and neither of us was sure what we'd find here. We didn't want to put her in danger.'

My heart warms that Bonnie came home for me.

'Thank you for—' I want to thank Kate for calling Bonnie and not bringing her here, but the adrenaline is starting to wear off. The world blurs. I fall against Leverett when I don't feel my legs for a moment.

He catches me, and together with Kate, he eases me to the ground.

I'm faintly aware of Kate rummaging through a bag next to me. 'I thought you might be hurt, so I whipped up a quick potion before we left. It's not much, I'm afraid, but we didn't want to wait too long. I can make you something stronger when you're home.'

I let her pour it into my mouth and swallow like a good patient. It's revolting. I don't even know what it tastes of, just... herbs and bitterness. I guess it's better than bleeding out, though.

Kate chuckles. 'I'm afraid I don't have anything to take the taste away. It will prevent the wound from becoming infected and will fight any infection that might already have begun to fester.'

I give her a questioning look. The world slowly comes into focus again around her.

'It doesn't look infected, no. But you should still move slowly until we can get your wound cleaned and treated.'

Leverett hasn't stopped staring at the puncture marks, assuming he can see them under all that blood.

'Are you okay?' I ask. My voice sounds quieter than I'd like, but I'm feeling stronger every minute. Whatever Kate gave me, it's good shit. Disgusting, but good.

I can't read his expression for a moment. Then whatever it was falls away, and concern replaces it. He takes my hand, a faint smile on his lips.

'Am *I* okay? Don't worry about me.' His smile disappears. 'I'm sorry she did this to you. I'm sorry a vampire put you through this.'

The look on his face and his initial reaction are starting to make sense. Is he wondering if I'm afraid of him now?

I squeeze his hand as much as I can. 'I don't blame you, if that's what you're thinking. I know you wouldn't...'

Words fail me. Safe with my friends, the adrenaline has well and truly worn off, and exhaustion is starting to set in.

'Let's talk later,' Kate says. 'I'll get you home, and Leverett can… deal with Chiara.'

I shake my head again. 'No.' I remember how she fell down the stairs, and my stomach churns. 'I mean, she's… I don't know if…'

Kate takes my other hand. It's odd to feel so vulnerable and so safe at the same time.

'What did she do?'

But I don't have to explain it myself. An outraged laugh rings through the air somewhere from my left.

'What did *I* do?' Chiara snaps. 'You should be asking *her* that!'

I feel a strange mixture of relief and fear at hearing her voice. I know Kate and Leverett won't let anything happen to me now they're here, but the sound of her voice may have forever scarred me. Still, I didn't kill her.

I don't mind admitting that I'm more relieved for me than for her.

Kate frowns. Leverett stands tall and extends his claws. He's in front of me, so I can only see part of Chiara.

'You know very well that she can't hurt you,' he growls. 'You're a coward, Chiara. I will end you for this.'

I shake my head again, but he can't see me.

'No, I… I did something,' I say.

Leverett doesn't take his eyes off Chiara when he says, 'What do you mean?'

'She used magic!' Chiara spits. 'Your human used magic and threw me down the stairs! Explain that!'

So I didn't imagine it. Can I still do it now? I don't feel any different except tired. Certainly not like there's magic running through my veins.

Kate looks at me like she's seeing me for the first time.

Leverett chooses to ignore everything Chiara just said.

'What do you want me to do, Esta?' he asks. 'You're the one she hurt.'

'Has Kate told you about the boggart?' I ask. Leverett nods. 'I think it used her, too. This isn't really her doing. It manipulated her.'

I imagine Chiara all but foams at the mouth when she says, 'Nothing manipulates me, witch!'

'Esta doesn't want you to die,' Leverett says. 'I'm sure you can't comprehend this kind of mercy and I'm not sure I agree with it, but I will follow her wishes.' He bends down, takes me into his arms, and stands with me folded against his chest. My face heats like I'm blushing, but after how much blood Chiara seemed to take, I can't quite picture my face anything other than deathly pale. Probably for the best right now.

Our eyes meet, he gives me a loving smile, and I feel like I'm going to melt.

'We should talk, when you're better,' he says. 'The boggart may have influenced my decision, too.'

I won't dare hope that he wants to be with me after all, but I'm overjoyed that he wants to reconsider, at least. The boggart messed with all of us. I imagine we'll all be revisiting the last few days to consider how much of them was us and how much was his influence.

Leverett turns around to Chiara. I try not to look too smug

in his arms.

'If I ever see you near Esta again, I will kill you.'

And with that, Leverett carries me away from her and towards Kate's car. Kate still looks slightly baffled by me having used magic. The confusion is mutual. But if anyone can help me make sense of it, it's her.

Leverett carefully places me in the backseat and lets me lean against him. Kate drives. I'm asleep in seconds and barely aware when Leverett carries me into Kate's house.

One crazy vampire lady down, one boggart to go.

CHAPTER TWENTY FIVE

I'm grateful to wake up comfortable and safe in Kate's living room. I think I remember her saying something about how I can go home again soon, but I was pretty out of it.

Something warm snuggles into me. My neck is so sore that I jolt wide awake when I try to look down. I suck in a breath, and the warmth against me shifts and lets out an upset whine.

'Sorry.' My hand slides around Lady and holds her close to me. I don't need to see her to know she's here and okay, but her beautiful face would have been as comforting as a hug.

Just behind my head and around my feet, Keano and Bruin are cuddled to me. I kinda want to move because the more I wake up the more I feel how much my feet have fallen asleep, but I can't disturb them. Besides, if these puppies want to cuddle me healthy, I won't say no.

So, I take a second to appreciate this wonderful, comforting living room and its dogs before I make myself get up. Without looking around too much, I think I'm the only one here. No idea where Kate, Leverett, and Bonnie are. It would have been even nicer to wake up with Bonnie sleeping nearby, but I guess everything we said to each other still hangs over us. That's fair. We'll need to talk through it when we get a moment.

'Hello?' I try. No one answers.

I make myself sit up. Now that I'm starting to stretch everything out, I can tell the wound isn't as painful as it was in Chiara's basement. I sat up more easily, for one. But I'm not sure if it's really healing that quickly or if it's just whatever Kate gave me numbing the pain, so I move slowly. After everything she's done for me, I'd feel rude bleeding all over her carpet. I gingerly touch my neck around the wound and am surprised to feel fabric. Someone bandaged my neck. It's a little flimsy, but I was probably lying on it and whoever bandaged me up likely didn't want to risk waking me.

I do take a moment to look into Lady's worried eyes. My dog is okay. A part of me was terrified that something might happen to her while I was dying somewhere else, but we're both here, and she's okay. Everything else will be okay, too.

It's all the motivation I need to pull myself up completely. The dogs don't look too happy that I've disturbed their nap after all, but I won't sleep completely peacefully until I know this final business is dealt with.

'Where are the others?'

Keano barks as he and Bruin jump up, their tails wagging like they were just waiting for a command, and then they both lead me through the kitchen and into the garden. Lady stretches and trots alongside me. I already see them from the window—Kate, Bonnie, and Leverett are sitting in the garden with drinks. I daydream about Bonnie being the first to see me, how she comes running and we apologise profusely and then everything is alright between us again, but of course Leverett sees me first. His vampire hearing probably picked up on me dragging myself through the house. His eyes are already on the door when I step out.

He says something, and Bonnie's head shoots around. Kate merely smiles like she already knew I was awake and on my way, like she's mentally linked with her dogs. I guess if even I have magic, anything is possible. Not that I feel a hint of it now except for the breeze on my skin, which always feels magical. Not sure that counts, though.

Leverett makes to stand but catches himself and stays seated. It reminds me of how he reacted outside Chiara's house—like he wanted to come to me but was worried about how I'd see him now. Or maybe it's just awkward because of what we feel for each other? Whatever the reason, he doesn't approach me first.

Bonnie runs over and stops just shy of throwing herself into my arms. As much as I want to hug her, I don't think my neck can handle the strain.

'You're okay!' she says, her eyes flying to the wound.

I carefully touch it and find the skin around the bandage crusted with dried blood.

'I will be,' I say. Once everything has sunk in, I… I don't know. Maybe the shock of everything will suddenly hit me in a week, or maybe I really will be okay. Maybe I'll need therapy. Or maybe I just need to not get threatened for a while.

I remember something the Dreamcatcher and the Mara said. Someone sent them. What if this same person sent the boggart? It'll be something to ask it, if we get along well enough by the time we're done pacifying it. But if it was the same person, my days of being kidnapped may not be over. I got lucky with Chiara. If Mischief hadn't activated my magic, or whatever she did, I'm pretty sure I wouldn't have escaped. If there's a way I can use it on purpose, I want to learn how, but I don't know how it's supposed to feel. I don't feel magical right now; I'm tired and in desperate need of a soak.

I look past Bonnie at Kate. 'Could I use your shower?'

She nods. 'Of course. Take as long as you want. We'll be here.'

With that, I excuse myself and lock myself in the bathroom. I take off all my clothes. I don't look at my reflection; I don't want to see my bloody neck in another mirror, and I don't want to see the wound. I turn on the shower and get in.

Then I sit on the floor, hug my knees to my chest, and cry.

I'm alive. I got out. I'm alright.

Why, then, do I feel so vulnerable?

I cross my arms and grip my shoulders. I sink against the shower wall. I must look pathetic, but I don't care. I know I need to actually scrub off the blood and sweat, but right now, I don't think I can stand. My legs are shaking. My whole body is rocking from the sobs. I'm glad the others are outside; I don't want them to hear. I also want Bonnie, at least, to get in with me and hold me. I want to be alone, but I don't want to be alone.

Mischief doesn't say anything, and maybe I'm imagining her here with me, but I feel soft fur brush around my legs, a weight climb onto my knees and cuddle into the unhurt nape of my neck. I even reach out, but there's nothing there. I think I hear purring, right in my ear. Slowly, gently, it soothes the pain inside me.

I don't know how long I sit like that, but eventually the tears stop, my body stills, and I feel strong enough to stand. I lean against the shower walls as I gingerly wash the blood off my neck. I do everything with one hand so the other can keep contact with the wall. There's no handle or rail or anything, but it makes me feel steadier. I know it's stupid. I still hold on.

The steam has just about softened the blood, so by the time I feel ready to wash it properly, a lot of it has already run down my neck and mingled with the water. The real challenge is the bite marks. They hurt. I take a deep breath and lightly touch one, because I'm curious and because I want to prove to myself that I'm strong enough for it. I hiss when fresh pain shoots down my neck, and let my hand fall away.

'You're okay,' Mischief says. 'Chiara isn't here. She'll never hurt you again.'

I swallow and take a moment to calm my breathing. Leverett threatened her, and she seemed plenty freaked out after I somehow used magic on her. Good thing she doesn't know I can't control it, but even so, Leverett *threatened* her. For me. He came for me. He and Kate both did. Bonnie came home for me. Even the dogs did their best to nurse me.

I realise with a strangled sob that I lied before. I'm not alright. But though I may always be scarred, I'll also always know that I made it through, and even Chiara can't take that away from me.

I feel better when I towel-dry myself and get into clean clothes. I didn't pick anything special when I brought a few things over, but I don't want anything special, either. The loose trousers and too-big shirt are perfect. It's comfort, just what I need.

I close my eyes. 'Thank you.'

I know Mischief knows I mean her, because I feel her soft fur around my leg again. She was there when I desperately needed someone—first in the basement, and again just now in the shower. I almost don't care how it works, I'm only grateful that it does.

'Let's discuss what to do about this boggart, hmm?' she purrs in my head. 'And then let's take a week off from the attempts on your life.'

Thanks to her, I can chuckle at it.

'Yes. Let's.'

I go back into the garden, where our dogs have found a shady spot under Kate's willow tree. My friends are still sitting around the table. They all look up as one, but it's Bonnie who hurries over to me and carefully takes me into her arms.

'I'm sorry we fought,' she says. 'We'll never do it again, okay?'

Tears burn my eyes again, but I blink them away. I'm not against crying and think it can be incredibly healing, but right now I need a breather from it. I'm ready to move on.

So, I hug her back. I only wince a little when the wound stings. 'I'm sorry, too. Can you forgive me?'

She playfully slaps me. 'Nonsense. We were both idiots, so there's nothing to forgive.'

I nod. Together, we join the others. Leverett gives me a heavy look full of unsaid things. I need to talk to him, too, but first we have a boggart to pacify. I don't want anything influencing us except our own judgment.

'How long was I gone?' I ask as I sit.

'We came as soon as we could,' Kate says. 'I reminded Leverett that we'd be foolish to rush after you without a plan, so you were there a few hours longer than we wanted. Chiara took you in the early hours of yesterday morning. We had you home by early afternoon. It's Sunday now.'

It felt so much longer, but I'm not complaining. I'm glad they didn't waste time, that they took a moment to discuss how to find me, how to get me out, that Kate made her medicine.

'Thank you,' I say again.

'How is your neck?' Kate asks. 'I'm preparing a salve and a tea for you, but there's another ingredient we need your approval for.'

'It hurts.' I want to ask Leverett if that's normal. All the dreams I've had of him biting me and it being the best, hottest thing ever seem beyond naïve now. But didn't he say something once about how a vampire's bite is like any other touch? That it can hurt or feel good? I'm not sure I'll ever be ready to test that theory now. 'What do you need my okay for?'

Kate and Leverett exchange a glance before his eyes fix on mine.

'I've no doubt that Kate's medicines will do wonders for you. There is, however, one thing that might speed up your healing even more.'

Kate nods. 'Vampire blood has incredible healing properties.' I pale. 'I was the one who suggested it. Leverett wouldn't agree without your consent.'

Bonnie frowns at them both and sits closer to me. 'How can you suggest that, after everything that monster did to her?'

'You need to see it like any other ingredient,' Kate says. 'In the tea, it'll be no different than the herbs or the water.'

'I understand your reservations after… everything,' Leverett says. 'Even if none of it had happened, you might still see it as a personal matter. We're suggesting adding a few drops of my blood to something Esta will drink, after all.'

I don't know who to side with. Leverett once told me that turning a human into a vampire is a risky thing that rarely ends well, but that's not what he's suggesting. I trust him; he wouldn't add so much that it would put me at risk. Being able to do anything without my neck reminding me of Chiara would be nice. But I always thought… I blush. I don't hate the idea of… But I thought I would, I don't know, lick it off his chest. But that's not what this is, either. It's just an ingredient like any other—Kate said so herself. So really, there's nothing to think about, is there?

But the idea of me drinking any amount of his blood feels too intimate, especially after he said that he can't be with me. I don't know if he's changed his mind, but it doesn't matter in this moment. Adding his blood to my medicine feels like a violation.

I start to shake my neck but immediately wince. 'No, that's fine. You don't need to do that,' I quickly add, because I don't want him to think that I'm opposed to the idea. 'It wouldn't feel right.'

He nods. I can't read his expression; it could be neutral, or he might see this as a rejection. Which it kind of is, I guess.

'I will finish the salve and the tea before you go home,' Kate says. 'You should feel better right away.'

'So,' I say, 'how do we placate this boggart?'

'Normally, we wouldn't,' Kate says. 'Boggarts are stubborn and not in the habit of changing their minds.'

My heart falls a little. 'Then what can we do?'

'I will talk you through offerings to make, and hopefully it will accept your honest apology.' She raises her eyebrows at me. 'Assuming it is honest, of course?'

I quickly nod and immediately regret it. Kate's medicines can't work soon enough.

'Of course! I didn't even know I was awake when I asked for its name.'

Kate nods. 'I will be with you when you make your offering and speak your apology. The brownie was likely already local when it moved in and so may well know my reputation.'

Bonnie looks at me. 'You can also name-drop the Dreamcatcher and the Mara, since that gossip apparently spread quickly.'

'That may not change anything,' Leverett says. 'As you said, the news spread quickly. The boggart is likely aware who you are.'

Bonnie scowls. 'Sure, but if it's not, she can try that.' She looks at Kate. 'Do I come, too?'

Kate shakes her head. 'It was Esta who offended the brownie and caused it to change into a boggart. The apology and offering need to come from her.' She turns to me. 'While they are stubborn creatures, we won't need much to appeal to it. We can go whenever you feel rested enough.'

I nod and stand. 'Then let's do it now.'

I'm ready to not be cursed anymore.

I feel strangely out of place, entering our house after everything that's happened. It's been so little time, but I feel like I've been away for weeks, if not longer. The new door isn't in yet, of course, so it's still the temporary wooden board. Was it the boggart's influence that made me forget to check the carpet? I doubt I'll ever know. Even the boggart might not know for sure—it's possible its influence is passive, that it doesn't pick individual moments throughout my day and throws some cursed energy at whichever ones it wants to mess up.

'We should avoid the stairs to be safe,' Kate says right behind me. 'The fire didn't spread into your living room or kitchen, so those rooms will be fine.'

I desperately want to curl up on my bed with Lady and sleep, but I get it.

'Where do boggarts, erm, live?' I ask as we step into the living room. How long did the brownie share this house with us, and we never knew? How many households have little helper spirits right now but have no idea? I shudder to think how easy it might be for any of them to slip up like I did.

Or maybe it's the brownie who slipped up, since it was in my kitchen when I came down. Surely it heard me come downstairs? Our stairs are old. They creak. I must have tipped it off, but if my secret enemy told it to be here…

I don't really care about the details or who ordered what. I just want it to leave so Bonnie and I can move back in, make up properly, and move on from all the nastiness.

'Many prefer kitchens or conservatories, though there are exceptions,' Kate says. 'It might sound counterintuitive, as these are spaces we use often during the day, but brownies are good at not being seen.' She ignores my raised eyebrow. 'Boggarts have the same talent. They are all but invisible during the day and only come out at night because they don't want to be seen. You will have to guess at the most likely place it's chosen as its home. The quietest, least-used place in your home is most likely, I think. Even if we choose the wrong place, brownies and boggarts have a deep connection to the houses they inhabit. It will know you've made the offering, even if you guess incorrectly.'

I think of our attic. We hardly ever go up there unless we're getting Christmas decorations down, and there are so many empty spots we don't use at all, but that's no use to us right now. We can't go upstairs while there's a chance the stairs might collapse.

'The small shed in our garden?'

We use it so rarely that I keep forgetting we even have the thing. Neither Bonnie nor I are gardeners. I have my small herb collection, but I don't remember the last time I cut the roses back. We only mow the lawn when it grows past our ankles, and then we fight over who needs to do it. We love having our garden, but looking after it and keeping it well-trimmed is another matter.

Kate nods. 'That sounds perfect. I suggest we start with your offering.'

'What do I do?'

I follow her into the kitchen.

'Do you have any milk in your fridge?' Kate asks. 'Cake or oats would be good, too. Even better if you have both.'

'We have milk and…' I check the fridge to make sure. 'Some unopened double cream, but no cake and definitely no oats.'

We've never been huge on oats, but it's a crime that there's no cake. Aside from it apparently being a great offering, Bonnie and I have earned some cake. It'll be the first thing I buy once this is over. Maybe, if the boggart chooses to hang around once it's a brownie again, we'll offer it a slice, too. Better late than never?

'Do you have any clothes you can spare?'

I look at Kate over my shoulder from the fridge. 'Only what I'm wearing since I can't go upstairs. Why?'

'All the things I listed make excellent offerings, but giving a brownie clothes is a good way to get them to leave. I imagine you'd prefer to not have a brownie at all?'

I start to nod but stop myself. It would be safer, but I can't pretend that having a helpful household spirit doesn't sound useful. It repaired my mug once, and I know better now.

I get the double cream out of the fridge and shrug. 'I guess I'll leave that up to it.'

For all I know, it's been here as long as we have, and we never had a problem. And what if it's lived here longer than we have? I wouldn't feel right kicking it out, even if it did get one of my old, worn shirts for it. Frankly, that sounds more like an insult than a present.

'Let's go to the shed,' Kate says. 'The actual offering won't take long. We'll know whether it accepted by tomorrow morning, though I advise against keeping an eye on the offering.'

I nod. I'm in this mess because I ran into it in the first place and questioned it about all the things it hates to be asked about. I got the point that brownies don't want to be seen just fine. What's the point in making a peace offering if I then spy on it through a window?

'So… how does this work if I can't see it or talk to it?' I ask as we reach the shed.

Kate gives me one of her smiles full of secret wisdom. 'Have you ever prayed before?'

I blink. 'No. I've never been religious or believed in God.'

I've invoked *gods* plenty of times, but that's mostly because I don't believe in God and therefore didn't feel right invoking him, as most other people do. I know it's used regardless of belief, but it's never felt right for me. I never mean any specific gods when I do it—it's just a habit I adopted that felt a little more natural and probably started in a rebellious phase.

Although, after everything I've read in my books lately, there could be an impossibly large number of deities around.

Kate laughs quietly to herself. I feel like a kid in primary school who got five-plus-seven wrong.

I raise my eyebrows at her. '*Are* there gods?'

Kate chuckles again. 'The important thing right now is how you approach this boggart. Learn how to treat a common household spirit before you mingle with deities, hm?'

Point taken. We had a friendly household spirit who was

here because it likes to help, and I managed to piss it off by complete accident. Fuck knows what would happen if I met a deity. Probably best if I stick to my own neighbourhoods for now or forever, actually.

'Fair point,' I say. 'So this is like praying?'

Kate nods. 'In a sense. We believe your boggart is behind this door, so this is where we will leave its offering. All you need to do is introduce yourself, then explain what you're leaving and why. Be honest—boggarts detest lies and will know when you're trying to deceive them.' She chuckles again. 'So do gods, in fact.'

I swallow. I can do that. I clear my throat, but instinctively feel Bonnie's and Leverett's eyes on me. They *are* in the garden right next door. But when I look behind me, the garden is empty. They must have gone inside to give us some privacy… or rather, to give *me* some privacy, since Kate is here to teach me the steps. She isn't the one who's about to talk to a door.

Except, I'm not really addressing the door but the boggart behind it. The creature responsible for… well, I don't know what exactly, but enough of the things that have gone wrong lately that I feel entitled to a bit of anger. The thought disappears as soon as I think it. The boggart has messed with me and my loved ones, but in its eyes, I committed the first crime by seeing it and questioning it. If I can hopefully end it all with a bit of double cream and an apology, why wouldn't I?

I sit in front of the door. It feels less like I'm lording over it and more like I'm talking to a friend. We're far from that dynamic, but who knows? Maybe it really will stay around and we'll get there after a few shared cakes.

'Erm… Hi. I'm Esta. I, erm, live here.' Strong start. 'I've brought you a present. Please accept my offering of cream.' I blush as I say it. By its very nature, the boggart won't respond, so there's a chance it isn't here and I really am just talking to a door. I open the double cream and place it in front of me. 'Sorry, I should have brought a bowl or a glass or something.' Just giving it the plastic container feels disrespectful, but it's too late now. 'I hope this is okay. I have milk, too, if you'd prefer that, though I suppose you won't tell me. I, erm…'

I'm very aware that I'm waffling, but it's not like Kate gave me a script. She said to be honest, so I figure it's better to spill every thought into the space between us than to hold something back.

'I'm sorry I disturbed you that night, and I'm really sorry I asked for your name and why you were there. I honestly didn't even know I was awake. I'm used to lucid-dreaming and asking other dream characters why they're there, and I thought you were one of them.' I blush deeper. Do I need to say this much? Maybe hearing how awkward I am will help. All this has got to reek of honesty. 'I offer you this cream in apology. I won't demand you leave us alone, but I'm happy to leave you regular offerings if you reconsider.' It feels right. This way, my life gets to return to relative normal, and the brownie gets something good out of it, too. 'So, erm… I hope you enjoy the cream, and I hope my offering is good enough. I…'

I *really* don't want to be cursed anymore.

So, I take off my shirt and place it next to the cream.

'Thank you for everything you did when you were our

brownie. I'm leaving you this shirt in offering, too. You don't need to leave if you don't want, though. Consider it a gift?' I clear my throat again. 'Erm, thank you for listening. Bye.'

It feels stupidly clumsy, but again—no script. I think I got my point across just fine.

I stand, ready to flee inside since I'm just standing here in my bra now, but Kate walks up next to me.

'And a small offering from me.' She places a small black stone covered in dog hair on the other side of the cream.

I give her a look. 'Boggarts like shiny stones and dogs?'

She gives me that smile again. 'Not as such.' To the door, she says, 'I trust you know what this means and that this will convince you if Esta's sincerity hasn't.'

The hairs on the back of my neck stand on end. It sounds suspiciously like Kate just threatened the boggart. She shut down the Mara, too. I don't remember what exactly she said, but— That's it. The Mara called her *Mother*, and Kate cut her off. I meant to ask her about it but forgot. I'd ask now, but...

'Can we go inside? Feeling a little exposed here.'

'Of course.'

I hurry back inside ahead of Kate. I try not to picture Leverett watching me from Kate's upper windows as I run half-naked through my garden. I'm so much more dressed than that, really, but I'm not used to being outside in just a bra... and trousers, yes, but still.

'How will I know if it worked?' I ask.

'The cream will be gone, as will our other offerings. If it decides to stay as a brownie, you may notice broken things being repaired overnight again.'

'And if it doesn't change back? If I'm stuck with a boggart?'

'You won't be.'

I don't ask how she can be so sure. Clearly she has more clout with the Veiled community than I realised.

I decide to be brave.

'Why did you offer the brownie anything? Bonnie asked if she should come, and you said the boggart's problem was with me alone. Why give it that stone covered in dog hair?'

Kate hesitates, and for a moment, I don't think she'll reply at all.

'That stone is obsidian,' she says. 'It's common amongst witches and was used for scrying in ancient times. You might say I left it to show the boggart that I'll keep an eye on it, and that I'll know if it troubles you again.' She gives me a slight wink that I don't believe for an instant. 'No one wants to anger the friendly neighbourhood witch, and everyone knows that dog people are good people, wouldn't you say? I've effectively told it that I mean well, and that I can and will watch its doings from here on.'

I want to point out that plenty of dog people are arseholes, but the moment is gone and it's no longer what I focus on. Her words sound like an excuse. She clearly doesn't want to tell me more, though, so I don't pry. Kate has helped me so many times that I have zero reason not to trust her. And anyway, maybe she did tell me the truth. Maybe I'm just paranoid now.

Only a month has passed since I stepped into the void lake. So many things have happened. If there's one thing I can be sure of, it's that Kate is on my side, and that's all I need to know. Besides, we're all entitled to our secrets. I decide to drop it.

'Thank you,' I say. 'For helping me with this, for teaching me, and for saving my life. I'll be a better student from here on.'

Kate gives me her patient teacher smile. 'No need to thank me, Esta. It's what anyone would have done. We can pick up your education again after next week, once you've had time to rest.'

I nod. That sounds wonderful.

When I visit the shed the following morning, the offerings are gone.

CHAPTER TWENTY SIX

Only two days after Kate and I left our offerings, it's clear just how much influence the boggart had not just on my life, but on everyone around me, too.

Bonnie and I are getting ready for a movie night, with her ordering the pizza and me preparing the cocktails. Things aren't all back to normal between us, but we've both apologised again and vowed to communicate better. Chiara kidnapping me taught us both a valuable lesson: We can't know what will happen tomorrow, but our last words to each other won't be hateful.

'Double pepperoni okay?' Bonnie shouts from the sofa.

'Yes, please! Tell them to murder it with cheese!'

'Got it. One death-by-pepperoni-and-cheese feast coming right up.'

I'm so, so grateful for this normality, and I'm even more grateful that Bonnie is embracing it with me. We both need this, especially after our last two failed movie nights.

Lady fusses around my legs as I mix our drinks. She was very busy stuffing her face with not only her own food, but

Kate's dogs' servings as well when we went back to hers. She's good as new. I don't know if it was definitely the boggart's influence or all the stress getting to her, but we're beyond relieved that she's okay.

Although, it *is* a little difficult to take the drinks to the sofa with her winding herself around my feet. I don't think the brownie fancies repairing another glass so soon.

We know the brownie decided to stay because Bonnie accidentally dropped a mug yesterday, we remembered that we still don't have any super glue, and it was fixed by the time we were back home from the shop. Both of us see this as the ultimate peace offering—the brownie came out during the day to repair it.

Bonnie giggles and takes the glasses from me.

'Did I tell you I found my necklace?'

My heart squeezes with mixed emotions as I sit next to her. I'm so happy she found it, but I accused Sunitha of stealing it. I was angry and hurt when I said it, but I suspected her before that. The boggart was likely to blame for it spilling out like it did, and I could have said it better, but the thought was my own.

'Where was it?' I sheepishly ask.

'You won't believe it—behind my nightstand. I don't even know how it got there. This morning I suddenly thought of it and checked, and there it was.'

A guilty smile twists my lips. 'That's great.' And then, because we promised complete honesty: 'I'm sorry I ever suspected Sunitha.'

Bonnie shakes her head. 'It did look suspicious. But it

doesn't matter now since I found it, right?'

My smile grows a little wider. 'Right.'

It felt so nice to sleep in my own bed again last night, and it feels even nicer to sink into this sofa with my sister next to me, an easy smile on my face and pizza on the way. Apart from the door, Kate's friends worked on replacing the carpets and general structural integrity of the staircase and ceiling while I took Lady for a long walk yesterday and Bonnie was at her internship. Kate had the whole thing arranged as a surprise, so by the time I got back they had already worked their literal magic. I especially love the door. Instead of the weird stained-glass boat we inherited from the last people who lived here, we now have a gorgeous triple moon greeting us home. There's a white full moon flanked by a crescent moon on each side, set against black glass. The door itself is a rich blue. Bonnie loves it all as much as I do.

Sadly, Kate's friends were gone by the time we got back, but she promised we could meet them if we wanted. They're simply busy people and couldn't hang out that day. Kate did ask them to do all this on short notice, so I'm not surprised.

'Since we're apologising…' Bonnie clears her throat. 'I'm really sorry I said that Leverett could never love you. That was stupid. If he doesn't want to be with you, he's an idiot.'

I lean my head against her shoulder, and she leans her head against mine. 'And I'm sorry I said that it could never work out with Sunitha. Obviously she doesn't live underwater. You could have moved in together.'

We give each other an awkward sideways hug. We did apologise before this, several times, but always in generic terms. It feels good to be specific.

'Drink to our forever friendship and sisterhood?'

Bonnie grabs the glasses and hands me one. 'Gladly.'

We clink our glasses and drink.

'Sisters forever,' I say.

'Sisters forever,' she agrees with a giggle. Bonnie glares at her phone when it buzzes. 'That had better not be the pizza people saying there's a problem. Hello?' Her eyes go wide and she blushes. 'Oh, hey, Sunitha. This is, erm— What's up?'

Honestly, it's amazing either of us ever managed to have a love life. We are not naturally skilled at flirting.

When Bonnie breaks into a huge grin, I know I should give them some space, so I excuse myself and go upstairs. I just about hear Bonnie explain something about the boggart and how she would love to go on a date next week when I reach the upstairs landing.

I'm glad they're working it out. Leverett asked me to stop by when I felt up to it; I'd probably go right now if pizza wasn't on the way. Instead, I sit on my bed and pull out my deck of cards. I shuffle, mostly to have something to do, but I can't very well ignore it when one card falls out. It feels like it's drawn itself. Like the deck needs to tell me something.

With a heavy sinking feeling in my gut—I really don't want to see anyone getting stabbed or any crumbling towers—I turn it over. I smile in relief when it's The Star. I even remember what it means: hope, and faith. I doubt it's the kind of faith Kate mentioned, though—the kind that involves prayers to deities. I think this means the faith that better days lie ahead. Even if it's not, I can cling to the message of hope. I give my deck a quick peck on The Star and put the cards back into their box. The doorbell rings and Bonnie shouts up that our pizza is here, so it's time to make my way downstairs anyway.

I squeal with Bonnie when she tells me everything Sunny said—how she wants to try again, how they're going on a date Friday night, and how she's pissed that a boggart made her afraid of their future together when they barely know each other. We both laugh and joke through the movie, and by the time it's over, I feel bold even though we didn't mix a second drink. It's The Star, our laughter tonight, my sister's second chance with Sunny.

And besides, it's only nine p.m. in early August. It's not even dark yet.

'Do you mind if I head out?' I ask Bonnie as she puts the empty pizza box away.

'Going to see Leverett?'

I blush. 'He asked me to come over when I felt ready, so…'

I have no delusions about him asking me out after everything he said, but The Star is literally giving me hope. It'll be good to know where we stand either way.

'Go,' she says. 'I'll stay up, we can talk when you're back.' She winks at me. 'Message me if you're staying the night, though, yeah?'

I wave her off but can't help smiling. It won't happen, but maybe… Maybe there's still a romantic future for us.

I think as I walk. The Dreamcatcher and Mara worked in my dreamscape. The boggart took it a step further and invaded my home. It influenced me and my friends, possibly even my dog. I have no way of confirming if the same person who sent the Dreamcatcher sent it, too, since I'd need to talk to it for that and it doesn't like that, but my gut says yes. I dread to think what she might send after me next, but I'll be better prepared next time. Under Kate's tutelage, I'll be ready.

My heart is in my throat when I reach Leverett's shop. It's closed, of course, but I knock anyway. He'll hear it.

Although, it occurs to me as I knock that he might not be home. For all I know he's out. He did ask me to stop by whenever, but did he expect me to come by this late when he said that? He probably doesn't—

He appears at the end of his shop, and our eyes meet. Two frantic heartbeats later he's unlocking the door.

'Esta. I wasn't expecting you so late.'

There's a strange look in his eyes, and I freeze. What if he's… not alone?

I pale. 'I'm sorry, I should probably have asked if it's okay first. If this isn't a good time, I'll come back tomorrow or something.'

He's shaking his head before I'm done. 'No, now is fine. Come in.'

I can't help feeling a little relieved. He wouldn't invite me in if he had a naked visitor on his sofa, would he?

'How is your injury?' he asks as I follow him. Maybe I imagine it, but I think his shoulders tense when he asks.

I roll my neck—lightly—to make my point. 'Better, thank you. Kate really knows her herbs.' Was he hurt that I didn't want him to add his blood to the tea? Did he see it as a rejection on my part? Our relationship has become so messy, but that's why I'm here. To fix it. For closure.

'I'm sorry I didn't come sooner. I…'

I was avoiding it, to be honest. Not because I'm scared of him now, but because I'm afraid to find out where we stand. Besides, it's only been a few days. If he's about to reject me, I wanted at least a small break from all the pain.

I stop in the doorway behind his till.

Leverett shakes his head again. 'You have nothing to apologise for.' He stands in front of me. In this small space between the door frames, he feels incredibly close. I want to pull him to me and kiss him. I want to wrap my legs around his waist like I did at the party. He said then that it was too public, but there's no one else here right now. Two steps, and we'll be in the storage room.

'I was worried you'd relate what Chiara did to me,' he says. 'That you'd look at me and relive the pain she caused you, but with my face.' He touches his forehead to mine. 'I'd never hurt you, Esta. Please know that. If you can't feel safe around me anymore, I understand.'

I briefly close my eyes to enjoy his skin against mine, then look up. I need him to see the truth of what I'm about to say. 'I could never compare you to her. I've never felt as safe as I did in your arms.'

I'm glad it's dark, because I blush furiously. I was too embarrassed to say things like this at the party, but I don't want to hold back anymore. I need him to know how he makes me feel.

Leverett touches his nose to mine. I tilt my head back a little, will him to lean in just a little more and kiss me.

'Esta—'

A slight moan escapes me at hearing my name on his lips.

But Leverett steps back. 'The boggart amplified my worries, but they are all valid nonetheless.'

My stomach sinks. He's had time to think, and he still doesn't want to be with me. I can't believe I just said what I did.

'I understand,' I say. My voice is steadier than the last time we had this conversation.

He leans in a little, cups my face with one hand, strokes my cheek with his thumb. 'You don't. Can I give this some more thought? I need to know that the way I feel about you isn't influenced by anything else. I need to know that I make this decision with a clear mind, not because the boggart affected me.'

I lean into his hand and nod. 'Of course. You know where to find me.'

I almost tell him that Bonnie will be on a date Friday night, but I don't want to rush his decision.

'Esta...' He touches his forehead to mine again. 'Never doubt how I feel about you. That's part of the problem. I never expected to feel as strongly as I do for a human. I... need to consider what that means. If it's possible.'

I stroke his cheek like he stroked mine just now. I stand on my tiptoes and place a small kiss on his forehead.

'You don't need to explain.' I'm grateful he did, though. 'I want you to be as sure as I am.'

And then I step away and leave him in the empty door frame. I don't turn back around until the counter is between us.

'I won't come by until you've decided. I don't want to make it awkward.'

He nods. 'Thank you.'

With that, I leave. I conjure the image of The Star and hold on to its message of hope. Maybe Leverett will decide that nothing has changed for him, but at least we'll both know that it's his decision. It'll still hurt, but I know now how much not being his friend would hurt, too. I'm prepared for whatever he decides. Either way, I'm on his side.

That's what I focus on as I walk home and the first stars appear:

Hope for the future, whatever it may bring.

The word 'scry' means to reveal something unknown.

Scrying is easier to get into than you might think, if you're as unfamiliar with it as Esta was at the start of this book (and, let's be honest, still is). It's so easy to try because there are an infinite number of ways you can scry (or it can feel that way, anyway, due to its amazing flexibility), and it doesn't take a lot of setting up if you're just dipping your toes into it. As Kate explained, it's also easy to hide if your living situation doesn't make it safe for you to scry openly.

Here are just a few ideas anyone can do if you want to try it:

- **Cloud scrying:** Even if you live in a densely populated city, you'll be able to see some sky! And where there's sky, there are clouds (and you can keep that incredible wisdom for free *ahem*). All you need to do is look up, find a cloud you like the look of, and let your gaze go soft—this is a must for all scrying techniques that require you to stare at something for a while. You basically don't want to try too hard. Let the shapes and ideas come to you. If you can, write down anything that comes to mind (also helpful no matter the scrying technique).

- **Water scrying:** If you're lucky enough to have a body of water (such as a lake or river) near you, you can do this next time you're there. Stare onto the water's surface and observe the forming images as they come to you. There are different variations you can try, such as dropping objects into the water and observing the ripples or circling a finger through the water. A bowl of water works, too. *Fun fact:* This was a preferred method of the Oracle of Delphi in ancient Greece! This is also called hydromancy.

- **Fire scrying:** If you can safely burn candles where you are, you can gaze into the flame and let images and visions come to you that way. You could also look at the shadows thrown by the moving flame and interpret them. This is also known as pyromancy.

- **Mirror scrying:** This is probably the most well-known type of scrying besides crystal ball scrying. If it's safe for you to do so in your circumstances and it wouldn't raise any questions with your family that might put you at risk, you might prefer to buy a picture frame, paint the underside of the glass black so the unpainted side faces up, and keep it in a black cloth when you're not using it. If you're just trying mirror scrying for the first time, though, feel free to experiment before you commit to basically defacing a perfectly good picture frame. It's easiest to do this in a dark room with minimal lighting—you want the mirror to reflect whatever images come to you, not the room around you.

Fun fact: I once did this in my bathroom mirror when I was younger. I stared at my reflection until I no longer looked like myself, and it scared the living daylights out of me.

- **Get creative!** If a room in your home has a plastered ceiling with specific shapes, like circles, you can stare up at that. A video game I love to play has a fishing mini-game, and I find my gaze naturally goes soft when I stare at the water for a short while. (This is, of course, easily interrupted when a fish takes the bait.)

As you can see, you don't need any fancy equipment to try scrying, and the options I've listed above barely scratch the surface. Scrying is not a small topic, so please see the above as a very brief introduction. The important thing (to start with) is that you have a more or less even surface to stare at, that you let your eyes go soft, and that you allow your mind to wander. That way, anyone can try scrying no matter where they are.

Brownies are helpful household spirits who come out at night to help with any unfinished household tasks (like broken mugs). They do belong to the wider fae family, though, so they're naturally mischievous and should be treated with the utmost respect—or else, as Esta learned the hard way.

They tend to attach themselves to one person in their household and become their personal helper. It's said that, if you have any troubles, you can tell your brownie and it'll make it go away—just don't address your brownie personally or it'll become one of your problems. They don't like meanness or lying, especially against their chosen humans.

As helpful as they are, it's easy to anger them. For all their hard work, they expect a small reward in return, and if their human misses an offering, the brownie will be offended. If you happen to see one, you can also offend it by asking its name, what it's doing in your house, or generally acknowledging that it's there. Since they prefer to work at night and out of sight, though, you're unlikely to stumble upon yours.

Should your friendly household brownie turn into a boggart, it will follow its victim around and make their life as hard as humanly (boggartly?) possible. Boggarts are hard to get rid of, so your best bet is to not anger your brownie in the first place.

Easy offerings include a bowl of cream or a glass of milk, oats or cake (though I'm sure it wouldn't mind both, either— who minds extra cake?), but don't address the brownie—just leave the offerings. If you'd rather not take the risk at all, you can also offer your brownie clothes, which will convince it to leave your household.

While they prefer to do their work unseen to their household's humans, they're not invisible. They're often described as roughly three feet tall with brown, shaggy hair and brown clothes, and they are said to be common throughout Britain.

Thank you so much for reading *A Dream of Stars and Curses*. This book means a lot to me, and your support does too. I hope you've had as much fun with Esta as I did! I'm really looking forward to writing the sequels—the whole damn decology—and hopefully, you're looking forward to reading them.

If you have two minutes, I'd be grateful for a review. This helps readers find their next favourite book, so your review or even just a rating makes a big difference. It doesn't need to be long, either! One sentence (or again, just a rating) is plenty. *Thank you.*

Like freebies?
Join my mailing list and receive my novella *Shadow in Ar'Sanciond* and the short story *Pashros Kai Zo* (which isn't available anywhere else!) for free. You'll also hear about upcoming releases, early cover reveals, exclusive giveaways, excerpts, and all other announcements. Join at:
subscribepage.com/sarinasbooks

If you'd like to hang out with me in an informal setting and get early peeks at new covers and maps, join my Facebook Reader Group 'Sarina's Sparrows':
facebook.com/groups/sarinassparrows

Let's connect.
sarinalanger.com
facebook.com/groups/sarinassparrows
twitter.com/sarina_langer
goodreads.com/sarinalangerwriter
patreon.com/sarinalanger

Me, after Book 1: wow, what a magical journey, I loved every second. Me, now: I'm tired and WHY are blurbs and acknowledgments the devil anyway??

Let me level with you: I'm writing these acknowledgments (and indeed the blurb) after a long academic year (I'm very fortunate to work in a university library—I'd say when I'm not writing, but I totally write there too), and I'm not quite sure where my head's at yet. My apologies if the below is confusing or in a weird order or reads like I need caffeine. It should provide you with a good look into my head, though I promise to hold back on the truly weird shit. I reserve that for Esta.

Given I said what I just said, I want to start by thanking my colleagues and managers for not only supporting me on my writer path but also egging me on during NaNoWriMo. I particularly remember Kathryn saying, 'Safety nets are there so you can build a bigger safety net. Finish that book, Sarina.' (I'm paraphrasing—I was reaching the end of NaNoWriMo and was *tired*, so my memory is a little hazy.) I'm aware of how incredibly lucky I am.

Thank you to my wonderful editor Rae Oestreich, whose insight and support never fail to amaze me. I'm so grateful I can message you with any concerns about any of my writing, knowing that you will make me feel better and be honest with me. I'm so grateful I can go crying to you over any beta feedback I'm unsure about, knowing you will say, 'No, you're right on this. It's your betas who are wrong.' (not really, she doesn't automatically side with me—we discuss everything I'm unsure about like professionals—but she does know how to make me feel better)

Thank you so much to Becky from Platform House Publishing for the beautiful interior. I really appreciate all your hard work, and I love showing off what you create for me.

Thank you to Diablerie GraphicArts for creating this incredible cover, which may well be one of my favourite pieces of art ever. Working with you is a pleasure and a privilege.

Thank you to Miri, my Bonnie, who read the first draft of this book and is still talking to me anyway. That's love and support, y'all.

Thank you to my early readers—Beverley Lee, Dana Fraedrich, Jules Appleton, TaniaRina Perri, Tasha Rogers, and Tris Prewitt. Whether you were a critique partner or a beta reader, know that I appreciate all your feedback and that you've made this book better.

I want to give a special thank you to Dana and Tasha, because your feedback gave me SO MUCH life. 'Shut your face, Esta! You're magnificent.' will forever be one of my favourite comments on anything ever.

I also want to thank my characters for being so damn vocal and for surprising me all the time. I consider myself a plotter, but you, dear reader, will never know how many of these plot twists were news to me, too. Chiara wasn't in my initial outline. That bitch just showed up and got angry at Esta out of nowhere, but I'm so glad she's here now! (Esta disagrees with me.)

And, always and forever, thank you for reading these books. They mean an awful lot to me, and seeing readers like yourself gushing over them and leaving wonderful reviews fills my dark heart with so much joy and sunshine. I hope you're excited for Books 3-10, because I can't wait to show you what's next!

Sarina Langer is a dark fantasy author of both epic and urban paranormal novels from the delightfully cloudy South of England.

She is as obsessed with books and stationery now as she was as a child, when she drowned her box of colour pencils in water so they wouldn't die and scribbled her first stories on corridor walls. ('A first sign of things to come', according to her mother. 'Normal toddler behaviour', according to Sarina.)

In her free time, she has a weakness for books, pretty words, and spends what's probably too much time playing video games.

She believes that the best books are those where every ray of light casts a shadow.